CRASH TEST

Also by Amy James

A Five-Letter Word for Love

CRASH TEST

A Novel

AMY JAMES

AVON

An Imprint of HarperCollins Publishers

CRASH TEST. Copyright © 2025 by Green Couch Writing Inc. All rights reserved. Printed in the United States of America. No part of this book may be used or reproduced in any manner whatsoever without written permission except in the case of brief quotations embodied in critical articles and reviews. For information, address HarperCollins Publishers, 195 Broadway, New York, NY 10007.

Avon, Avon & logo, and Avon Books & logo are registered trademarks of HarperCollins Publishers in the United States of America and other countries.

HarperCollins books may be purchased for educational, business, or sales promotional use. For information, please email the Special Markets Department at SPsales@harpercollins.com.

FIRST EDITION

Interior text design by Diahann Sturge-Campbell

Race car illustration © Pekosman/TheNounProject
Part illustrations © Winderfull Studio/Stock.Adobe.com

Library of Congress Cataloging-in-Publication Data has been applied for.

ISBN 978-0-06-339905-1

25 26 27 28 29 LBC 5 4 3 2 1

For Gillian

CRASH TEST

Sector One

Travis

1

After

NO ONE THINKS TO TELL ME ABOUT THE CRASH, NOT UNTIL
an hour after it's happened. Even then, no one goes out of their
way to tell me directly. Why would they? No one knows we're
friends, let alone . . . whatever we are.

I'm caught by a reporter on my way out of a press conference, a
bright red microphone pushed into my face.

"Got a second, mate? Great."

Obediently, I stop walking and plaster on a look of interest. If it
were anyone else, I might have made an excuse and kept on walking, but James Riley is a retired F1 driver, one of the greats from
the eighties.

"Well done out there today, Travis," he says, in his bright English accent. "P4, you must be pleased with that."

"Yeah," I say, swallowing down the uncomfortable prickle of
nerves that always surfaces when I have to talk on camera. "We
had a few issues in practice yesterday, but yeah, a bit better today."

"Talk to us about that," James says. "You and Matty—" He
moves aside as a man and woman in Crosswire Racing gear step

past us. "You and Matty both had some problems out there yesterday—"

"—see the replay?" the woman asks. "Nichols' car—"

At the sound of his name, my entire body goes cold, like someone's doused me in ice water. Her tone is tight and horrified, as if something awful has happened. I turn toward them, panic spiking my pulse, but James' question drowns out most of the man's response. I only catch three words.

"—killed on scene."

"—if the weather holds out," James finishes. He's holding his mic expectantly, waiting for my response, but all I can hear is—all I can think is—

Killed on scene.

They can't mean—

He can't have been—

James is staring at me, a bemused look on his face. I know I need to answer, but I can't hear anything beyond the rushing in my ears. The man's words are stuck on repeat. Killed on scene. Killed on scene. Killed on scene.

"Did something happen?" I blurt out, in a thin voice that doesn't sound like mine. "Did something happen in F2?"

James looks around, his forehead wrinkling. "I don't know, mate. I've been in a meeting all morning, just stepped out two minutes ago." He glances at his camerawoman, but her face is as blank as his.

"Excuse me." My words come out harsh and strangled. I push past them, my fingers clumsy as I fumble for my phone. It takes three tries to open the F2 live timing app, and another three to navigate to the updates. I feel sick, literally sick, as it loads, then my brain sort of freezes when I see what's there.

Nothing.

The last live update was forty-three minutes ago. Martinez gets past Rourke to claim the lead on lap one. #livewithf2 #formula2 #circuitpaulricard.

After that, nothing.

I refresh.

Nothing.

My feet start moving again, carrying me toward the outside. If it were a minor crash, they would've posted about it. If they aren't posting about it—if they aren't posting *anything*—

It means dying. It means death.

Killed on scene, the man said.

Nichols' car, the woman said.

There's a roaring in my ears, drowning out all other sound. Someone tries to approach me. I push past them. Someone calls my name. I ignore them. A door opens and I'm momentarily blinded by sunlight. Sunlight and silence. The F2 sprint race was supposed to start after F1 qualifying—a change in the usual order of things, to try to entice more fans to stick around and learn about Formula 2—but right now, the whole track is eerily silent. How long has it been like this? I went into a press conference right after qualifying, but surely I should've noticed the silence fall?

My stomach lurches as I remember the end of the press conference. I thought it had ended sort of abruptly, but I hadn't bothered to wonder why. I'd just been grateful it was over. I even laughed at some smart comment my teammate, Matty, made about it.

I force myself to keep moving forward. The grid is almost empty, and that's not right, either. I look to one of the big screens, and it's blank.

Dear god, it's fucking blank.

The few people left in the pits are huddled in twos and threes, arms crossed and faces somber. No one's smiling. No one's laughing. I pass a group of fans on a pit lane tour and they swing their phones around to take pictures of me, but even that reaction is strangely muted, as if they aren't sure they're being appropriate.

My eyes seek out a familiar face, finally latching on to a mechanic in Harper clothing. He's talking to a blond girl whose forehead is lined with concern.

"What happened?" I demand. The girl blinks at me, startled.

"Huge crash in F2," the mechanic says. "They airlifted, like, six drivers out."

An icy wave crashes over me, numbing me to my fingertips. Six drivers. There are twenty-four drivers in F2 this year. That means there's a one-in-four chance that one of them was—

"Five drivers," the blond girl corrects. "One of them was cleared by the medics here."

"Who—" The word doesn't come out right. I swallow and try again. "Who was airlifted?"

"Parrot," the mechanic says, at the same time the girl says, "Nichols."

"Yeah, Parrot and Nichols, Costa, Theriot . . . and McDougall, I think," the mechanic finishes.

I walk away from them. Stumble away, maybe.

There's a horrible searing pain spreading through my chest. My lungs won't work right. It's like I've forgotten how to breathe. No, I *have* forgotten how to breathe.

For a minute, a full minute, I stand there totally paralyzed. Then a little voice rises in the back of my mind, the same voice that hollers at me when I've done something stupid in my car, or when I've snapped at the team over something that isn't their fault.

What the fuck are you doing? the voice demands. *Get to the hospital!*

I start moving again, pushing back through the doors and pounding through the halls to get to my room. By some miracle there's no one around, not my trainer, not my teammate, not anyone. I grab my jacket and car keys and then freeze with one hand on the door. I can't roll into the hospital in race gear. Someone could see—someone could realize—

It takes me two minutes to strip out of my Harper gear and climb into jeans and a gray T-shirt, and it's only as I'm sprinting through the parking lot and jumping into my car that I realize those two minutes might mean the difference between seeing him alive and seeing him dead. My heart starts hammering even harder, and as I wait for the security guard to let me out of the lot, my brain is stuck on the thought that I might've just thrown away my last chance to see him alive, all because I'm terrified someone might guess why I'm there.

I'm out onto the highway before I realize I have no idea where I'm going. My hands shake as I punch in the numbers for the only radio station that might give me some news. Sky1 turns on mid-sentence, and I feel the first words as a thud in the center of my chest.

"—with live updates from Circuit Paul Ricard. Lisa, tell us what's going on," says the reporter.

"Well, John, it is very quiet, very quiet here as we try to come to grips with what we've just witnessed. Absolutely devastating crash in Formula 2, and as you know, five drivers were airlifted out just over an hour ago."

Airlifted *where*, I want to scream. A car honks behind me, and I realize I'm driving like a maniac, straddling two lanes as I type "hospital" into my GPS while trying to catch every word Lisa says.

I pull over, because I think I might kill someone if I don't. The GPS is coming up with two—no, three hospitals nearby. Hôpital Aubagne, Hôpital Maisonneuve-Talon, Medical Center Les Oiseaux . . . god, the further I zoom out, the more hospitals pop up.

"For folks at home who might not know," the male reporter says, "Formula 2 is the motor racing league just below Formula 1. The cars are slower than Formula 1 cars, but can still reach speeds of nearly two hundred miles an hour, isn't that right, Lisa?"

"That's right, John," Lisa says. "We've just heard that two of the drivers at Hôpital Nord have been triaged with only minor injuries, but there's no word yet on the other three—"

I punch in the hospital's name before she's even finished the sentence, and the radio is interrupted by Siri, who tells me to stay straight for thirteen miles. I force myself to look around at traffic before I pull back onto the highway. Hôpital Nord is thirty-five minutes away. I take another breath as Lisa's voice starts up again. I want to kiss this girl, whoever she is. I want to drain my bank account and send it all her way. Two drivers with only minor injuries.

I force a deep breath into my lungs, then another. The male reporter is asking Lisa to tell us what she saw, and I turn the radio up higher to hear.

"Well, all five cars were quite close coming off the straight. It looked like Parrot locked up just after turn one, then his car was hit by Nichols and Costa, who were wheel to wheel. It looked like Costa was trying to overtake Nichols when they hit Parrot, and then Theriot and McDougall were caught up in the wreckage—"

The *wreckage*. I'm gripping the steering wheel so hard, my knuckles are white. In my mind's eye, I try to imagine the crash. Parrot's car locking up, then getting hit by two cars going a hundred and fifty out of the straight . . . he must be one of the drivers who's in trouble. But if Theriot and McDougall were just "caught up in the wreckage" . . . if they were coming up behind the crash and had to swerve out of the way . . . does that mean they were the two that walked away with minor injuries?

Fuck, I think I might be sick.

"He's fine," I say out loud, as though that can make it true. "He'll be fine."

Siri interrupts the broadcast again to tell me to make a turn, and for the next twenty minutes I can barely hear any of the radio as Siri guides me through a series of complicated roundabouts and side streets. By the time I'm back out on open road, Lisa is signing off, and John is promising to keep us updated as more information is available. I hit the off button as a news broadcast starts up, and Siri tells me that in seven minutes, my destination will be on the right.

In seven minutes, I tell myself, I'll find him waiting for me with minor injuries. I can already picture it—he'll be in some awful, sterile hospital room, and there will probably be all sorts of people at his side, but he'll see me come in and crack a smile, crooked and subtle and just for me. I'll keep my distance until I can get him alone, and then he'll make some smart comment about me worrying about him and roll his eyes like I've been foolish. He's like that, always playing things off, never admitting weakness or defeat. But if Parrot and the others are as bad off as it sounds, he'll be shaken. I probably won't have much time to be alone with him—fuck, his parents flew in for this race, didn't they?—but I'll take his hand and kiss the very center of his palm—

"In three hundred meters, your destination is on the right," Siri says, jerking me out of my thoughts.

As I turn into the hospital, I'm thankful for the bits of French I've learned over the years. Stationnement, that's the parking lot, although I'm not sure if it's quite the right one. The hospital seems to have several different buildings, and I drive past three separate entranceways before I find a parking spot.

I find the closest entrance and walk into a small, quiet waiting room with a registration desk. I get a horrible sense of déjà vu as I walk in. I haven't been inside a hospital since my dad died. He was already dead when I got there. The ER doctor had called to tell me. For a moment, I feel a flicker of hope—Jacob can't be dead yet, because no one's called to tell me.

Then I shake my head at my own stupidity. Even if he's dead, I'm the last person anyone would think to call.

The sign by the registration desk says "Enregistrement—Chirurgie Cardiothoracique," which doesn't sound right at all. The woman behind the desk is speaking in rapid French to an elderly gentleman holding an appointment card. I wait behind him for about five seconds before I spot a sign on the hall to the right that says "URGENCES." I take off at a run—that must be the ER.

There are a few more signs along the way, but the hospital is so big I keep getting lost. It doesn't help that they're doing construction on some of the buildings. I'm getting increasingly desperate, typing "Hôpital Nord emergency room directions" into my phone when I spot a hospital volunteer wearing a bright red vest.

"Est-ce que je peux vous aider?" she asks cheerfully.

"Emergency room?" I blurt out, too anxious to remember what it was called in French.

"Ah, oui," she says, before switching to heavily accented English. "You will go down this hall, just here, then you are turning left, down the long hall, then there is a door that leads—away? Non, outside," she corrects herself. "You are walking straight across, there is main registration."

"Thanks," I choke out, already hurrying away. Down the hall—left—down the long hall, which is so long I start to worry I've lost my way. But, no—there's the door that leads outside. I emerge onto a sunny sidewalk. Across the road is the entrance to another building, with a bright red sign that says "URGENCES."

Someone honks as I sprint across the road and through the doors. The air conditioning is bitterly cold after the heat outside, and the waiting room is filled with people, some of them looking pale and sickly, others red-faced and impatient.

At the registration desk, one of those red-faced, impatient assholes is berating the clerk, who wears a thin, beleaguered smile. I don't understand a word of his rant, but I don't have to. He's being a dick about the wait, never mind the fact that there are people here with actual emergencies.

The girl behind the desk purses her lips as the jackass finally stomps away, and yet after he's gone, she gives me a patient smile and gestures me forward. She says something in French, too quickly for me to understand.

"Er—Anglais?" I say awkwardly.

"Oui, a little," she says, still smiling kindly. There's a line forming behind me now, but she looks me right in the eye, as though she'll wait as long as it takes to help. People like her don't get paid enough, I think.

"I'm looking for someone who was brought in," I say. I have to swallow twice on a paper-dry throat before I can spit out his name. "Jacob Nichols."

"Ah." The girl types something into her computer and squints at the screen. When she looks back at me, there's something terribly pitying in her gaze. "And you are—friend? Famille?"

"Family," I lie.

She nods. "He was in emergency, but he is transferred now, to USI. You take the elevator—là—to ninth floor. Press the bell and tell them who you look for."

"USI," I croak. "Is that—is that bad?"

Her eyes soften even more, and I think I might vomit. "It is—" She hunts for the words. "L'unité de soins intensifs. Intensive care."

Intensive care.

I don't remember to thank her. I just stumble away, those two words ringing in my ears.

The elevator ride takes a year. There's a middle-aged woman riding with me who asks me something in French and then looks offended when I don't answer. She gets off at the fifth floor with a little huff of irritation, and I ride the rest of the way alone.

The doors open right into the intensive care waiting room. I don't need to speak fluent French to know that's what it is. The walls are painted a depressing shade of gray, and everyone sitting in the expensive-looking chairs has the same pale, tight look on their face. These people look just how I feel. Like they might fall apart at any moment.

At the far end of the room is a door with a buzzer next to it and a placard of complicated-looking instructions. I press the buzzer and then wait, in perfect silence, for the door to open. No one in the waiting room looks at me or makes a sound. Just like me, they live in bubbles. Nothing exists outside of their fear.

The door finally opens on a thin guy in pale blue scrubs.

"Oui? Est-ce que je peux vous aider?"

I clear my throat. Behind him, I can see a long row of glass-walled hospital rooms.

"I'm looking for Jacob Nichols," I mumble. Trying to keep my voice down, even now.

"Vous êtes famille?"

I hesitate this time, but only for one heartbeat. "Yes."

"Oui, entrez," he says, waving me forward. "Salle neuf cent vingt-quatre."

I follow him, moving on autopilot. "Is he okay?" I manage.

"He is not my patient," the guy says, switching to accented English. "Voilà, c'est là."

He points to a room up ahead and then hurries away. I stumble along a bit farther—I can see "924—neuf cent vingt-quatre" engraved on one of the frosted glass doors just ahead. Time slows down as I walk forward. I can hear voices from inside. I can see shadows moving.

The door is half open. Someone is crying inside, a woman. His mother, maybe? My heart thuds painfully. I've never met his mother. She doesn't know that I exist.

I step closer, and then I can see him.

My whole body goes numb. I have to clutch the doorframe to stay upright.

I had hoped—

I had thought—

I know it's stupid, but a small part of me still hoped he was one of the ones with minor injuries. I was expecting . . . I don't know. A split lip. A gash in his forehead. I was so stupid, I hadn't even thought of broken bones.

He looks so, so much worse than I could've imagined.

One leg is casted and hanging from some medieval-looking contraption on the ceiling, and there's a catheter draining bloody urine into a bag, and another tube coming out of his chest. IVs are dripping fluid into both arms, and there's a heart monitor beeping over the bed, and another, bigger IV dripping stuff into his neck.

And . . . he isn't breathing on his own. I've seen enough medical TV shows to know that's a breathing tube sticking out of his mouth. There's a bag attached to it, and tubes running into a massive machine on the side of the bed, and rhythmically, the bag inflates and deflates.

His face isn't bruised or cut up, but that almost makes it worse, somehow. He looks so fragile. So breakable.

There's a middle-aged woman with short blond hair sitting at his bedside, her face puffy from crying and one white-knuckled hand pressed to her lips. A thin, middle-aged man stands behind her, clutching her shoulders. On the other side of the bed, a brawny guy in his mid-thirties is talking on his cell phone, one hand pressed to his forehead.

"I don't know—I don't *know*, Lil, they haven't come to talk to us yet. No, not since downstairs—"

His voice is tense and vaguely familiar. He must be Jacob's older brother, Paul. He calls Jacob a couple of times a month. He has a huge, booming voice that always comes through the phone like it's on speaker. He's a businessman of some sort, and he's always asking if Jacob has a girlfriend, or if he wants to be set up with one of his own girlfriend's "hot friends."

The girl on the other end of the phone must be Jacob's older sister, Lily. I've seen pictures of her. She's twenty-seven, with dirty blond hair just like Jacob's. She works as an event planner somewhere in America, always frantically busy with a hundred different weddings and bar mitzvahs and things. She only calls Jacob about once a month, but when she does, she keeps him on the phone for hours.

His family's like that. All of them, thick as thieves. No drama. No secrets.

No secrets except me, I mean.

I stand there stupidly until they catch sight of me. For a moment, their eyes light up, like they think I'm the doctor. Then they see my jeans and T-shirt, and their faces drop.

"Can we help you?" Jacob's father says in a tight voice.

It takes me a second to push out an answer. I can't think, with Jacob lying there. All he has on is some stupid hospital gown. He'll be so cold. He's *always* cold. Irrational fury clenches my chest. Why haven't they put any blankets on him?

"I'm sorry," I mumble. "I'm . . . he's a friend of mine. From racing."

Jacob's dad nods, but honestly, I'm not sure if any of them have even heard me. They're staring at Jacob again, just like me.

Then Paul looks at me, his phone still clutched to his ear. "No, it's not the doctor," he says impatiently. "I don't *know*, Lil."

He stares at me again, his mouth twisting down, and I just know he's going to ask me to leave. But before he can, the heart monitor starts going off.

I can't understand any of it, there are so many numbers and lines, but the thing's definitely going off, and there's some sort of alert flashing on the screen. About two seconds later, I'm edged out of the doorway by a nurse, this one tall and female. She goes straight to the monitor and pushes a button. The machine starts spitting out a long strip of paper, and the beeping stops but the flashing alert doesn't go away.

"What's happening?" Jacob's mom asks.

"His heart rate is a little fast, that's all." The nurse's English is flawless and her tone is calm, but there's something in her eyes that makes me sick to my stomach. The machine starts beeping again, and Jacob's mom rises out of her seat. The nurse turns to the machine again and shuts the beeping off, but this time, when she turns back, the worry in her eyes is obvious. "I'll be right back with the doctor. If you would like to go to the waiting room?"

"We'll stay right here," Paul says loudly. "We're his family."

The nurse nods and hurries from the room, and this time, when Jacob's family looks at me, there's something beneath their grief—something like hostility. I am an intruder in this deeply private moment.

I choke out an apology and fall back out of the way just as the nurse returns with an older woman wearing dress clothes and a stethoscope. There are two other nurses following close behind, and as they enter the room, the heart monitor starts going off again. The door slides shut and I'm left standing in the empty hall.

They only want family inside.

I'm the one who woke up next to him this morning. I'm the one who made him his coffee. I'm the one who wished him luck on his race, the one who kissed him and tried to work up the nerve to tell him I love him before chickening out for the hundredth time.

But I'm not family.

And so, while he dies behind frosted glass walls, I lock myself in the first bathroom I can find and cry until I'm sick.

2

Impress Me

I'D HEARD OF HIM OVER THE YEARS, BUT ONLY IN THE WAY that I'd heard about all the Formula 2 drivers. He was a name I'd hear every now and then on the racetrack speakers—"Nichols will take his first victory at Monza!" or "What a race for Jacob Nichols!"—without a specific face attached. We never really overlapped in the racing world. I was already in single-seaters when he started karting, and I moved up to F1 the year before he got a spot in F2. Even though some of the F1 and F2 races take place on the same weekends, the drivers don't interact much. We're busy with press, busy with training, busy with racing. I watched F2 now and then, out of interest, but even so, Jacob was just another driver in a car. Utterly uninteresting, until one Friday at the Austrian Grand Prix.

It was the last race weekend before the summer break, and it was supposed to be FP1—the first free practice session for Formula 1—but it was pouring buckets outside. Rain was bouncing six inches off the ground and the wind was howling through the grandstands. Even the most dedicated fans had left the stands an hour ago, and it seemed inevitable practice would be canceled.

F2 qualifying was scheduled to take place after FP1, but there was little chance that would be happening. Still, no one could leave until things were officially called off, and the stewards were taking an age to decide. Everyone was bored and waiting, and almost all the reporters and interviewers had packed up their gear or moved inside.

I was too restless to wait in my room. I did some weights with my trainer, Brian—an obnoxious, sleazy fellow I'd unhappily inherited from the previous Harper driver—and then ditched him in the cafeteria. I don't think he noticed, honestly. He was too busy bragging about his gluten-free diet to one of Harper's race engineers.

I put my headphones on, loaded up my usual pre-race playlist, and began wandering aimlessly, going over the track in my mind. I'd only been in F1 three years—two decent years with Torrent, a midfield team, then this year with Harper Racing, the second best team in the league. The car was a hell of a lot faster, and I was running third in the championship. Halfway through the season, the championship was still theoretically in my sights. Every time I thought about it, I felt this little shiver of excitement. Winning an F1 championship was all I had ever wanted. And with rain forecast on and off all weekend, the Austrian race was anyone's game.

Secretly, though, I thought it was mine. Rain is the great equalizer of F1, a chance for drivers in objectively slower cars to snag a surprise podium or race win. I'd gotten my own first win for Torrent in a wet race three years earlier. For years, I'd made a point of practicing on rainy days. Not just in my F1 car, but in street cars, rally cars, anything with four wheels I could get my hands on. I'd torn up a few cars in the process, but after a while I got the hang of it. I knew in my gut, if it rained this weekend, I could win.

I bit down hard on my lip and forced myself to recite the track again. I passed a few people, mostly bored employees on their cell phones, but for the most part I was alone. Then I took a left turn and walked right into the middle of a TV interview.

It was for a smaller network I'd never heard of, and the interviewer was a dark-haired woman with a nervous smile. Her eyes lit up when she saw me, and the cameraman swiveled my way.

"Travis Keeping!" The reporter beamed at me. "Join us for a word?"

I reluctantly took off my headphones. Harper's press team had rules about impromptu media—"Don't talk to anyone without us" was their mantra—but the camera was already rolling and the reporter looked desperately hopeful. Still, I hesitated a moment, until the driver she was interviewing shot me a crooked, white-toothed grin.

I'll admit, I felt it like a lightning strike. It's stupid and cheesy and was in no way reciprocated—Jacob told me later he initially thought I was a dick—but that's how it felt for me. He was just . . . god. He was every fantasy I'd never let myself have, wrapped up in dirty blond hair and gray eyes and strong forearms. I still remember the shirt he was wearing, soft gray cotton with his F2 team's logo printed in black.

In the five seconds it took me to (1) imagine stripping the shirt off his back, (2) realize what I'd just thought about another driver, and (3) freak the hell out about it, the reporter came up with her first question.

"If you're just joining us now," she said to the camera, "I'm here with Formula 2 driver Jacob Nichols and Formula 1 driver Travis Keeping, both of whom are waiting impatiently, I imagine, for the rain to stop." She smiled at us. "Boys, what do you think about this weather?"

"It's nuts out there," Jacob said, with another slanted grin. "Shame they won't let us race in it."

He was standing so close to me that I could smell his shampoo, something dark and earthy and masculine. My brain was going completely haywire at that point, but fortunately I was already known for being quiet in interviews.

"Yeah," I said.

The reporter nodded like I'd said something profound. "The weather's supposed to clear up a bit tomorrow, but the forecast still calls for showers on and off. This would be the first wet race of your season, Travis. How do you feel about that?"

I cleared my throat. "Not bad."

There was a beat of silence while they waited for me to elaborate. When I didn't, Jacob raised a single eyebrow. That's probably about the time he was thinking I was a dick.

The reporter, though, bless her, was not so easily beaten. Her cheeks were a little flushed from nerves, but she swallowed hard and changed tack.

"Tell you what," she said, with newfound vigor. "We've got a few minutes to kill—why don't we do a rapid-fire quiz?" Without giving us time to answer, she barreled on. "I'll say two things, you pick one. No hesitating, just say the first answer that comes to mind. Got it?"

Jacob smiled encouragingly at her, a bright, confident smile that I felt deep in my stomach. "Go for it," he said.

The reporter took a breath and launched in. "Early bird or night owl?"

"Night owl," Jacob said, at the same time that I grunted, "Early."

"Beach or mountains?"

"Mountains," I answered, while Jacob said, "Beach."

"Rap or techno?"

"Neither," I said, at the same time that Jacob said, "Both."

The reporter laughed. "It's a good thing this isn't the newlywed game, or you two would be headed for divorce!"

Jacob's laugh was warm and infectious. One corner of my mouth turned up, entirely without my permission.

"Tea or coffee?" the reporter continued.

"Coffee," we answered together, and I was rewarded with a flash of Jacob's smile.

"Cat or dog?"

"Dog," we both said.

The reporter chuckled. "Alright, maybe you'll stave off divorce for a little while. Last one—rain or shine?"

"Rain," I answered automatically, while Jacob said, "Shine."

The reporter grinned. "We'll call it a rocky relationship, then, shall we?"

"We have our ups and downs," Jacob deadpanned, squeezing my shoulder. I felt the warmth of his fingertips through the thin cotton of my shirt, and for a moment I honestly couldn't breathe.

"Thanks so much, boys," the reporter said. "We'll leave you to it."

The camera turned off and she shook both of our hands and thanked us for playing along. "It's my first week," she admitted. "Sorry if I was rubbish."

"No, you were great," Jacob said, and a pleased flush spread up her neck. She thanked us again and then headed off with her cameraman in tow. Jacob and I were left alone in the narrow, white-walled hallway. He could've just walked off, but instead he crossed his arms and leaned back against the wall. His smile was sharp and confident, and his eyes danced as he looked me up and down.

"You're really good at interviews," he said.

Warmth crept up my neck. I reckon I was just as flushed as the reporter. I cleared my throat, my mind completely blank. Later, I would think of something to say, but I was never someone who could be clever in the moment.

"Right," I managed.

I felt his laugh as a warm shiver down my spine. "It helps that you've got such a great smile," he said. "Really puts people at ease."

My mouth twitched up reluctantly. It was true, I wasn't known for being particularly friendly. It wasn't that I was trying to be rude, I just always felt . . . out of place, I suppose. Uncomfortable. The only place I didn't feel like that was inside a race car. In the real world, with people, I was rubbish. Luckily, it seemed to have translated into a "strong, silent type" sort of image in the media.

Right now, though, I wasn't feeling particularly strong. Jacob was grinning at me, and I felt like he could see everything, from the flush on my neck to the unsteadiness in my hands. Not just that he could see it, but that he knew the root cause.

"What are you listening to?" he asked, nodding at my abandoned phone. Without waiting for me to answer, he took my phone out of my hand. He pressed the home button, then raised a surprised eyebrow as the home screen popped up. "You don't have a passcode?"

I shrugged. I'd never needed one. I didn't have any social media, despite the Harper press team's longstanding campaign to convince me to set some up. The only texts in my phone were work-related.

I waited for Jacob to open my music, but instead he blinked up at me. "Did you just get this phone?"

I cleared my throat again. "It's a few years old."

"Your background is the default home screen," he said slowly.

Color was spreading farther up my face. I felt off-balance, nettled and pleased by his attention. "So?"

"So you must have one picture you can put as your background." He tapped the Photos icon and then stared at me in horror. "You've never taken a *single* picture on your phone? Are you a robot?"

I grabbed my phone back, my heart twitching nervously as my fingers brushed his. "I don't use it much."

He barked out an incredulous laugh. "You fucking weirdo." He snatched the phone back. "Let's see if your music has a personality, at least."

He looked down at my phone again, and I leaned closer under the slim pretense of looking at the screen. My eyes traced the lines of his neck, smooth tanned skin and strong muscle disappearing beneath the soft collar of his T-shirt. I had a sudden, overwhelming urge to put my mouth there.

At the same time, my mind was skittering. It wasn't just that Jacob was another driver. It was also only the second time I'd thought something like that about anyone *real*. I was aware of my sexuality, in a distant, inconvenient sort of way, but it was something I kept firmly relegated to the corners of my mind. For years, I told myself if I didn't pay any attention to it—if I kept my fantasies vague and faceless, never attached to a real person—then it couldn't really matter.

Then, on a flight from Montreal to London a few years earlier, I sat next to a guy who spent the whole flight typing some research paper on his laptop. I spent the first hour plotting his death—he typed loudly and inconsistently, so every time I started to doze off, I was woken up by an abrupt burst of clacking—but then he pushed his sleeves up to his elbows, and I spent the next five hours sneaking glances at his forearms and fantasizing about feeling his fingers moving over my skin. That night, in my bedroom in London, I could hardly sleep for thinking about him.

Then I woke up the next morning, completely horrified, and vowed never to think about a guy like that again.

I took every thought and desire and shoved it into the darkest corner of my mind. Every time a feeling threatened to arise, I pushed it into racing instead. It was the first time I realized the sheer force of my own willpower. I told myself I wasn't attracted to anyone, and I was so convincing, I think I actually believed it.

Then Jacob stepped into the picture, and it was like I was back on that plane, shivery and wrung out from five hours of longing.

"I've never heard of any of these bands," Jacob said, wrinkling his nose. "'Race playlist'—what is this, like, pump-up music?"

He clicked play and listened for a minute with one earbud. I bit into my lip, fighting the smallest smile, because I knew it wasn't exactly pump-up music. It was just calm, mellow indie stuff, most of which was only instrumental.

Jacob pulled the earbud out and stared at me. "This is the kind of music they play at *spas*," he said in horror.

I frowned. "I've never been to a spa."

He ran a hand over his forehead. "Good god, Keeping. You really are a robot. Someone needs to teach you how to live."

He dug into his pocket and pulled out his phone, a battered iPhone with a splintery crack in the screen. His background image was a group of ten people grinning at the top of a mountain hike. They were all squished close together with their arms wrapped around each other. I'd never been in a picture like that in my life.

"See?" Jacob said, holding up his phone for me to get a closer look. "This picture says something about me."

"It looks like an ad for some sports clothing company."

I won't pretend it was a particularly clever thing to say, but it was an attempt at a joke, and my heart was racing at my own boldness. I was rewarded for my bravery with a crinkle at the corner of Jacob's eyes.

"I do look like a model, thank you," he drawled. "No, it says I like hiking, and being outdoors, and being with friends."

"What does mine say?" I asked.

"Yours?" He raised an eyebrow. "I don't know. 110101. Robot speak."

He laughed at his own joke, and I smiled without thinking about it. His eyes dropped down to my mouth, then back up again. Something shifted behind his dark gray irises, and a beat of loaded silence fell between us.

"'Scuse me!" The moment was broken as a man appeared from around the corner, lugging a heavy crate on one shoulder. I stepped forward to get out of his way, and suddenly I was about six inches from Jacob. When I stepped back again, my legs were unsteady. I understood, now, that stupid saying about knees going weak. It turned out it wasn't stupid at all, just an accurate assessment of how it felt to want someone so badly.

He watched me for a long, drawn-out minute and then grinned. "Yeah, someone definitely needs to teach you how to live. Here." He handed me his phone. "Give me your number."

I know he saw how clumsy my fingers were as I thumbed my number into his phone. My heart rate ratcheted up again as I was doing it. I felt like I was having some crazy out-of-body experience, like I'd been drugged or something. Or like I was drunk—drunk on sandalwood and stubble and forearms.

"Thanks," Jacob murmured as he took his phone back. He took a step toward me, and for one brief, insane moment I thought he might kiss me right there in the hallway, all of five minutes after we'd met. My eyes dropped to his mouth, and when I finally dragged them back up to his eyes, he looked exceptionally smug. He brought a hand up to his neck and rubbed it absently—months later, he would admit he knew exactly what he was doing to me with that single, casual motion—and my brain went totally blank. I think I may have actually leaned toward him, but suddenly he stepped back.

"Good luck tomorrow," he said. He strolled away, hands in his pockets, and threw his last words over his shoulder along with a challenging grin. "Try to impress me."

3
Touch and Go

AFTER A FEW HOURS HIDING OUT IN THE ICU BATHROOM— one of the staff bathrooms, I learn, after about ten irritated nurses knock impatiently on the door—my face is presentable enough to emerge. I walk past Jacob's room, but the doors are closed. I can see shadows moving inside, and I hover for a minute, trying to work up the nerve to go in. But then a nurse walks by and frowns at me, and I'm forced to retreat.

The waiting room is still half full. I sink into a seat, only to spot Jacob's brother, Paul, in the far corner, cell phone pressed to his ear. I search his face desperately for clues. He's nodding and talking in a quiet voice, then he cracks a thin smile and all the breath rushes out of my lungs. He wouldn't be smiling if Jacob were dead.

A painful lump is forming in my throat. I get up and flee into the stairwell before Paul can spot me.

Compared to the pristine waiting room, the stairwell is muggy and dingy but mercifully quiet. I dig my phone out of my pocket and my breath hitches at the sight of the background picture. It's from the top of a hike on the Isle of Harris, in Scotland. Jacob set it as my background photo nearly a year ago.

I squint at the time. Ten forty-seven p.m. I have fifteen missed calls and ten texts. I ignore all of them, except the ones from my teammate, Matty. He's been with Harper for three years already, with seventeen podiums and six wins under his belt, and he's something of a media darling (his words, not mine).

F1 teammates aren't really teammates at all—your teammate is the only one on the grid in the same car as you, so they're your biggest competition, as well as the only driver your performance can be properly measured against—but Matty's always been really friendly to me. He kind of reminds me of Jacob a bit. Always joking, always up for anything.

Yo, did you see the F2 crash? his first text reads. Media canceled for the rest of day. I know you'll be disappointed lol.

Two hours later, there's another text. Shit, did you hear about Parrot?

My blood runs cold. I open up Google and type in "Parrot formula 2 crash." The first result that comes up confirms my worst fears. "Formula 2 Driver Ellis Parrot Dies After Tragic Crash," reads the first headline. I open the article and learn that Parrot died in hospital—*this* hospital—at eight thirty p.m. The article goes on to state that drivers McDougall and Theriot were released with minor injuries, while Jacob Nichols and Antony Costa remain in critical condition.

I clutch my phone so hard, I think I might break it.

Ellis Parrot *died*.

Just like Jacob might die.

The door swings open behind me and a young doctor in green scrubs and a long white coat emerges, phone and coffee in hand.

"Pardon," she says in French, spotting me on the steps. Then she does a double take. For a moment, I think she's recognized me, but instead her face softens and she says gently, "Pardonnez-moi . . . est-ce que ça va?"

I open my mouth to lie, but instead I blurt out, "Do you know how Jacob Nichols is?"

"Jacob Nichols?" she repeats.

"Room 924," I say, flushing. "He was in a car accident?"

"Ah." She nods. "The racing car driver. Oui." A drop of suspicion creeps into her eyes. "You are—media?"

"No, I—" I shake my head. "He's just . . . a friend. I don't want to disturb his family."

"We are not supposed to give information, only to family," she says. The painful lump in my throat grows a little bigger. I swallow it down and force a nod.

"Right. Sorry."

I wait for her to leave, but instead she gives a little sigh. A moment later, she sits down beside me on the steps.

"It is, how you say, touch and go," she says quietly. "He has suffered injury to—" She pats her stomach. "Organs inside. La rate. Ah, comment dire en anglais?" She rubs her forehead and then opens up some French search engine on her phone and types into it. "Ah! Ici. Spleen. La rate. And liver. You know?"

I nod a little uncertainly.

"He has done surgery to stop the bleeding," she continues, "but . . . la tension artérielle—blood pressure—is low. He is taken back to surgery soon."

"He's had surgery?" A hollow feeling spreads through my chest. "He's going for *more* surgery?"

She nods. "I am sorry."

"No, thank you," I say. "Thank you for telling me."

Her phone buzzes in her hand. She ignores it, and studies my face a moment more. "You are . . . good friends?"

The beat of silence is entirely too telling. She knows—or at least, suspects. The first person in the entire world to know. Maybe I should be freaking out, but in light of everything else, I can't bring myself to care. And something in the girl's steady gaze tells me our secret is safe.

"I am working all this week," she says. "I give you information when I can, yes?"

I manage a tiny smile. "Yes. Thank you."

She nods again and continues on down the stairs. My phone buzzes with a text from one of Harper's press people.

> Race still on for tomorrow, will send
> updated press schedule shortly.

The race. Jesus. I'd completely and totally forgotten about it. Qualifying seems like it happened a hundred years ago.

I scroll through all the texts I've missed, mostly notifications from the team about canceled press events. With an F2 driver dead, no one will be doing interviews. But they won't cancel the F1 race. There's too much money on the line. Which means tomorrow morning, I'll be expected to be in my car, driving around the same track where Jacob's car was . . . what?

Gritting my teeth, I open up Google again on my phone and slowly type in "Formula 2 crash circuit paul ricard video." A YouTube clip pops up. The thumbnail looks a little grainy, like it was shot on someone's phone, but it was posted a few hours ago and has sixty-seven thousand views. It must be the real thing.

Taking a breath, I click play. It takes a few minutes to load, and every second steals another heartbeat out of my chest.

The video was filmed by a fan in the stands. It opens on a section of empty track, with motors roaring in the distance. A car zooms through the frame, then five more cars zip past in rapid succession. It's too quick to tell which car is which. They must be going one-fifty, maybe faster. The camera shifts to the left and suddenly it's all smoke and flying cars. There's a collective cry from the crowd, and the video jars. Someone nearby says, "Oh my god!" and then the camera swings back to face the big screen nearby.

There's a replay showing—they always replay crashes, because usually there aren't any injuries—and the track cameras have picked up a perfect shot. Parrot is coming out of the corner when his front left tire locks. His car swerves erratically at the exact moment that Costa tries to pass Jacob on the outside of the corner. Wheel to wheel, the two cars slam into Parrot, and all three cars shatter and fly. I rewind the video, my breathing quick and shallow as I watch Jacob's car tumble through the air, over and over, before skidding upside down into the barrier. Three of the tires have come off of it, and the chassis is a mess of torn-up carbon fiber.

Touch and go, the doctor said. Seeing that video, I'm surprised Jacob survived this long.

I feel strangely numb all of a sudden, strangely distant from it all. I turn the video off and climb up one more flight of stairs, settling myself on the top floor, just outside the door to the roof. I can't imagine anyone will come up here. And there's no way in hell I'm leaving.

Instead, I open up my text messages and find Jacob's name. I scroll back, all the way to the very first text he sent me, almost a year ago to the day.

4

Second Place

THE RAIN EASED UP THE NEXT DAY, SCATTERED SHOWERS turning the F2 race into a slippery, dangerous melee. I watched it all on one of the big screens through the window of my changing room, while my trainer, Brian, prattled on about a party he was going to that night. Jacob got a bad start from P10, but as the laps ticked by, he overtook car after car and finished second. He's a damn good driver, Jacob. Great instincts, aggressive pace. The camera showed him getting out of his car after the race, and for about three seconds I was transfixed by his crooked, cocky smile.

I was fighting a grin of my own as I got into my car and headed out into qualifying. I breezed through Q1 in third and Q2 in second. Then, in Q3, it all went wrong. I pulled out with ten minutes left, but before I'd even started my flying lap, I started to lose power. "Anti-stall" flashed on the steering wheel as I maneuvered the car off the track.

I started the race the next day from the pit lane, after the engineers spent the night repairing the car. I checked my phone once more right before the race started. My stomach leapt when I saw

I'd missed a text message. I swiped it open eagerly, but it was only a text from Brian. Feeling sick, be there next weekend.

God, he was an asshole. There was no way he was sick. He'd been bragging all day Saturday about the "lit party" he'd been invited to. No doubt he was hungover somewhere. I turned my phone off and headed for my car, swallowing down disappointment. It had been two days since Jacob took my phone number, and there had been nothing but radio silence. I couldn't even text him, not that I'd have ever had the nerve. He hadn't given me his number.

I pulled on my helmet and climbed into the car. Outside, the rain was starting to fall again, heavier than it had been all day. It would be a wet race after all.

Try to impress me, Jacob had said.

A feeling like cold water washed over me, and my senses seemed to sharpen. Impress him . . . I could do that.

For two hours, it was like I could do nothing wrong. My mind was as focused as it had ever been. I wasn't even thinking, really, just reacting. Car after car disappeared behind me, until there was one lap to go and only two cars left in front of me. Mahoney and Clayton were first and second in the championship, two of the best drivers in F1's best cars. But they didn't have as much experience in the rain as I did—or at least, Clayton didn't. I overtook him on the last corner of the race and crossed the line in second place. From a pit lane start to second place, in a wet race. It was a record—or at least, that was what my race engineer was saying in my ear.

I climbed out of the car, grinning beneath my helmet, and threw a cursory wave to the crowd. I shook Mahoney and Clayton's hands, waited for Clayton to finish his interview, and then stepped up, obediently, for my own. I answered the reporter's

questions with a few one-word answers and wondered if, somewhere, Jacob was watching.

For the next four hours, I went from press conference to team
debrief to press conference again. By the time I got to check my
phone again, it was past six. I had one missed text from a number
I didn't recognize. My stomach tightened in anticipation.

> Second place? I thought I
> said to impress me.

I grinned stupidly at the screen, then looked at the timestamp.
He'd only sent it a minute ago. Biting my lip, I started typing an
answer, then promptly deleted it. I made five or six false starts,
cursing my own inability to come up with anything clever when
it mattered.

I was about to give up when three dots appeared on the screen.
He was typing something.

You could ask what would impress me, he prompted me.

Heart pounding, I snatched a breath.

What would impress you? I typed.

Three dots appeared instantly. I grinned at my phone, glad that
no one could see me behind the walls of my room. When his answer appeared, all the air rushed out of my lungs.

> Hotel Hofwirt, room 723. Nine o'clock.

I DIDN'T MAKE it back to my own hotel room until eight p.m.,
and by that time, I'd worked myself into something of a frenzy. I
jumped into the shower as soon as I got home and scrubbed the
day's dirt and sweat from my skin. Afterward, I spent a humiliating

five minutes staring at myself in the bathroom mirror, wondering what people saw when they looked at me. Wondering what Jacob might see. It had never occurred to me to wonder if I was good-looking before. It had never mattered, so I'd never cared. But right then, it seemed like there were a hundred things I should've paid attention to before.

Over the next twenty minutes, I filled my Google search history with the most embarrassing things I'd ever typed, starting with "Travis Keeping Formula 1 driver handsome"—which turned out to be quite reassuring—all the way down to "first time gay sex"—which was far less reassuring. Twice, I picked up my phone to text Jacob and cancel, but both times I thought of the smell of his skin and the strong lines of his forearms, and I put the phone down again.

I got stuck in traffic and arrived at the hotel twenty minutes late. I pulled my baseball cap down over my head as I crossed the lobby and found the elevators. I scrubbed my palms over my jeans as I rode up to the seventh floor. Fuck, but I was nervous. Really, really nervous. I tried to reassure myself that, as a fellow driver, Jacob would have just as much to lose as I would if this got out. Still, as I raised my hand to knock on door 723, my stomach was in knots.

Someone laughed loudly behind the door. In fact, there were several voices echoing from inside. I was double-checking the room number in my texts, certain I was at the wrong room, when the door swung open. Jacob looked surprised to see me, his eyes widening for a moment before he gave me the most devastating smile.

"Well, well," he said. "You came. I *am* impressed."

I glanced behind him. There were at least ten people in the room, all of them smiling or laughing or pouring drinks. In a chair near the door, a girl was sitting on some guy's lap. I vaguely recognized him as one of the other Formula 2 drivers.

Jacob followed my gaze. "C'mon in," he said. "We're playing a drinking game."

I stared at him for five whole seconds, feeling like I'd missed a step coming downstairs.

I felt so stupid for thinking—for imagining—

I remembered my Google searches and my cheeks burned red-hot.

But I could hardly just turn around and leave. Swallowing hard, I followed Jacob inside.

"Guys, we've got a straggler," Jacob announced. "Poor F1 drivers have no fancy parties of their own to go to, so they're stuck crashing ours."

He raised a glass to someone in the corner as he said it, and I recognized another face—another F1 driver, Josh Fry. He drove for Torrent Racing, and at the time, he was something like sixteenth in the championship. My stomach dropped even further to the ground. I couldn't *believe* I'd been so stupid.

The hotel room was pretty small, and filled with more people than I'd initially thought. There were probably twenty people, and most of them looked half wasted already, including Josh Fry.

"Travis Keeping, as I live and breathe!" he said. He held his glass up to me, sloshing liquor onto a pretty girl's dress. She laughed and smacked him across the head. "Grab a drink, mate."

"The bar's out on the balcony," Jacob told me. Then he picked a drink up off the television stand and turned away to talk to a beautiful red-headed girl in a sparkly gold dress. He must've said something funny, because she laughed and hit him on the arm. Her fingers lingered on his skin a half second longer than the action required.

Fuck.

I went out onto the balcony alone and found the bar, which was just a table covered in half-empty liquor bottles and plastic cups. I filled a cup with soda. I didn't really drink much back then, though that night seemed like it would be a good time to start. Sighing, I threw a few ice cubes into my glass. Just because I'd been an absolute idiot didn't mean I should make it even worse by getting drunk. I figured I'd just stay for twenty minutes, make up an excuse to leave, and then never think of this humiliating night again.

I was about to turn back inside when the sliding door opened and Jacob stepped out onto the balcony.

"You found the bar," he said with a grin.

I nodded, utterly unable to look him in the eye.

"What are you drinking?" he asked, stepping closer to add more scotch to his drink.

"Just soda," I muttered.

"Good call," Jacob said cryptically. He waited till I finally looked at him and then shot me a small, secretive smile that sent shivers running down my skin. "This could be a long night."

He leaned forward again, to get some ice, and for a moment his strong, warm arm was pressed up against mine. As he pulled away, he gave me another sharp grin, and a warm rush of blood flooded through me.

"See you in there," he murmured.

When he was gone, I let out a careful breath.

I might not have been wrong after all.

FOR FOUR HOURS, I played card games with Jacob's friends and watched as everyone but me and him got progressively drunker. I didn't contribute much to the party, but once or twice I found myself smiling at everyone's antics, and about once an hour I got up to refill my drink. Every time, Jacob followed me. The first time, his fingers brushed against mine as he passed me a soda. The second time, as he leaned past me to get a bottle of whiskey, his whole body pressed up against mine.

"How long do these parties usually last?" I asked hoarsely, as he added a shot of whiskey to my soda. "I don't usually drink," I added.

"Make an exception for me," he said. "Everyone should be leaving soon."

Sure enough, everyone stumbled home over the next half hour. Josh and the pretty girl he'd spilled alcohol on—his girlfriend, Becca, it turned out—were the last two to leave. Jacob had to practically push them out. Between the two of them, they'd downed nearly a full bottle of vodka, and before they left, Becca had climbed onto Josh's lap and kissed him deeply, giggling as his hands slid down her back.

I watched them covertly, as though I could pick up tips or something. God, I was in well over my head.

Finally, Jacob closed the door behind them. It shut with a very firm click, followed by a heart-stopping rattle as Jacob slid the chain over the lock.

He turned to face me with a grin. As he walked toward me, my heart started thundering in my chest.

"Help me clean up?" he asked.

Biting my lip, I nodded and started collecting discarded plastic cups and beer bottles while he tracked down loose playing cards that had fallen on the floor. Then I followed him out onto the balcony and helped him put caps on all the half-empty bottles. Afterward, he leaned onto the balcony railing, staring out at the twinkling lights of town.

Swallowing hard, I walked over and leaned next to him. I was far too cowardly to brush my arm against his, however much I wanted to. We stared at the lights for a few minutes, then he spoke without looking at me. "Good race today."

In a rare moment of genius, I found a good answer. "I thought you said it wasn't that impressive."

His smile was veiled in the moonlight. "It wasn't bad."

"Your race was good, too," I said.

"You watched it, did you?"

I flushed, caught out. The silence stretched out. I wished I had a drink again. I needed something to do with my hands.

Finally, Jacob chuckled and turned toward me. "You've never done this with a guy before, have you?"

Grateful for the darkness, I shook my head. "Not really."

"Not really," Jacob repeated. He moved closer and suddenly his fingers were trailing up my arm.

"Never," I corrected, forcing the word out over a dry throat.

"Never." Jacob repeated my words again. His fingers traveled farther up my arm, leaving prickles of electricity everywhere they touched. They slid up to my neck as he stepped closer. Two more inches and his body would be pressed against mine. I couldn't breathe. Every bit of my body felt like it was on fire.

"Let me get this straight," Jacob murmured, his lips twitching at his choice of words. "You've never had a guy do—this." He leaned forward and brought his lips to my neck, a brush of warmth against sensitive skin.

I shook my head unsteadily. He shifted closer. "Or this," he said, and pressed another kiss to my jaw. I shook my head again. My brain had completely shut off by that point, and my mouth was paper dry. It was taking every scrap of willpower not to pull him closer, or push him away.

He leaned back again and tilted his head, looking at me.

"Well?" he said.

"Well, what?" I asked, hating the way my voice cracked.

He grinned and leaned forward, and then suddenly his whole body was pressed up against mine. I could feel the hard planes of his chest, and the hardness farther down, pressing against me. Honestly, the feel of it made me seriously consider fleeing. This was madness—absolute fucking madness.

"Impress me," he murmured, sliding both hands around my neck.

His mouth was inches from mine. It should've been nothing to close the gap, but instead it took every ounce of courage I had. It was the first time I'd ever kissed anyone, and I didn't have the guts to do anything but brush my lips once over his. Still, it was devastating. Life-altering. I kissed him again—I couldn't help myself—and this time his hands slid into my hair and pulled me closer. The first sweep of his tongue against mine was like a hot brand pressed to my spine. He pressed himself against me, his hips moving against mine, and within ten minutes of his hands and lips and tongue, my breathing had gone ragged. I was—close. Embarrassingly close. And by the little chuckle Jacob gave as he pulled away, I think he knew it.

"It's alright," he drawled. "I'll give you a free pass this time. Next time, though . . . next time, I'll set the bar a little higher."

Then he slid his arm around my waist, pulled me tight against him, and kissed me so hard I saw stars.

5
Race Day

I DON'T USUALLY GET SCARED BEFORE A RACE. THERE'S always a sense of anticipation, always some nerves, but never all-out fear. But today, as I wait for the lights to go out, I'm icy with it.

Jacob survived the night. Survived the second surgery. My doctor friend from the stairwell, Dr. Ines Martin, told me that just before I left the hospital. I should've been more relieved, but her eyes were worried and her voice was cautious, warning me not to get hopeful. It's still bad, she said. Still very bad.

I tried to get in to see him around six a.m., family be damned, only to be told politely but firmly by a ward clerk that the nurses were doing their morning rounds, and no one, not even family, was allowed in.

Now, I'm going two hundred miles an hour down the straight at Circuit Paul Ricard, and it's a good thing I've driven this track before, because my brain sure as hell isn't telling my body what to do.

I tortured myself all night on my cell phone, reading every article I could on the crash, but they all said the same thing, so I started stalking Jacob's friends on Instagram instead. His clos-est friends said nothing, except some who'd known Parrot and posted photos of him. Some of Jacob's more distant acquaintances posted long, narcissistic posts about how devastated they were. His ex-girlfriend, a model, posted a photo of the two of them on a beach together, arms wrapped around each other, with the caption "You never know what you've got until you might lose it."

It got two thousand likes and about three hundred comments. A news site even reposted it with the caption "Nichols' girlfriend mourns as F2 driver remains in ICU."

Girlfriend. The whole world thinks she's his fucking *girlfriend*. She and Jacob dated for about three months, nearly two years ago. But now everyone thinks she's his goddamn girlfriend.

In desperation, I even tracked down his friend Nate's e-mail address and sent him a message asking if he'd heard anything. He answered within a half hour—Sorry man, nothing yet. He prob-ably thought it was weird I'd even asked. None of his friends know about him. About us.

My car barrels around turn one and an image flashes in my mind, Costa's and Jacob's cars smashing into Parrot's. We held a minute of silence for Parrot before this race. His younger sister and his father were there, and the two of them cried silently through the whole thing. In a horrible, despicable way, I was jealous of them. At least they got to show their grief.

Meanwhile, all morning, people asked me what I thought of the crash, and I had to pretend to feel nothing. Or at least, to feel no more than any other driver who hadn't known the racers well. Matty, my teammate, was one of the first to find me.

"Did you get my texts, man?" he asked, the minute I saw him. His expression was unusually grave. "It's so fucked up. I know all those guys."

"Nichols and Costa might still be fine," one of Harper's engineers chimed in.

Matty's face was grim. "Even if they pull through, though, there's no way they come out of it without some kind of brain injury. At those speeds?" He shook his head. "No way."

It's stupid, I know, but until that moment I hadn't thought about brain injuries. Something must've shown in my face, because Matty frowned at me. "You alright, man? You look like shit."

"M'fine," I muttered.

But I'm not fine. I'm not even close to fine, and I'm definitely not safe to be racing right now. The g-forces in F1 cars are always intense, but I'm so exhausted right now that my vision is going spotty in the corners, and my head feels like it's clamped in a vise. I'm driving so poorly that my race engineer is asking if something's gone wrong with the car. I pick up my pace automatically, but I've already been overtaken by two cars, and there's a third coming up close behind me.

Brain injuries. It's all I can think about. It's what Parrot died from. That isn't public knowledge, but I overheard the track medics talking about it earlier. They weren't gossiping, just talking about it in these low, hollow tones, like they'd never seen anything so awful.

Fifty-two laps later, I cross the line in tenth place. It's my worst finish this season, and I'm grateful for a reason to look pissy and miserable as I step out of the car. I disappear into my trailer for a few minutes, but there's no escaping my obligations. I've got a press conference to do, and I just know all the damn questions they're going to ask.

There are only five of us being interviewed—Mahoney and Clayton from Crosswire Racing, Josh Fry from Torrent, me, and Matty, who wound up finishing third from P7. The reporters settle in front of us in unusual silence. No one feels like celebrating today.

"Alright, first question from Sky1," someone says. A beleaguered-looking reporter with gray hair stands up. I think his name's Pat.

"Tough race out there today," he says. "Tough race. Obviously it's hard to be out there today, after yesterday. Talk us through your feelings coming into today."

Talk us through your feelings.

Well, Pat, my boyfriend's lying unconscious in a hospital right now, possibly dying as we speak, and I'm not allowed to set foot inside his room. I haven't slept in almost thirty hours and if someone asks me a single question about it, if someone so much as says his name out loud, I might break down right here and now.

Eric Clayton answers for all of us. "Yeah, it's not easy. No one wants to be here right now. I'm sure none of you want to be here. But we have to be, so we are. It's definitely not easy, but yeah. I think we were all racing for Ellis today."

"Josh, you knew Ellis Parrot quite well," the reporter says. "How are you holding up?"

Josh scrubs a hand over his head. He looks almost as bad as I feel. "Yeah, I knew him from F2. It's definitely hard."

"You raced with Nichols quite a bit, too, didn't you?"

My heart twists. I know he doesn't mean it the way I'm hearing it, but the way he says it makes it sound like Jacob's already dead.

Josh nods, and the reporter continues, "Have you heard any news about him or Antony Costa?"

"I spoke with Jacob's brother this morning," Josh says, and my head swivels toward him so fast, I get dizzy. "They can't give out much information, obviously, but . . . yeah. It's not good. It's a really tough time for all of us. And I haven't heard anything about Antony, unfortunately."

Matty is giving me an odd look. He leans toward me with his hand over his mic, like he's going to ask me something, but another reporter interrupts.

"Travis, I have to ask—starting from P4 and ending up in tenth, your worst finish this season. Do you think yesterday's crash was playing at all on your mind? Did you know Ellis Parrot well?"

All eyes move toward me, and I hear myself answer as though from far away. "No, I don't really know any of them."

Matty frowns at me, but luckily the reporter moves on to him, leaving me to feel disgusted with myself. I should've said I knew them, I realize belatedly. Then I'd have an excuse to go back to the hospital. I should've *said* I was going to visit them, that way no one would be surprised when I showed up. But no, instead I sat there on television and said I don't know the only person in the world who means anything to me. The only person I've ever loved.

Not that he'll ever know I loved him. I've wanted to tell him for months now—I've felt it for even longer—but I kept chickening out. I had a hundred opportunities. A hundred chances. Now, even if he wakes up, he might not be in any fit state to understand me. God, why did Matty have to mention brain injuries?

Matty grabs my elbow on the way back to our trailer after the press conference.

"Yo, Keeping, are you okay?" He punches me hard on the arm when I weasel out of his grip. "Seriously, man, you look like hell and you raced like shit. Do you need to see the team doctor or something?"

"I'm fine," I say. "Slept like shit, that's all."

Matty grimaces. "Yeah, I know what you mean. It's so fucked up. Ellis was a really good guy."

I grunt in acknowledgment and then escape into my room. I pull on my street clothes without bothering to shower. I catch a glimpse of myself in the mirror and see that, yes, Matty is right. I look appalling. The dark circles under my eyes are almost violet, but more than that, I look like I've aged ten years overnight.

I can't blow off our team debrief without calling attention to myself, so I trudge over to the motorhome meeting room and spend an hour reassuring the team that no, the car doesn't have any issues, and no, I'm not sick, just tired. Matty shoots me suspicious looks from across the table, frowning even deeper every time I repeat my lies. My temper starts to fray by the end of the hour, and I snap at one of my favorite engineers, Katie.

"I just had an off day, alright? I'm not allowed one fucking bad day?"

I regret the words even as I'm saying them. Forget about being unprofessional, I sound like an absolute dick. Katie raises a sharp eyebrow but mercifully doesn't call me out on it.

"I think that about wraps things up," says our chief engineer, Freddie, after shooting me a frown.

Harper's team boss, Stefan, who sat silently through the meeting, corners me afterward. He's a gruff, bearded fellow who's usually about as talkative as I am, but today he thumps me on the shoulder like we're old friends.

"It isn't easy, racing after a bad crash," he says in his thick Swedish accent. "You rest up the next two weeks."

"Yes, sir," I mumble.

"And you talk to your team like that again, I send you packing, yes?"

He's probably not kidding. "Yes, sir," I say quietly.

I escape to the parking lot, avoiding every microphone and camera and fan in sight, and then drive alone back to my hotel room.

Our hotel room.

Not that it was really ours, technically speaking. Jacob always had his own hotel room, several miles away and several hundred dollars a night cheaper, but when our race weekends overlapped, without fail, he'd show up past dark with a duffel bag and a smile, and we'd spend the nights together.

It takes me a few minutes to work up the nerve to go inside the room. I wouldn't have come back at all, except I can't exactly leave all my things here. I can't leave all his things here.

I flash my key card over the lock and step inside. I walk through the room, moving like I'm in slow motion. I thought I'd cried myself out in the locked ICU bathroom, but I'm not prepared for this at all. Housekeeping hasn't been in—I always leave the "Do Not Disturb" sign on the door—so everything is just how we left it yesterday morning. Jacob's half-empty coffee cup is on the table, with his laptop beside it. His hoodie is thrown over the back of the sofa. His toothbrush is in a cup by the sink.

I sink onto the edge of the bed, holding onto control by a single, rapidly fraying thread. With shaking hands, I pull out my phone and open up my texts from Jacob again, this time staring at the last one he sent me. It's from early Friday morning, right after he flew in.

> Just landed. Headed to track now, soo tired lol. Pizza tn?

Pizza was definitely not on the list of approved foods for my strict diet, but whenever I pointed that out, Jacob would grin and say we'd work off the calories afterward. We didn't, though. Not Friday night. He was totally beat from traveling, and I'd strained my shoulder a bit during free practice. Our last night together, and we spent it watching old MotoGP videos on YouTube and eating takeout.

I don't even remember if I kissed him before we fell asleep.

I don't remember the last thing he said to me the next morning.

I've been racking my brain since the accident, but I still can't remember. I know I made him coffee, and I remember asking him where he and his parents were planning to go to dinner that night, but I don't remember what he said before he left. I was so focused on working up the nerve to tell him I loved him, I wasn't listening to the last thing he said to me.

The lump in my throat is a vicious thing, and if I'm going to break down again, I should do it now, in private. But even as the thought pops into my mind, someone raps on the door.

I freeze, hoping they'll go away, but whoever's out there knocks again.

"Yo, Keeping!" Matty hollers.

I bite down so hard on the inside of my cheek that I taste blood, and then force myself to go to the door.

"What?" I say unhelpfully.

"You left your ID at the track," Matty says, holding it out to me. I take it from him with a muttered "Thanks." Matty studies me— really looks at me—and my stomach turns over. "What the fuck is wrong, man?" he asks. He tries to step inside, but I move to the side, blocking him. The last thing I need is for him to see Jacob's things everywhere.

"I told you, it's nothing," I snap. Then, almost immediately, I realize my mistake and backtrack. "I just have a brutal migraine, that's all. Need to lie down," I add pointedly.

"Ah shit," Matty says, frowning. "I didn't know you get migraines. My sister gets wicked ones. I think she takes Imitrex for 'em. You have any of that shit around?"

Of course Matty would have a sister with migraines. "Yeah, I've got something," I lie. "Really gotta lie down, though."

"Right, of course. You need me to get anything for you?"

The offer sounds genuine, and for a moment I feel awful. I've been brushing Matty off since I joined Harper, but that's never stopped him from being nice to me, or texting me, or generally being a good person. Even in the last few months, with some of the media running snarky stories about how much I'm out-performing him, he's never once been anything but pleasant to me.

"I'm good, but thanks, man." I try to close the door in his face before I can do something stupid, like burst into tears, but he catches it just before it closes.

"Did you hear the good news, though?" he asks. "Antony Costa's conscious again. Totally fucked up his legs, but he's completely with it. The doctors think he'll turn out okay."

"That's great," I croak.

"Yeah. Doubt he'll be racing anytime soon, but at least he's going to make it."

I nod twice, blinking quickly. "No word about Jacob?"

I'm such a mess, I forget to call him Nichols. I don't think Matty notices.

"No, nothing. Still critical, that's all it says online."

"Right."

"Anyway, I'll let you crash. You text me if you need anything, yeah?"

"Yeah," I say, already closing the door.

I wait until I hear the telltale ding of the hotel elevator, then I curl up on Jacob's side of the bed, hug his favorite hoodie into my chest, and cry like I'm a fucking toddler.

6

Fireside

AFTER THAT FIRST NIGHT, IN JACOB'S HOTEL, I WASN'T SURE I'd ever hear from him again. His alarm had gone off at five a.m., and he'd groaned and reached over me to turn it off, cursing strong liquor and early flights.

"I bet they never make you fancy F1 drivers take the red-eye," he grumbled.

"Isn't a red-eye an overnight flight?" I asked groggily, still half asleep.

"You might be right," he said. Then, without warning, he crawled over me and kissed me hard. "So clever," he murmured against my lips. His hands were sliding around my neck, his weight settling against me, and suddenly I wasn't tired at all anymore. He chuckled as my hands moved down his back.

"No time, Keeping," he said. "No time."

He hopped off me, laughing at whatever he saw in my face, and then disappeared into the shower. I sat up, feeling turned on but also awkward. I'd never been in a situation like this before, and I wasn't sure what the etiquette was. Was he expecting me to leave while he showered? Or was he expecting me to follow him in?

While this idea worked its way through my body, the shower turned off and Jacob reemerged with wet hair and skin and a towel wrapped around his waist. He rummaged through his suitcase, pulling out a T-shirt and jeans and cursing as he stubbed his toe on the bed.

My eyes caught on the hotel room coffee machine. I bit my lip. "Do you want me to make you a coffee?"

He blinked at me, like he was surprised, and then grinned. "Definitely."

It felt much better to have something to do, so I busied myself making him coffee while he dressed and packed. When that was done, I made the bed—just because it always stressed me out, leaving a bed unmade. When I finished, Jacob was watching me.

"You know a housekeeper is just going to strip that," he commented.

I flushed. "I know."

Two seconds later, he was in my arms again, kissing me so hard my lips felt bruised when he pulled away. "You are such a fucking weirdo," he said, and pushed me backward onto the bed.

"I thought you said there wasn't time," I said on a dry throat.

"No time for you to fuck me again, no," he said. "Maybe just enough time for me to suck you off."

He pulled my boxers off as he said it, and before my brain could process his words, his mouth was on me. A strangled noise slipped out of my lips. He'd touched me last night, and let me fuck him, but he hadn't used his mouth. It was all tight, wet heat and pressure, and when I hit the back of his throat, my whole body pulsed, and a strangled noise slipped from my lips. He withdrew with a chuckle.

"You are too easy," he said, his voice dry and slightly smug.

I rose up on my elbows, my blood throbbing hard at the sight of him kneeling fully clothed on the floor, his hands on my thighs and his mouth just above me. He seemed to be waiting for some sort of response to his words, but all I could manage was "Yeah."

His grin widened, then he leaned forward and took me in his mouth again, a steady, rhythmic slide. I dug my fingers into the bedsheets, resisting the urge to grip his hair. My whole body felt like it was on fire. It was taking every ounce of strength I had not to move my hips, but after a few moments, he pulled back again abruptly.

"Well, go on, then," he said, looking up at me with those blown-out pupils and that crooked, confident smile.

It was a challenge, and not one I was sure I was equal to. But I'd be damned if I could've done anything but thread my fingers into his hair and thrust into his mouth, trying to be as gentle as I could. He moaned around me and that was all it took.

"Fuck," was all I was capable of saying when it was over. "*Fuck*."

He grinned again, watching me. I was about to offer to reciprocate—I'd never done it before, but the mechanics didn't seem overly complicated—but before I could speak, he was on his feet saying, "Christ, now I'm *really* going to be late."

He brushed his teeth and finished throwing clothes in his suitcase while I tried to remember how to breathe again. As he pulled his baseball cap on, I heard myself say, "Will I see you again?"

I sounded pathetic, and I knew it. Jacob laughed. "'Course you will. We both have a race in September. That's, what, four weeks away?"

My disappointment must've shown on my face, because he cackled. "You're too much fun. Tell you what—I'm going to this cabin in Harris next week with some friends. I might be persuaded to stay a few days extra if you happened to show up after they left."

"Harris?" I asked.

"It's an island in Scotland. I can text you the details." His phone buzzed impatiently, someone calling him. "I've got to run." He brought his hand to my jaw and leaned forward, but just as his lips were about to touch mine, he stopped and pulled back with a grin. He grabbed the coffee I'd made him and headed for the door. "See you."

A WEEK LATER, I drove a battered old rental car along a dirt road in Scotland, hunting for the cabin that Jacob had described in his text as "really fucking hard to find." His friends had left the day before, and the whole flight from Glasgow to Stornoway I'd worried I'd made a huge mistake. It was the F1 summer holidays—no press, no obligations for an entire month—and I usually spent it at my house in London, walking dogs from the animal shelter up the street and doing some extra training. When I'd booked the flight to Scotland, my heart had been going about one-eighty. I couldn't believe I was committing to seeing Jacob again. I was afraid of what would happen if it got out, but even more than that, I was afraid of spending a prolonged stretch of time with him.

My whole life, I'd been sort of a loner. It's a strange thing to say, because looking from the outside, I'm sure it didn't seem that way. Racing is not a solitary sport, and I was constantly surrounded by people. There was my awful trainer, Brian; my manager, Aaron, who managed my contracts and sponsorships; all the mechanics and engineers and social media managers and press people at Harper, not to mention the constant presence of fans, many of whom had no qualms about throwing an arm around me in the paddock and pushing a camera into my face. But I didn't have much in the way of friends. I was burned a few times in my early racing years, friendly chitchat with people around track turning into pushy requests for free race tickets or publicity appearances—or, in one particularly irritating case, a bald-faced request for money. I grew to be more cautious, and in doing so, created a layer of distance between myself and the people around me. And maybe it sounds a bit sad, but if I'm being honest, I never really felt like I missed out. As long as I could race, I had everything I needed.

Still, when I finally pulled into the driveway of the cabin Jacob had rented, I was uncomfortably aware of my own isolation. I wished I knew what to expect, if we were supposed to spend all our time together, or go out together, or what.

The cabin was large and rustic-looking, nestled in the foothills of a mountain and completely isolated from any other buildings. It was late afternoon when I arrived, and the crisp, cool air smelled like burning wood. I could hear a fire crackling somewhere behind the house, and Jacob emerged from the side of the building wearing jeans, sneakers, a gray sweater, and a flannel jacket. His face split into a grin when he saw me, and I think right there and then he had me for good.

"You found it," he said, smiling at me from twenty feet away. "Throw your things inside and come around back, I've got a fire going."

Inside, the cabin was old-fashioned but inviting, with plaid blankets thrown over squashy couches, thick rugs underfoot, and about a million potted plants. I put my bag by the kitchen table, taking note of the half-empty bottles of liquor on the countertop. There was a deck of playing cards strewn over the coffee table and a dartboard that looked well used. Jacob and his friends must've spent the whole week partying.

In the back of the house, there was a fire roaring in a huge fire pit. The sunlight was bleeding away rapidly and fireflies were zipping around, drawing little lines of light in the night sky.

Jacob had a beer in hand and was poking at the fire with a stick, I think for no other reason than to make little bursts of sparks jump into the air. He glanced over his shoulder as I stepped out of the house, and I saw the corner of his smile.

"I'll admit it, you've impressed me again," he said. "I didn't think you'd show."

My cheeks were red as I stepped closer to the fire. "Yeah, well," I said, because apparently that was the best I could come up with. I bit my lip and tried again. "Did you have a good week with your friends?"

He grinned, like he knew how much effort it took me to get the question out. "Yeah, this place is awesome. There's a beach a little ways up the road and some crazy hikes up the mountain. We can do some of them while you're here, if you want."

A little spark of excitement leapt inside my chest. "Yeah," I said. "I'd like that."

He watched me for a second and then laughed and shook me by the arm. "Relax, Keeping. This is going to be fun."

I cleared my throat. "Right. Sorry."

"It's okay," he said, grinning. "I think it's cute, how weird you are. You want a beer or something? There's stuff in that cooler."

I grabbed a soda, and he settled into a chair by the fire, motioning absently for me to do the same. We talked about racing for a while—he must've known it was the easiest thing for me to talk about—then he asked what my summer plans were.

I shrugged. "Nothing really. Training."

He laughed. "Doesn't that defeat the very purpose of a break? Don't you have plans with family or anything?"

"No." I hesitated, then added, "I don't really have any family."

He frowned. "What about your parents?"

"My mom died of leukemia when I was a baby," I said. "And my dad had a heart attack a few years back."

He winced. "Shit, I remember reading something about that. Sorry. That was before you started F1, wasn't it?"

"Mm. A few months before."

"Fuck. That sucks. I'm really sorry."

"It's fine," I said automatically. Then, when he made a doubtful face, "I mean, it sucked, yeah. I miss him." I fiddled with my soda can for a moment. "I don't know. It happens."

He tilted his head. "What'd you mean?"

"I don't know." I shrugged. "Plenty of people have lost a parent, right?"

Something in his face changed, then, and I felt a rush of nerves, certain I'd said the wrong thing. But it was true, wasn't it? Most people lose their parents in their lifetime. It's not like what happened to me was unique. It's what I told myself after my dad died. It was natural to be sad, natural to miss him, but throwing myself a pity party wouldn't do anything to change it.

"What about your grandparents?" Jacob asked, after a moment.

I shook my head. All four of them had died during my childhood, when I was too young to understand death, or be upset by it.

"I have an uncle," I offered. "My father's younger brother. He hung around for a few weeks after my dad died." I grimaced at the memory. "He's a prick."

I left it at that, because Jacob was looking at me with pity and faint alarm, and I didn't think he'd enjoy hearing about my uncle's brief but contentious struggle to get more money out of my father's will, or the restraining order I had to take out against him to put an end to it.

I cleared my throat. "What about you? Do you have a lot of family?"

He stared at me for another second before he nodded. "Yeah. Parents and grandparents and all that, and an older brother and sister."

"That's cool. Are you close with them?"

He shrugged. "Oh, you know." He took a sip of beer and added, "They put me through racing."

"Yeah, that's what my dad did for me."

Jacob hesitated. "What was he like?"

I blinked. I don't think anyone had ever asked me that before. "I don't know," I said, stupidly. I thought for a moment. "He was a good dad. He loved cars. He raced a bit when he was younger." I paused, then added, with a rueful smile, "I don't think he was very good. He always said he started too late. He was too poor growing up to do karting and stuff. But the company he started got really big in the nineties, and he put, like, all his money into my racing."

"He must've been really proud of you getting into F1."

I smiled again. "Yeah, he freaked out." I was quiet for a moment, remembering. I hadn't thought about it in a while, that day when my F1 contract was officially announced. We'd known about it for weeks before the actual press release, but my dad was kind of a nervous guy, and he was convinced that something was going to go wrong at the last minute. He said we couldn't celebrate until the official announcement, so we wouldn't jinx it. "I wish he'd lived long enough to see a few races."

"Was he sick for a while?"

"No, not at all. He just dropped dead at work. Massive heart attack."

"Fuck," Jacob said. "That really sucks."

"Yeah."

For a moment, I thought about the phone call, the one from my dad's ER doctor. I was in my apartment when she called, just getting out of the shower. The first thing she said after she introduced herself was, "Are you driving right now?" I thought it was a weird question—did she know I was a race car driver, or something?—but then I realized she was asking because she was about to tell me something horrible, and she didn't want me driving off of the road in shock.

I shook my head against the memory. There was no point reliving it. It wouldn't change anything. I stared at the fire for a few moments, casting my mind around for something else to talk about.

"The friends that were here with you," I said. "You know them from racing?"

"Mm." Jacob was quiet for a moment. Then he took another swig of beer and said, "I'm really sorry about your dad. That's really shit."

I shrugged. "It was a long time ago."

"Still."

I shifted in my chair, slightly uncomfortable under his steady, dark gray gaze. "Thanks," I said finally. "It's nice to talk about him."

It was true, and slightly surprising. I hadn't thought I wanted to talk about my dad. But I suppose no one had ever asked.

"You can talk as much as you want," Jacob said.

The firelight flickered over his skin as he spoke, and I had a sudden, overwhelming urge to reach for him. I licked my lips and took a brave stab. "Yeah," I said. "Or we could go inside."

His lips curved into a smile, and a heat stirred low in my stomach. "Or we could do that," he agreed, and rose to his feet.

IF I'M HONEST, I think I fell in love with him that week. It sounds stupid, I know. But being with Jacob . . . it was like coming alive. I had never considered myself an unhappy person, but up until that weekend, my whole life had been consumed with racing. Even when my dad was alive, all we talked about was cars, and racing, and getting into F1. And honestly, I wouldn't have had it any other way. But that weekend in Scotland, it was like a door opened, and suddenly I could see there was this whole huge world outside of motorsport.

I'd never been a chatty person, but it was easy, somehow, to talk to Jacob. We talked while we went hiking, and while we drank coffee in the mornings, and while we lay on the empty, white-sand beach a few miles away.

There were silences, too, but they never felt awkward. At the top of a mountain hike, we sat for an hour in silence, watching the sunlight shift over the island. I noticed him shivering about two minutes in, and when I shucked off my jacket and gave it to him, he smiled and shifted closer to me, and I remember thinking something like, What the hell had I been doing all this time? What had I been wasting my life with before him?

We were only supposed to stay for three days together, but on the night before we were supposed to leave, Jacob came into the bedroom where I was reading and chucked his phone down before settling in beside me.

"I told the owner we're staying a while longer," he said, shifting the bedsheets so he could slide his legs underneath them. "Unless you have somewhere else to be?"

A strange, shivery sort of warmth spread through me. "No," I said, trying to match his offhand tone. "I don't."

"Good." He shifted even closer. "I have so much more to teach you."

His hair was damp from his shower, and his shampoo smelled like sandalwood. "Oh yeah?"

"Mm. We've already done mountain climbing and selfies and hand jobs." He counted them off on his fingers. "Tomorrow we'll get you an Instagram account and teach you what YouTube is."

"I know what YouTube is," I retorted. "And I don't want an Instagram account."

"C'mon," he wheedled. "People would love it. Throw a few car pictures on there, add a shirtless pic from the beach, and voilà— you'll be drowning in followers."

"I don't want an Instagram account," I repeated. "What else've you got?"

His smile shifted. "Well, now that you mention it . . ." The subtle change in his tone made my heart beat differently. "I haven't taught you anything about blow jobs, have I?"

The words worked their way over me like a warm wave of water. "You've taught me a little," I said, as he leaned close and pressed his mouth to the soft patch of skin below my ear.

"Please." His dismissive breath shivered over my neck. "One quickie in a hotel room does not an expert make."

I put my book down and turned toward him. "I'm listening."

He grinned. "Oh, silly boy," he drawled, pushing the comforter aside. "I wasn't going to teach you by *talking*."

7

Cold

THE WEEK AFTER THE CRASH IS THE LONGEST AND DARKEST of my life.

I'm supposed to be doing a hundred different things—scheduled interviews, sponsorship appearances, meetings with the team—but instead I flesh out my migraine excuse and beg the team to give me some time off. They send the team doctor up to see me the day after the race, and I look like such shit he barely even examines me before calling up Stefan, Harper's team boss, and telling him I'll need to be off for at least a week. He gives me a bottle of sumatriptan and naproxen for my "migraine" and advises plenty of fluids and rest. I need to be ready to race again in Austria in two weeks.

The team pays for me to stay in the hotel suite an extra week, and after the doctor leaves, I fall asleep for the first time in two days and sleep for almost fourteen hours. When I wake, there's an awful, stupid moment of confusion where I forget what's happened. I stretch my hand out to Jacob's side of the bed, and when my hand hits the cold sheets, I remember all over again.

I can't bring myself to move any of his things, except his sweater, which I can't seem to let go of. I almost wear it to the hospital, but then I worry it might start smelling like a hospital instead of him. I tuck it under the sheets, put the "Do Not Disturb" sign on the door, and then go to the front desk to double-check that no one will go into my room. They look at me funny, but I don't care. I have to get back to the hospital, and if I come back and find some housekeeper's moved Jacob's coffee cup, or something, I think I might lose it.

I manage to find the right hospital parking garage this time, following the signs for USI, and as I ride up the elevator to the ninth floor, a rich-looking couple riding with me exchange a furtive look. For a second I wonder if they've recognized me, but then I catch a glimpse of myself in the elevator doors after they step out on the seventh floor. I still haven't showered—I couldn't bring myself to do it, not when I saw Jacob's shampoo sitting on the shower ledge—and I look absolutely disgusting. My hair is dirty beneath my ball cap, and my skin is pale and rough with stubble. I must smell like garbage.

There's no one in the waiting room today, and the door to the unit is open. A ward clerk is on high alert just inside the doors.

"Bonjour," she says. "Qui êtes-vous venu voir?"

"Er—Jacob Nichols?" I say, cursing my rudimentary French. Her mouth purses into a frown.

"No press," she says firmly. "No media."

"I'm not press," I say. "He's a friend." She still looks doubtful, so I force myself to add, "I'm a driver."

"Hm," she says, still frowning. "ID, s'il vous plaît?"

I dig out my driver's license and hand it over. She pulls out her own phone, and I see her type my name into a search engine. A moment later, she looks up. "Ah. You drive in Formula 1, yes? Allez-y." She waves me onward. "Room nine-two-four."

My feet slow as I approach the room. I don't know what I'll do if Jacob's family is in there. But the door is ajar and by some miracle there's absolutely no one inside. A rough noise slips out of my throat as I rush to Jacob's side.

"Hey," I choke out. "Hey, you."

I snatch up his right hand in both of mine. His fingers are limp and unmoving. Fuck, his skin is cold. And he still has that stupid breathing tube in, making that awful rhythmic noise.

"Don't die, okay?" I say, even though I know he can't hear me. "Don't you dare fucking die."

I'm desperately close to crying again, and I know I have to let go of him before someone walks in. I squeeze his hand tightly, then lean forward and press my lips to his temple.

"Don't die," I repeat in a whisper. "Promise you won't die."

The sound of footsteps in the hall outside gives me just enough time to drop his hand and step backward before a nurse walks in. He's got a pinched, arrogant sort of face, and he scowls at me straight off the bat.

"Qu'est-ce que vous avez fait?" He waves me out of the way and peers at Jacob's hand. The IV in it is bleeding around the edges. Fuck, I must've done it when I squeezed his hand.

The nurse looks at me like I'm trash and says something in rapid French. Then, to make things even worse, Jacob's brother, Paul, walks in.

"What's going on?" he demands, his sharp eyes taking in me, the nurse, the bleeding IV. "Why's his IV bleeding?"

I take another step back, wishing I could melt into the wall.

Paul's eyes narrow. "You were here yesterday, weren't you? We aren't talking to the press."

"I'm not with the press," I force out. "I'm one of the drivers."

His scowl fades a little. "Oh. Which one? Josh? Patrick? Auguste?"

Cheeks burning, I shake my head. "No, I'm—Travis? Travis Keeping?" I don't know why I say it like a question.

Paul's eyes narrow again. He doesn't watch Formula 1, I remember. He once told Jacob it was "overrated." "I don't remember hearing your name before," he says. "And I talk to my brother all the time."

There's no mistaking the suspicious tone in his voice. He must think I'm a real piece of shit, sneaking in here to get dirt on his dying brother.

"I'm . . . not in F2," I say throatily. "I'm in F1. With Harper Racing?" I clear my throat. "You can look it up."

"I will," Paul says. He whips his phone out and taps at it for a minute, then looks up again, his frown a fraction smaller. "We can't be too careful," he says, not quite an apology. "Stupid reporters have been trying to get in all weekend. And I haven't heard him mention your name before," he adds sharply.

I don't know what to say to that. I doubt he'd believe the truth, even if I blurted it out right here and now.

"What happened with his IV?" Paul asks the nurse, forgetting me for a moment. "Does it have to be changed?"

"No, I have fixed it," the nurse says in English, shooting me a dirty look. "The doctor will be here any moment."

"Good, thank you," Paul says briskly. The nurse leaves, and Paul parks himself in a chair by Jacob's side. He gives me an expectant look. "Nice of you to visit."

It's an obvious dismissal, but now that I'm here—now that I've touched Jacob's skin—there's no way in hell I'm leaving.

"Everyone's wondering how he's doing," I say, as steadily as I can. "All the other F1 drivers. I'm sure they'd all like to hear an update."

Paul opens his mouth—to disagree, I'm sure—but he's too slow. An older lady with gray hair and dress clothes, the same one I saw the first night, steps into the room.

"Ah, Monsieur Paul, bonjour," she says, holding a hand out for Paul to shake. "And who is this?"

She holds out her hand to me.

"Travis Keeping," I say, shaking it. "I'm a friend."

Paul shoots me a swift, skeptical look, but the doctor nods, unaware of the tension between us.

"Very good," she says. "I'm Dr. Kajetanowicz—Dr. K, you can call me."

"How's Jakey doing?" Paul asks. My jaw tightens in irritation. Jacob hates when Paul calls him that. He's only told him about fifty times.

"Let me take a look," Dr. K says.

She steps up to the bed and begins her exam. There's something in her manner that makes me trust her implicitly, but watching her examine Jacob is profoundly unsettling. She lifts his eyelids up and flashes a light in his pupils, listens to his heart and lungs with her stethoscope, and lifts up his hospital gown to examine some terrifying bruising all over his stomach and sides. I get my first look at the tube in his chest, stuck in between two ribs and secured with a bunch of white gauze and paper tape. She peers at the machine his breathing tube is connected to, looks at his catheter, examines his legs. The whole time, I want to step in and stop her. I want to wrap Jacob up in blankets and tell them all to leave him the hell alone.

Finally, she steps back and moves to stand at the end of his bed. She gestures for me to sit on the other side of the bed, opposite Paul, and I sink gratefully into the chair.

"As we discussed the other night," she tells Paul in her gentle accent, "Jacob has suffered an extreme traumatic injury. There are the obvious issues—his broken leg and hip, broken ribs and punctured lung. Those will heal with time. But it is the injuries we cannot see as easily that are causing the most trouble."

She moves to the side of the bed again and lifts up his gown to show us the bruises. "These bruises are not from impact, they are from internal bleeding. Jacob had a bad laceration to his spleen. The surgeons removed his spleen yesterday. He does not need it to live, though its absence will make him more vulnerable to certain infections. Down the road, he will need extra immunizations to prevent against those types of infections. He also had a deep liver laceration, which is more difficult to fix. The surgeons think they've stopped the bleeding for now, but his blood pressure is still too low, and his blood counts are not good. He will need another blood transfusion this morning."

All the color is draining from Paul's face. "Another one? But . . . didn't you say it could be bad for his lungs to give him more blood?"

Dr. K nods. "You've pinpointed the problem exactly," she says. "We need to have Jacob on this medicine"—she points to one IV bag—"to keep his blood pressure up. He needs this one"—she taps another bag—"to prevent infection, and this one to keep him sedated. Unfortunately, all of this means pushing fluid into his body. When you have a pulmonary contusion—bruising to the lungs," she adds, seeing my confusion, "fluid can leak out of the tissues and cause pulmonary edema—fluid on the lungs. Adding a transfusion on top of these three means more fluid, and more risk of respiratory failure."

"But—can't we do the transfusion tomorrow, then?" Paul asks.

Dr. K shakes her head. "Jacob's blood count today is sixty-eight. It should be around one hundred and forty. Without enough red blood cells, he can't get enough oxygen to his organs."

Paul catches my eye—he's forgotten, in his fear and grief, to be suspicious of me—and we share a helpless glance.

"We will give him a medication through his IV to help push off fluid, before and after the transfusion," Dr. K continues. "This may help protect his lungs."

She sighs heavily, her eyes on Jacob's face. This is probably an awful case for her. People in the ICU should be eighty-year-olds with cancer and heart disease and diabetes, not twenty-three-year-olds who were previously in perfect health.

"His situation remains very critical," Dr. K finishes quietly. "Do either of you have any questions for me?"

Paul hesitates, so I jump in. This may be the only chance I have to get any information.

"You said—" My voice is thin and hoarse. I clear my throat and try again. "You said one of these medicines is to keep his blood pressure up?" I wave a hand at the IV bag she pointed out.

She nods. "Yes. It's called a pressor."

"But . . ." I lick my lips. "That machine says his blood pressure is ninety-two over fifty, doesn't it?" I Googled "heart rate monitors" last night, and I know a normal blood pressure is something like one-twenty over eighty. "That's still low, isn't it?"

"It is," she confirms. "Quite low."

"So . . . can't you increase the medicine to make it better?"

Her mouth tightens. "Unfortunately, that medicine is already maxed out."

I swallow this news down. The urge to reach out and grab Jacob's hand again is almost overwhelming. "And do you think—is there a chance he has a brain injury?"

Paul flinches. Like me, I'm guessing he hadn't thought about brain injuries yet.

Dr. K considers her words carefully before speaking. "Unfortunately, we won't know until he wakes up. We did a scan of his brain when he came in, and another yesterday when his heart rate dipped, and neither showed any sign of swelling or bleeding within the brain. But we won't know for sure until he wakes up."

"You said one of these medicines is a sedative, too?" I press. "It's . . . keeping him out of it?"

She nods.

I swallow hard. "So he's not—in pain?"

As soon as the question leaves my lips, I realize it sounds too personal, too intimate, not at all the type of question an acquaintance would ask. But Dr. K's expression doesn't waver.

"There's no reason to believe he's in any pain right now, no."

She waits patiently while I frown at the bed, trying to think what else I can ask. My eyes catch on the bare skin above his casted leg, and another question slips out. "Should he have a blanket over him? He's usually—he's always cold."

Paul snaps out of his daze. "No, he isn't," he says.

It hurts so much, it takes my breath away. I'm not sure why. In the grand scheme of things, it shouldn't matter. But the way he says it, like I'm such an idiot, like he knows Jacob so much better than I do. And maybe they talk on the phone a couple times a month, but it's always Paul talking at Jacob, not the other way around. How would he know that Jacob always sleeps with two extra blankets on top of the comforter? How would he know that Jacob always brings a hoodie when he goes out, even in the middle of summer?

Dr. K's expression remains calm and pleasant. "Either way, it would be good for him to be covered up, yes. His skin is a little cold. I'll have the nurses bring some warm blankets in."

She smiles at Paul and then at me, and I don't know if I'm imagining it, but I think there's an extra twinkle in her eyes when she meets my gaze. I give her a small, grateful smile in return.

"Do you have any other questions for me?" she asks.

"What are his chances, really?" Paul asks. "Give it to me straight."

The words are harsher than his tone, and I remind myself that for all his bluster, he's probably just as scared as I am. Dr. K's smile is apologetic.

"I wish I could answer that, but I'm afraid it's not something we can put into numbers. We're doing everything we can. For now, we can only take things day by day."

Paul doesn't seem thrilled by the answer, but he nods grudgingly. "Thank you."

"Yeah, thanks," I add quietly.

"Of course." Dr. K smiles again and then slips out of the room.

Paul and I are left in awkward silence. My hand twitches. I almost reach out for Jacob's hand again before I check myself.

"That was a good question, about the brain injury," Paul says finally, surprising me. "I hadn't thought of that."

His tone is a bit hollow, and I feel a sudden wave of empathy for him. He may not be perfect, Paul, but he's here, isn't he? And he's scared of losing Jacob, just like I am.

The door slides open again and Jacob's parents step in. They both look surprised to see me.

Reluctantly, I rise to my feet. "I was just leaving."

His dad nods, already moving past me to his son, but his mother lingers.

"What was your name again, dear?" she asks.

I swallow. "Travis Keeping."

"Travis." She nods. "It's nice of you to visit again. You're a good friend."

She smiles at me, but I can hardly look at her, I'm so ashamed. Both of Jacob's parents have been nothing but supportive of him. They've poured buckets of money into his career and have flown all over the world to cheer him on at his races. But he's never, ever told them he's bisexual. The few times I asked him about it, he got irritated or changed the topic. The most he ever said was that it "wouldn't be worth the headache." And I never pressed him on it. It would have felt a bit hypocritical. After all, I never told my dad I was gay.

Now, I wish I'd pushed him a little harder.

"Thanks," I mumble. "Sorry."

I step outside the room and slide the door closed behind me. My limbs are so heavy, I think I might sink through the ground.

I'm so out of it, I take a wrong turn on my way to the waiting room. I'm looking around, trying to get my bearings, when someone calls my name.

"Travis Keeping?"

I turn. I know this man. Not his name or his face, but I know who he is. He isn't wearing a press tag, but the eager look in his eyes is so out of place here, he can only be a reporter.

"Yes," I say warily.

"Ryan Simmons, *Daily Post*." He sticks his hand out, but I just stare at him.

"I don't think press are allowed back here," I say, looking around for a nurse.

"Antony Costa's family agreed to an interview," he says. "I was just looking for the way out . . ."

He feigns looking around, and I just *know* he's looking for Jacob's room. And Antony's family may have agreed to an interview, but Jacob's family sure as hell didn't.

"I can show you the way out," I say coolly, and walk toward the waiting room without giving him time to argue.

"So, what are you doing here, then?" he says as we walk. "Visiting Nichols?"

There's absolutely no suspicion in his tone, but my stupid brain goes from zero to panic in half a second. "Costa and Nichols," I say. "Both of them. Just . . . offering support to their families, from the F1 drivers."

"Antony's family didn't mention," he says. "I did ask, if anyone had reached out—"

"I haven't been there yet," I say irritably. "I went to Nichols' room first. I'm headed to Costa's now."

"Ah." He nods. "I see."

We've reached the waiting room. I pull the door open for him expectantly.

"Well, thanks, mate," the guy says.

I close the door behind him and mutter to myself, "I'm not your mate."

But now, I think I have no choice but to go visit Antony Costa. What if the reporter comes back and asks his family about it?

I know I'm being paranoid, but I can't help it. It's like my default setting nowadays.

The ward clerk gives me his room number, 907, and I drag my feet there. I'm dreading every second of it, but when I nervously slide open the frosted glass door, I find something like a party going on inside. There are cards and balloons and about fifteen people crammed into the room. In the middle of all of it is Antony Costa, sitting up in his hospital bed looking weak but conscious.

"Travis Keeping!" A girl no older than ten squeals my name. "Pedro, look! It's Travis Keeping!"

An even younger boy spins around and gapes at me. A pretty, middle-aged woman beside him turns toward me.

"Well, hello!" she says brightly. "I recognize you from the TV. You're that Formula 1 driver!"

"Yes, ma'am," I mumble. "I was just . . . passing by. I thought I'd come visit."

"Hey, man," Antony says. He looks very surprised to see me—which makes sense, since I've spoken to him maybe once in my life—but not unhappy. His voice is hoarse but pleasant, and although he has a few IVs running fluids into him, he looks a hell of a lot healthier than Jacob.

I open my mouth, not sure what I'm going to say, but it turns out, with Antony's family, I have to say absolutely nothing. The two kids start talking rapidly about Formula 1, asking me a hundred questions without stopping for breath, Antony's father offers me some coffee, and his mother squints at me, pronounces me "Too thin!" and sends two of Antony's cousins running off to the nurse's station to bring back some of the homemade food they brought in for the staff. Before I know it, I've been pushed into a chair with a steaming cup of coffee and a plate of Brazilian truffles called brigadeiro.

"You look tired," Antony's mother chastises me. "Are you sleeping enough?"

Antony laughs. "Leave him alone, Mom."

"Nonsense," she says briskly. She waves her hand at the young girl who squealed my name when I came in. "Quinn, give him some more food."

"Shouldn't you be training or something?" Antony asks me, while Quinn eagerly piles more food onto my paper plate.

Probably I should come up with some excuse, but for some reason I can't lie to him. I think he's reminding me too much of Jacob. Instead I just shrug and say, "Should be."

Antony gives me a swift, searching look, but luckily he's distracted by his grandmother's arrival. She comes bearing more food and a vase of flowers.

"You can't have flowers up here, avó, the nurses told you that," Antony chastises her halfheartedly.

"Ah, you will be downstairs tomorrow," she says, waving him off.

"He's being moved out of the ICU," his mother says proudly, before I even have to ask. Her face sobers for a moment, and she puts a sudden, unexpected hand on my shoulder. "Did you know the boy who passed away? Ellis?"

I shake my head. "No, ma'am."

"Ah." She closes her eyes and touches a silver cross hanging from her neck. "God keep his soul. It is too awful."

"How's Jacob?" Antony asks me. "Is he okay?"

There's something in his tone, something a lot like guilt. Antony was trying to overtake Jacob when they crashed, I remember. But even I know it isn't his fault.

"He's still critical," I say.

Fear skitters over his face, but in an instant, his mother is by his side, clutching his hand. "We'll pray for that boy. It was a terrible accident. No one's fault."

"Yeah," I say quietly. "It wasn't your fault."

Antony's mom shoots me a swift, approving look. Then she strokes Antony's hair and kisses his forehead, and I busy myself signing autographs for the kids while Antony clears his throat a few times.

"Are you good friends with the other boy, Jacob?" Antony's mother asks me.

I open my mouth to lie, but instead part of the truth slips out. "We're friends, yeah," I mumble.

"They're really tight," Antony tells his mother. "Jacob's always talking him up."

It's probably the nicest thing I've heard since the crash. A lump forms in my throat, sudden and painful. Antony's mother makes it ten times worse by swooping in to give me a tight hug.

"Poor darling," she says. "You need anything, you come to us, yes?"

She holds my face between her palms until I nod. "Yes, ma'am."

"Good." She nods. "Now come with me, help me get the rest of the food out of the car."

"Mom," Antony protests. "He's got things to do, don't make him help."

But I don't mind. I follow Antony's mother out through the waiting room and into the elevator, and the whole time she talks nonstop about how she's always been terrified something like this would happen, and how awful it must be for Ellis Parrot's parents. It should be hard to hear, but the whole time she has her arm wrapped tightly around mine, and it's like she's holding me together, holding me up.

"That other boy is going to be okay, too," she tells me, as we get back onto the elevator with our arms full of Tupperware. "I just know it."

Then she starts talking about Brazilian desserts, and how have I never tried them before, and what on earth have I been eating instead? She doesn't seem to expect an answer, as if she knows it's just the rhythm of her voice that's helping me. She holds on to my arm again, and I hold on to her hopeful words. When we get back to the room, she releases me and swoops in to give Antony a hug.

"I love you," she says firmly, kissing his cheek.

Antony looks slightly embarrassed, but he hugs her back just as tightly. "Yeah, yeah," he says. "Love you, too."

Hearing the words physically hurts, like someone's clamped a vise around my chest. Antony's family tries to offer me more food, but I back away from them, my voice growing thin. "No, sorry, I have to go now, really."

"You come back again soon, yes?" Mrs. Costa says.

"Promise?" Antony's little cousin, Pedro, adds.

"Yes," I croak. "I promise."

I escape to the staff bathroom again, but this time, although my throat is aching terribly, the tears won't come. I grip the edge of the sink and take shallow, unsteady breaths. Mrs. Costa's words are spinning through my mind.

I love you, I love you, I love you.

8
Sorry?

I TOLD JACOB I LOVED HIM ONCE BEFORE, BUT IT DIDN'T count.

We'd been together for about four months, and I was still amazed at how easy it was to be with him. I didn't have to pretend to be chatty or funny or clever. For whatever reason, he found me interesting just the way I was. He told me that all the time, always prompted by the most random things, like when he saw the way I arranged Nespresso pods (in a spiral on the center of my kitchen table—don't ask why, I just liked the way it felt taking one after another, watching the spiral grow smaller), or when he found out I donated two thousand dollars a month to the animal shelter down the street from my house.

"It's not a big deal," I said that day, scrubbing a hand over my head and turning to the sink to wash out my coffee mug. "They need money for food and stuff."

It was the middle of the week, and he was staying at my house between race weekends. He claimed it was because some of his friends were in London, but it had been two days and he had yet to go out to see them.

He breathed out a laugh. "Stop being so fucking brilliant, will you?"

He came up behind me as he said it and wrapped his arms around my chest. He pressed his mouth to the back of my neck, and even after four months together, that single, casual touch made my pulse change.

"It's really not a big deal," I repeated, embarrassed.

I'd always felt sort of weird about money. My father's business had made him reasonably wealthy, but he'd grown up poor and had strong opinions about people who spent money wastefully. He left me a good chunk of money when he died, but I put it in a separate bank account without touching it. It would have felt too weird to spend it, like I was profiting off his death, or something. I didn't really need it, anyway, since I started F1 the year he died. My contract with Torrent was pretty big—my manager got a bidding war going between them and a few other teams—and after my first year in F1, I bought my London townhouse and a vintage Porsche. After that, money just built up pointlessly in my bank account. I didn't care about fancy clothes or private planes or anything like that, and the only real traveling I did was for races, which was paid for by the team.

I was going to say something about the donations to the animal shelter being self-serving, since I liked walking the dogs there, but I was distracted by the slide of Jacob's hand down my chest, and the warm press of another kiss to the back of my neck. A second later, his teeth grazed my skin, and a pulse started up deep inside of me.

"You're going to be late," I pointed out. He was supposed to be heading out for a run with one of his friends.

I felt him shrug. "So, I'll be late."

One of his hands slid lower, his fingers deftly undoing the front of my jeans. He rose on his toes to fit his mouth over my earlobe, a weakness I never would've guessed I would have. All of five minutes later, I was panting and clutching the edge of the counter, his breath hot and heavy on the back of my neck. I came with his hands on me, and his mouth on my skin, and when I turned around to return the favor, it only took a few strokes before he was shuddering and crying out.

"*Fuck*," he breathed, dropping his forehead against my shoulder. He stayed like that for a few seconds, his chest rising and falling. Then he let out an incredulous, almost frustrated laugh. "You're so hot."

It almost sounded like a complaint, or an accusation. I'd heard the tone before, and I couldn't help associating it with an offhand comment he'd once made about how he never dated guys. "Not my thing," he said. I think what he meant was, he didn't want anyone to know he was bi. I understood that—the last thing I wanted was for anyone to find out I was gay—but I was way too into Jacob to let that stop me. And I liked being the first guy to make him break his rule.

"And you're gorgeous," I told him.

He rolled his eyes. "You're so cheesy." He laughed and batted me away when I tried to kiss him again. "I have to go change."

I watched him walk away, loving him so much I couldn't stand it. I grabbed his water bottle and filled it up for him, and all the while I was psyching myself up. I drove cars at two hundred miles an hour, for fuck's sake. I could tell Jacob that I loved him.

He came back to the kitchen dressed in his running clothes, then disappeared into the entranceway for a minute.

I snatched a quick, steadying breath. I could do this.

He reappeared with his iPhone and earphones in hand and took his water bottle from me with a grin.

"See you later."

"See you." I stared down at my hands, clenched tightly around the edge of the marble countertop. I told myself again, I could do this. I took a breath, forced down my fear, and pushed the words out. "Love you."

It was a bit of a cop out, "love you" instead of "I love you," as though dropping the "I" made it less life-changing, somehow. I looked up at Jacob, my heart in my throat, to see him pulling one earphone out of his ear.

"Sorry?"

My stomach plummeted. He hadn't heard me. I could hear the tinny music blaring out of his earphone.

"Nothing," I blurted out. "Just saying bye."

He grinned at me like I was being a weirdo. "Bye."

Then he was out the door.

I dropped my forehead to the countertop and thought, *Fuck*.

9
Allies

OVER THE NEXT SIX DAYS, JACOB GETS ANOTHER TWO BLOOD
transfusions and develops a kidney injury from poor perfusion.
My friend from the stairwell, Dr. Ines Martin, explains it like a
tap with bad water pressure. Jacob's blood pressure is too low to
push enough blood through his kidneys, and they wind up getting
starved for oxygen.

Dr. Martin's been working every night, and I've learned she's
a fourth-year internal medicine resident who reports directly to
Dr. K. She speaks decent English, and I speak broken French. Between that and Google Translate, we get by. She makes a point to
find me in the stairwell every night, usually well past midnight.
Once, she comes by around nine to tell me Jacob's family has
stepped out. It's the only time I get with him that whole day, and
while I'm in there, I make another unexpected ally.

It's the obnoxious-looking male nurse, the one who glared at
me when I messed up Jacob's IV. I want to throttle him for in-
terrupting. I barely got two seconds with Jacob before he barged
in. He's got a pile of blankets in his arms, and he waves me out
of the way to spread them over Jacob's frame. One of them gets

caught on Jacob's cast. Without thinking, I step forward to fix it. The blankets are nice and warm, even if they are made of scratchy hospital cotton. I tuck the edges carefully around Jacob's feet, and when I'm done, I look up and find the nurse staring at me.

"Sorry," I mutter, certain I've pissed him off again somehow. But instead, he just studies me a moment longer and then leaves. Two minutes later, he returns with a cup of coffee. He sets it on the bedside table next to me, without a word, and then leaves again.

From that point on, whenever Jacob's family leaves, either Dr. Martin or the nurse, Jean, come and find me. I stay in the hospital about twenty hours a day and barely get to spend a tenth of that time with Jacob, but now, at least, I'm getting a tiny stream of information, and short stretches of time when I get to sit with him and hold his hand.

I visit Antony Costa and his family a few more times, secretly enjoying his family's care and attention, but on my third visit, Antony asks me again if I shouldn't be training, and the puzzled look on his face lingers long after I lie. After that, I stay away, too frightened he'll put it together somehow.

But none of that really matters, because on the seventh day that Jacob's in hospital, Dr. Martin gives me the first scrap of good news.

"His blood pressure is very good all day," she says, an hour after she's started her night shift. She hands me a cup of tea and a granola bar with a smile. "They have turned down the pressor. Tomorrow, if it is still good, we will turn off."

After she leaves, I put my head in my hands and force myself to take several deep, steadying breaths. I don't want to get too hopeful, but for the first time, I let myself imagine him waking up. I haven't let myself think about it, not even once since the first drive here. I didn't want to jinx it. But now, for five full minutes, I imagine him sitting up in his hospital bed, pale and weary but just as conscious as Antony, smiling at me and reaching for my hand.

It keeps me going through the rest of the day, even though I don't get to see Jacob at all. His sister, Lily, has arrived, and between her, Paul, and his parents, he isn't left alone for even a minute.

I hunt down the nurse Jean around three in the afternoon. I have to meet with the team doctor at three thirty at my hotel room.

"Family is still here," he says, in his heavy accent, as I approach him by the nurse's station.

My heart sinks. "I know. I . . . have to go soon. Maybe for a whole week."

He watches me a moment. "They are looking for his laptop," he says. "They cannot find it in his things."

My blood runs cold. Of course his parents can't find his laptop. It's still sitting in my hotel room.

"I'll bring it by before I leave," I say. "You can tell them . . ." I trail off uselessly. I don't know what he should tell them.

"I will say it has turned up," Jean says with a shrug. "Some of his other items are in storage," he continues, in leading tones. "I happen to go there now."

I follow him to a small room at the end of the hall filled with a bunch of lockers. He unlocks the one labeled "924" and pulls out a big plastic bag with "JACOB NICHOLS" written on it.

"I will come back in five minutes," Jean says.

He closes the door behind him and I'm left alone with Jacob's things. His parents would've gotten all his things from his own hotel room. This must be the stuff he came to the hospital with. His racing suit is long gone, probably cut off in the back of the ambulance, but his racing shoes and gloves are here, and his wallet. He wouldn't have had that with him in his car, but someone must've thought to bring it in. The hospital might have needed his health card, or something.

I take the wallet out and turn it over in my hands. It's such a small, trivial piece of him, but I'm stupidly grateful for it. I open it up and thumb through the cards. I think Jean brought me here thinking there might be evidence of my relationship with Jacob in his things, but it's not like there will be a card in his wallet that says "Hey, Mom and Dad, I'm bisexual—oh and by the way, I'm dating Travis Keeping!" Still, there's a strange comfort in touching things that belong to him, like little bits of proof he's still alive.

His debit card, credit card, license, and health card are there, along with an international license he must've picked up on his travels. My heart twists painfully as I pull out the card behind it. It's a coffee card from the café near my house in London. Jacob went there all the time to get this massive cappuccino that he loved. He never let me go with him. He was worried that people might recognize me, or him, and wonder why we were together.

I wish I'd gone with him anyway. I regret every stupid moment that I wasn't at his side.

There's a sharp pain in the back of my throat. I swallow hard and keep flipping through cards, until my fingers reach a stack of tiny pictures shoved in a slot behind his money.

The first few are soft and creased, as though they've been in there a long time. There's a picture of him as a kid with his karting friends, a picture of him in F3 with his friend Nate, and a picture of him with a pretty blonde I recognize as his high school girlfriend.

The last three photos are newer, their laminated edges still sharp. My breathing changes as I look at them. The first is a picture from his hotel party in Austria, the first night we spent together.

Josh Fry and his girlfriend, Becca, are caught mid-laugh, and Jacob is grinning at them while I sit nearby, holding a red plastic cup. I don't even remember the picture being taken.

Next is a picture of the cabin we stayed at in Scotland, the building silhouetted in a pale purple sky, then a picture of two pairs of feet hanging over the edge of a cliff. I recognize it immediately. It's from a hike we did a couple months ago. I almost told him I loved him that day, sitting up on the edge of a mountainside. I knew he took a picture of our feet hanging over the edge. I didn't know he printed it off and kept it in his wallet.

Gritting my teeth against the awful searing pain in my throat, I take all three photos out and put them in my pocket. They're ours, and I know he wouldn't want his family to see them. Then I drop his wallet back into the plastic bag, put it back in his locker, and make my way alone out of the hospital.

I DOUBLE BACK to the hospital to give Jacob's laptop to Jean, then I return to the hotel to meet with Harper's doctor. He clears me, like I was afraid he would. I don't look as bad as I did last week, though I'm still running on about four hours of broken sleep a day. The doctor is more thorough this time, asking me question after question about my "migraine," even talking a bit about ordering an MRI. I bluff poorly through it all, and finally he frowns and gives me a prescription for something to take if I get a migraine again. I'm thinking he's a bit of an idiot—not a very nice thing to think, but like I said, running on four hours of sleep—when he pauses at the door and looks at me for a long moment.

"It isn't uncommon for drivers to get . . . overwhelmed." His gaze flicks around the room. I still haven't let housekeeping in, and the garbage is overflowing with mostly-full takeout containers, my pathetic attempts at meals from the last week. "Would you like me to make you an appointment with a psychologist?"

Will a psychologist let me stay here in France with Jacob? I want to ask.

"No, sir," I say, because I already know the answer to that question. No psychologist in their right mind is going to tell Harper that their ten-million-pound driver should skip a few races. Even if they did, there's no way the team would listen.

"Are you sure?" the doctor asks.

"I'm sure."

He frowns. "Well, if you change your mind . . ."

When he's gone, I collapse on the hotel bed, pull Jacob's sweater out from under the pillow, and breathe in the familiar smell. Fatigue is hitting hard, and with Jacob finally doing a tiny bit better, I think I might actually be able to sleep a few hours. But the moment I close my eyes, my phone buzzes with a message from Harper's travel coordinator, Connor.

> Heard the doc cleared you, great news. Booked you a flight out tonight. Sending ticket through now, Clara will send you an updated press schedule.

A minute later, an e-mail pops up with a ticket from Le Castellet, France, to Spielberg, Austria. It's only a two-hour flight away, and I suppose I should be grateful the next five races are all in Europe, but I'm not. A two-hour flight away from the hospital . . . I might as well be on a separate continent.

The flight Connor booked me leaves at seven, but the airport's only about ten minutes up the road, so I let myself sleep for two hours. I take pictures of the hotel room before I finally start packing. It's stupid, but I can't help it. If Jacob dies, I'll probably go mad staring at these pictures, trying to remember our last moments together.

I steal the coffee cup he used, too, which is idiotic, but I can't bring myself to leave it there. At the checkout desk, I tell the smiling clerk I broke a cup and to put it on my bill.

"No problem," she says brightly. "Have a great day!"

I nod stiffly, unsmiling. I drive to the airport, drop off the rental car, and find the PA the Harper team sent. I vaguely recognize her from my years on the team. Her name is Heather, I think, and she's got long dark hair and hundreds of freckles. She greets me politely but doesn't try to chitchat as she guides me to some private waiting area. She vanishes for a spell and returns with a burger and a milkshake, neither of which is on my dietary plan. Not that I'm worried about gaining weight. I've eaten maybe one full meal in the last week.

"Your trainer sent me a four-page e-mail about acceptable foods," she says, sitting down opposite me and opening a laptop. "Let's just pretend I didn't get it, shall we?" She pulls her hair back and clicks at her computer before glancing at me again and adding, "Besides, you look like you need it."

I manage a thin smile. She types rapidly while I eat, though I get the feeling she's watching to make sure I finish everything. She nods in approval when I'm done and whisks away the garbage. Someone tries to approach me as she returns—a drunk-looking jackass in a business suit who seems like he has every intention of sitting down and talking to me—and she waves him away while speaking in very loud, rapid Spanish. The guy looks utterly flustered and retreats. I find myself giving her the smallest smile. I wonder if this is what it feels like to have an older sister.

The airplane is small and barely half full. Heather and I sit in the front, with her in the aisle seat to scare off anyone who might approach me. As the plane lifts into the sky, I put on headphones and close my eyes, but no matter how hard I try, sleep doesn't come for me.

10

Insomnia

JACOB WAS NEVER A GOOD SLEEPER UNTIL HE STARTED sleeping with me.

The first time he told me that, I tucked the fact away like a treasure, iron-clad proof that he was meant to be with me. We'd been together for something like six months, stealing days in London here and there and spending nights together on over-lapping race weekends. It was early December, and the F1 season was about to end. I'd managed another three wins since Austria, but then had a spell of bad luck with engine trouble and poorly timed safety cars, and Mahoney had won the championship two races ago. The lowest I could finish was third, even if I crashed out of the last race. No one else was close enough in points to get past me.

"Next year," Jacob told me, the night before the last race of the season. "I can feel it."

"Yeah, maybe."

Secretly, I was thrilled by his belief in me, but I was just barely cool enough to hide it. I pulled off my shirt and crawled into bed, fighting a yawn. "You staying tonight?"

Sitting on top of the covers beside me, Jacob glanced at the clock. It was only ten p.m., but I always tried to get to sleep early before races. Plus, we were in Abu Dhabi, and my internal clock was completely messed up.

"Mm, sure," Jacob said finally, standing to pull off his own jeans and shirt. "I always sleep better with you."

My heart stilled for just a moment. I had to force myself to match his casual tone. "You sleep like the dead. I don't think I can take any credit."

"I'm actually a total insomniac." Jacob crawled under the covers and slid an arm around my waist. "I've lived my whole life on, like, four hours of sleep."

My arms went around him automatically. "I've seen you sleep twelve hours before."

"Mm." He pushed his head into the crook of my shoulder. "All you, Keeping. You're, like, Ambien for my soul."

My heart skittered foolishly in my chest. "You're ridiculous."

"Mm-hm." I felt his smile against my skin. While I lay there, trying not to grin at the ceiling, he let out a sigh. "I'm not that tired right now, though."

He said it with a grin and a subtle press of his hips.

"I should really get some sleep," I said, just to bug him.

"Sleep is for losers. Plus, I'm good luck. We've proven that."

Grinning, I shifted so I was lying on my side, facing him. "I guess I can't argue with that." The last three races I'd won, I'd spent the night with Jacob beforehand. "Plus, Brian's always saying I need to do more cardio on race weekends."

Jacob pulled a face. "Jesus, don't talk about that douchebag in bed, I'll never get hard again."

I chuckled. "Oh, I don't know about that."

I wrapped a hand around his back and pulled him closer, capturing his mouth in a rough kiss. Jacob was the only person I'd ever slept with, but we'd been together for months, and I'd paid attention. When he was drunk, he liked to be in control, crawling into my lap and dictating his desires in rough, breathless orders. The rest of the time, he was—not *shy*, exactly, but he liked for me to take the lead.

I tangled my fingers in his hair and kissed him hard and deep, then pushed his arms up over his head, pressing his palms into the mattress.

"Keep your hands there," I said.

He chuckled. "Bossy jackass."

I shifted back so I could pull off his boxers and then knelt for a moment at the foot of the bed, admiring the picture he made stretched out on the sheets. Featherlight, I traced my fingertips up his legs, earning a soft hitch of breath when I reached the sensitive skin on the insides of his thighs. I crawled forward and settled my weight on his hips, continuing the slow, gentle trace of fingertips over his chest and neck and jaw, then brushing one thumb over his lower lip. I kissed him once, soft and open-mouthed, then traced my mouth down the same path my fingertips had taken.

I could feel the steady thud of his pulse under my lips, and when I finally put my mouth on him, he made a soft noise at the back of his throat. I moved slowly, without any intentional rhythm, enjoying the building tension in his frame, the quickening breath and increasingly impatient squirms. I stepped away for a moment to rummage through my bag, returning with slick fingers that set him shifting even more helplessly against me.

After a few minutes under my mouth and fingers, there was an urgency building in the rhythm.

"Travis," he panted, and I pulled back obediently. A shiver ran through me when I saw he still hadn't moved his arms from over his head, and I had to bite sharply into my cheek to refocus myself.

He groaned when I pushed inside, his back arching, his fingers grasping at the sheets. My eyes were on his face; his were on my shoulders, my chest, my abs. It was the one tiny thing that always felt strange to me—he never quite made eye contact when I fucked him. It was as though it was too intimate for him, like I might look into his blown-out gray eyes and see too much.

Regardless, it had been over two weeks since I'd been with him, and with every tight, hot thrust I was hurtling closer to the end. I shifted positions so I could hit that sensitive spot inside him every time, and he started panting, a sure sign he was about to fall apart.

He came about a second before I did, crying out and clutching at the sheets. The sight of him pushed me over the edge—I came deep inside him, gripping him tight as the last aftershocks ran through me. For a few seconds, it was very quiet, the only noise the thump of my pulse in my ears and the rough sounds of our breath.

Jacob was always odd during those moments immediately after, too. He was quick to shift beneath me and slip away to the bathroom. But he would always emerge with a crooked smile and chuck a roll of toilet paper or a washcloth at me, so casual that I never bothered bringing up those few strange moments. And once we were under the sheets with the lights off, he would curl up with his chin tucked into my shoulder and his arm wrapped around me. I figured those little quirks were just normal parts of sex. I'd never had anyone fuck me before, not that I hadn't offered Jacob the chance. Probably I would feel just as shy after.

And anyway, I thought, as his breathing evened out and he drifted into a heavy sleep, he only slept well when he was with me. I was like Ambien for his soul. He'd said so himself.

11

Antony

THE WEEK LEADING UP TO THE AUSTRIAN GRAND PRIX IS A blur of press appearances and meetings. My days are booked from dawn to dusk, and in a bizarre way, the distraction is helpful. Every night when I get back to my hotel, I phone the hospital for news. The first night, I made the mistake of asking the ICU clerk how Jacob Nichols was doing. She told me coldly that no information was being given out over the phone, and that the family would release a statement to the press when it was appropriate. I didn't dare call back straightaway, in case the same clerk picked up, and spent the night worrying about Jacob and cursing my own stupidity.

The next morning, I called and asked for the nurse Jean, and by a stroke of luck was put straight through. Once he realized who I was—which took a lot of very rapid Google Translate searches on my end—he told me that Jacob's pressor had been stopped, and that his blood pressure was doing well, and that the doctor planned to do something called "spontaneous breathing trials" in the next few days, to see if he could get the breathing tube taken out.

Every day since, the news has gotten better. His blood counts have been holding steady without any more transfusions, his kidney injury has resolved, and yesterday Jean said Dr. K told his family they had "reason to be hopeful."

I cling to this notion all through free practice on Friday, and my race engineer, Freddie, slaps me on the back as I get out of the car and tells me he's glad I'm finally getting over my illness.

A lot of the press ask me about my migraine, because it's news, at least in F1, when a contender for the championship gets a headache.

"I get brutal migraines once or twice a year," I tell some reporter after practice on Friday. "It's not a big deal, this one just knocked me out a few days."

"So you're not expecting any difficulties this weekend?" the reporter asks.

"Nothing out of the ordinary."

"And tell me—" The reporter pauses mid-sentence, cocking her head to one side like she's listening to something in her earpiece. "Tell me—"

She breaks off again, her smile dropping, and murmurs into her earpiece, "You're sure?"

All around us, a strange silence is spreading through the press, and my blood turns to ice in my veins.

"Sorry," the reporter tells me. "Sorry about that. Thank you for talking with us, Travis, and good luck tomorrow."

"Thanks," I say through numb lips. The reporter has hauled out her phone and is typing rapidly, muttering "Wait for confirmation" to her cameraman. I glance around, already reaching for my phone, but before I can get it, another reporter steps up to talk to me, with a face like death warmed over.

"Travis, give us a word," he says, pushing his mic in my face. "I don't know if you've heard, but we've just learned that Antony Costa passed away about an hour ago."

It's so unexpected—so horrifying—that for a moment I'm paralyzed. I stare at the reporter, who's reminding viewers that Antony was one of five drivers involved in the Formula 2 crash in France two weeks ago.

"He was improving initially, and doctors had hoped for a full recovery, but unfortunately the family has just released a statement confirming his passing." He looks to me. "Travis, what do you make of this devastating news?"

I stare at him blankly, my mind jerking back and forth, until words spring forth from somewhere in my brain.

"It's horrible," I choke out. I remember Antony's mother, and the way she'd stroked his hair in the hospital, like he was a little kid. "It's . . . I can't imagine what his family is going through."

The reporter opens his mouth to ask another question, then seems to think better of it. "I think we'd best leave it there. Our thoughts and prayers go out to Antony Costa's family during this tragic time. Travis, thanks for speaking with us."

Dimly, I realize the other reporters are wrapping up interviews around me, the other drivers being led off by their trainers or PAs, all of them frowning, some of them shaking their heads.

"Motherfucker," my trainer, Brian, says. "That's crazy. Two deaths from one crash."

He's texting on his phone while he walks, pushing me forward with one irritating hand. I can tell he's just dying to go gossip about this with the rest of the team.

"I'm going back to my room," I snap, striding ahead of him without waiting for an answer. I weave my way through the crowds, flinching from fans who try to approach me for a selfie. I close the door to my room and sit down on the small, padded bench across from the closet. I put my head in my hands and close my eyes.

Antony is dead.

I can't believe it. I saw him days ago, and he looked so good. He was weak, sure, but he was talking and laughing and sitting up in bed to eat the food his family brought him. What the hell happened?

I rub my arms and punch the temperature up five degrees on the thermostat. It doesn't help. I'm frozen with terror. I had always thought that if Jacob woke up, that would be it. He would be safe. Antony looked so much better than Jacob, I was actually jealous of his family. A small, awful part of me had almost resented them for their good fortune. If a driver could recover that quickly, I wanted it to be Jacob.

Now, even if Jacob does wake up, he *still* might die.

I thought I'd already learned the depths of fear and grief, but now I've plummeted to some new, darker level. My insides are cold and hollow, and there's a horrible static filling my mind. I sit in my empty room, staring at nothing, and the hours tick by, one after another, until I finally fall asleep.

I WAKE UP stiff and disoriented, slumped uncomfortably on the tiny bench in my room. For a moment, I'm not sure what's woken me, then someone raps sharply on the door. Heather, the PA who flew with me from France, is standing outside. Her brown eyes widen when I pull open the door.

"Are you alright?" she asks, looking me up and down with faint alarm. "People have been looking for you all morning."

"I'm fine," I say shortly. "Where do I have to be now?"

She raises an eyebrow at my tone and then clicks her tongue. "Brian is 'sick' again"—she traces her fingers around the word—"so I'll be with you today. There's a quick bit of press to do, then they're having a ceremony and a minute of silence for Antony Costa before qualifying."

Great.

I blunder through the press, handing out stilted, one-word answers until the reporters give up and move on to more well-spoken drivers, then everyone gathers for a ceremony at the front of the grid. I pull my cap low over my eyes and speak to no one, but I'm still put in the front row, where I have an unobstructed view of Antony's racing helmet.

As a band plays his national anthem, I stare at his helmet, an inexplicable fury spreading through me. I can't stop thinking how unfair it is that he died. How pointless. If he hadn't tried to pass Jacob on that corner, if Parrot's brakes hadn't locked up, or if they'd locked up a half second later . . . it was the sum of a thousand random things, any one of which done differently could have prevented all of this from happening.

The minute of silence ends, and someone gives a speech, but all I can hear is the slow, angry thud of my pulse. I head to my car and sit in it silently while I wait for Q1 to start. I'm so angry, if anyone talks to me, if anyone even *looks* at me, I'm going to lose it. Antony's death has erased all the progress I thought Jacob was making. How can Jacob survive, if Antony couldn't?

He can't. He can't survive. Which means every moment I sit here is a moment I should be at his side.

When I go out onto the track, I feel entirely disconnected from my body, like I'm watching myself from ten feet above. I don't hear anything my engineer says over the radio. Later, I'll thank god the track was almost empty, because I'm not sure I would've had the wherewithal to avoid other cars on their out lap.

I end up in P1, somehow, at the end of it. I sit in my car in the garage, fury burning a pit in my stomach, and wait for Q2. When it starts, I go out for another lap and set a new track record. No one speaks to me as I sit in the garage again, waiting for Q3. I beat my Q2 time, setting another new track record, and end up taking pole position.

I wish I could go back to the garage, throw my helmet off, and head home, but that's not how things are done. I pull my car in front of the "1" flag and get out of the car to a roar of applause. I know my every move is being broadcast on live TV, and on every enormous screen around the track. I ignore the crowd and pull off my helmet, swallowing the urge to fling it angrily to the ground.

Someone touches my arm and points me to James Riley, the TV reporter who was there when this whole shitshow started. He's waiting for me with a camera and microphone.

"Travis, congratulations," he says. "Another pole position—your first in Austria, and your tenth, I believe, overall. How do you feel?"

"Fine," I say.

He looks surprised by my curt tone, but after a second he recovers. "Hard to celebrate after yesterday's awful news, I'm sure."

He's giving me an easy out. He must know what it's like to have a mic shoved in your face when you don't feel like talking. Still, that's not how most drivers feel after landing their tenth pole position.

"Hard to celebrate," I repeat.

"How do you feel about your chances for a win tomorrow?"

I couldn't give a shit, I think.

"Alright," I say out loud.

James hesitates, studying my face. I'm sure he has more questions to ask, but after a moment, he gives a small shake of his head and says, "Well, congratulations again and good luck tomorrow."

Mahoney from Crosswire Racing comes forward to take my place. As I walk away, I nearly collide with Josh Fry. He must've finished P3, an impressive feat in a midfield car. He doesn't look very happy about it. In fact, he looks as miserable as I feel, and I remember he was friends with Antony.

"Good drive, man," he says, offering me a thin smile.

All the anger rushes out of me as I look at his face. "Yeah, you too," I mutter. "Sorry about Antony."

He shrugs stiffly. "I guess Jacob'll be next."

I can't think of anything to say to that. James Riley beckons him forward for his own interview, and I melt away, grateful to be out of the cameras.

Somehow, I get through the press conference afterward, then Heather the PA drives me to my hotel and escorts me up to my room. I'm annoyed at her presence, until it occurs to me that she's the one who kept people away from me all day.

"Thanks," I say before she leaves, trying to inject some gratitude into the word.

Her mouth crooks into a smile. "I'll come get you tomorrow morning. Get some sleep."

It's good advice, but I don't even try to follow it. Instead, I sit on my bed and watch F2 videos on YouTube. There are some tribute videos for Ellis and Antony, and I watch all of them, even the poorly made fan videos. F2 is not as publicized as F1, so a lot of the videos use the same clips. There's one of Ellis Parrot getting a second-place trophy on the podium. Jacob's standing next to him in first place, and even though the clip only lasts about two seconds, every time I watch it my heart clenches.

Dawn arrives, and I still haven't slept. I watch the sun rise, sipping coffee from Jacob's mug, heavy-limbed and empty of emotion. When Heather arrives, she looks at the bed, my clothes, and my face, and grimaces.

"Come on," she says bracingly. "We'll get you a coffee on the way."

She hands me off to Brian at the track, who's back from his brief illness looking like someone who's been lying on a beach all day, and who raises an eyebrow at my coffee and tells me caffeine isn't good for me. Somehow, I manage not to punch him in the face.

He and I join Matty at a table in the Harper cafeteria. A murmur of whispers follows us to the table, and Matty looks up a little guiltily from his cell phone.

"Did you see this?" He slides the phone toward me. It's open to some trashy-looking news site called *The Weekly Starz*. There's a grainy picture of me leaving Hôpital Nord below the caption "Star F1 driver Travis Keeping—mourning secret lover's death?!"

My blood runs cold—I think it might actually stand still in my veins—then a sickly heat spreads over my flesh as I read the poorly written, sensationalized article claiming I was dating Antony Costa.

"It's just some garbage tabloid," Matty says. "None of the legit networks are running it. I think Stefan's already on top of it."

I scrub a hand over my face. "It's fine," I mutter.

"That's such bullshit," Brian says, pulling the phone toward him. His face creases in disgust as he reads it. "You should sue them or something, seriously."

Matty frowns at him but says nothing. When Brian gets up to get more food, I look up and find Matty watching me with an uncharacteristically thoughtful look on his face.

"Keeping," he says.

"What," I say, flatly.

"I don't want to pry—"

"Then don't."

Matty drums his fingers on the table, watching me. The silence stretches out until my palms start to prickle.

"I wasn't dating Antony Costa," I say finally.

He nods slowly. "Okay."

Just as he takes a breath to speak again, Brian reappears and pushes some noxious-looking green drink toward me.

"Let's go," he says, without looking up from his phone.

For the next hour, I'm stuck listening to Brian brag about his diet while I do some strength training. Every time I think about the article, I go cold all over. For all that Matty called it a garbage tabloid, some of it hit disturbingly close to the truth. They mentioned my poor performance in the race after the crash, called out my crappy migraine excuse the week after . . . they even had a picture of my stormy face from yesterday's moment of silence, and quoted some nurse who saw me helping Antony's mom carry food up from her car.

It's all so insane. A full year of worrying someone will find out what's been going on with me and Jacob, and now this.

About five minutes before the race, just as I'm about to get into my car, Brian grabs my arm.

"There's some French chick on the phone for you," he says, waving my cell phone at me. "Iness or something. Sounds hot."

For a moment, I stare at him blankly. My first thought is that he really shouldn't be answering my fucking phone. My second thought is that it's some reporter trying to get information after that stupid article. Then something clicks into place.

"Ines Martin?"

Brian shrugs. "Yeah, maybe."

I almost trip as I scramble out of the car and snatch the phone from him. My race engineer, Freddie, gives me an incredulous look as I sprint past him into the hallway.

"Hello?" I say. My hands are shaking, and my heart is thundering in my ears.

"Oui, Travis? C'est Ines Martin."

"Yes, hi," I say urgently. "Is everything okay?"

"I am sorry to be disturbing you, I only wanted to give you good news," she says. I press the phone harder to my ear, my pulse doubling. "Jacob's breathing tests went very well today. Dr. Kajetanowicz thinks of removing the breathing tube tonight."

"Tonight?" My voice breaks on the word. "Does that mean he might be awake tonight?"

"Keeping!" Freddie appears around the corner, giving me an impatient glare. I wave him away. The race is nothing compared to this.

"Oui, maybe," she says. "I thought you would like to know."

"Yes, thank you," I breathe. "I'll try to get there."

"Keeping!" Freddie roars.

"I've got to run, thanks," I say quickly, then hang up, chuck my phone to one of the engineers, and hop into the car about half a second before I'm waved out onto the pit lane.

For the entire formation lap, I keep breaking out into stupid, nervous laughter. I feel lightheaded with hope, almost drunk with it.

Jacob might be awake tonight.

It feels dangerous to hope, especially after Antony, but I can't help it. Ines has never given me hope before. That means it must be real.

I'm grinning as the starting lights turn on, one after another. In the second before they go out, I take a deep breath and let it out. When I see Jacob tonight, I don't want him to think I've been falling apart. I want to have something positive to tell him, something to make him smile.

A race win will do just fine.

12

Truth

AFTER THE PODIUM AND THE PRESS, HARPER'S TEAM BOSS, Stefan, calls me to his office. I'm still in my race gear, and I'm itching to get out of here and hop a plane back to France. It's only four thirty now. I figure, if I'm lucky, I can get there by nine. I should've asked Ines what time they were thinking of taking out the breathing tube. I'll have to call the hospital again after I'm done with Stefan.

I'm expecting a quick congratulations or a chat about our game plan for the rest of the year—I'm only twenty-seven points off Mahoney now, still well within championship range—but instead, after a brief greeting, Stefan slides his cell phone toward me. It's open to the same damn article that Matty showed me this morning. I'd honestly forgotten about it, after the call with Ines and the race.

I let out an impatient breath. "I don't have time for this."

Stefan frowns. "I only need to confirm that it isn't true, before we request a retraction." He shakes his head. "It is despicable, what these people will do in the wake of a tragedy."

"I wasn't dating Antony Costa," I say.

Stefan nods. "I didn't think so."

He pulls his phone back. He never believed that article, I can tell. This is just an item on his to-do list.

The next words spill out of my mouth entirely without my permission. "I am dating Jacob Nichols."

Stefan blinks, and my heart stutters to a stop.

I can't *believe* I just said that.

"Well," Stefan says. Then he clears his throat and tries again. "Well."

He stares at me for such a long time that my palms start to sweat. Somehow, I manage to hold his gaze.

"You . . . don't have migraines," he says finally.

Color rises to my face. "No, sir."

He rubs a hand over his mouth, back and forth. "I . . . need to think about this."

I swallow hard. "Yes, sir." I rise to my feet and then turn back at the door. "His doctor called earlier, from France. They think he might wake up tonight."

Stefan looks at me for a long moment, then he clears his throat again. "We'll get you a flight out."

I almost leave, only to turn back once more. Stefan raises an eyebrow expectantly. "Something else?"

"I want Brian fired," I blurt out. "Or—replaced, or whatever."

This, somehow, seems to surprise him more than anything. "Fine," he says.

"Really?"

He shrugs. "He is not well liked."

I blink. "Alright. Thanks."

He nods and watches me steadily until I mumble a goodbye and slip away.

HEATHER THE PA accompanies me back to the airport. She doesn't question our return to France and stays mercifully silent on the plane, putting in earbuds faster than I do and opening her laptop to an old episode of *The Office*.

The whole flight, I replay my conversation with Stefan. I can't believe I told him about Jacob. An awful sickness spreads through me every time I remember it. What was it that he said? *I need to think about this.*

Think about what? How to deal with the press if it ever gets out? Or . . . my future with Harper?

Fuck. *Fuck.* What have I done?

By the time we start to descend, my hands and feet are numb with nerves, and a cold sweat is prickling the back of my neck.

"I'll get you a rental car," Heather says, once we're in the terminal. "Did you bring any clothes with you at all?"

"Er . . ." I glance down at my bag, which I know for a fact only contains my laptop, Jacob's coffee cup, and his hoodie.

"Didn't think so. I'll run to the shops and get you some stuff, then I'll check us in to the hotel. I'll text you your room number."

"Thanks," I say.

Fifteen minutes later, I'm on my way to the hospital in a rental car. Siri guides me back to Hôpital Nord. As I step into the familiar lobby, my pulse quickens. I'm trying to remember the hopeful tone of Dr. Martin's voice, but being back here, all I can remember is the fear I felt two weeks ago.

God, has it really been two weeks?

The USI waiting room is empty. It's almost nine p.m., and the hospital feels unnaturally quiet. I take a moment to center myself before I press the buzzer. Beyond this door, Jacob might already be awake.

After a few minutes, a harried-looking nurse lets me in without asking any questions. Breathing quickly, I stride toward Jacob's room. I don't care if his family's there. I have to see him.

The door to his room is half open, and there's an alarming beeping sound echoing from beyond the doors. A nurse hurries out of the room, speaking rapid French over her shoulder. Heart in my throat, I rush through the doors.

Three nurses are crowded around Jacob's bed while his mother stands against the wall in the corner, her eyes wide and frightened. Jacob is moving—actually *moving on his own*—and fighting the nurses at his sides. He's trying to pull the breathing tube out, I realize, and by the frantic way the nurses are acting, he isn't supposed to do that himself.

I don't stop to think, I just push my way to his side. His eyes are open, but they're hazy and confused.

"Hey—look at me," I order, putting my hand on his cheek. "Look at me, okay?"

He twists toward the sound of my voice, and when his frightened eyes lock on mine, something shifts in my chest, something undoable, something forever.

"Stay really still for me, okay?" I say. The nurses have stopped fighting, but they're keeping a tight grip on his arms. His eyes are on my face, and he makes an awful retching sound, like he's trying to cough the tube out.

"I know," I say. "I know. Just try to stay still for me, okay? Just for a little bit."

"The doctor is here," one of the nurses says, stepping back. Dr. K walks into the room, pulling on a pair of blue gloves and wearing a calm, soothing smile.

"Ah, Monsieur Travis," she says pleasantly, nodding at me like it makes total sense that I'm here. "What have we here?"

"He's trying to pull the tube out," I say, while the nurses elaborate in French. Dr. K nods at all of us.

"Well, let's get that tube out, then, yes?" she says pleasantly.

There's a flurry of activity while the nurses gather equipment. One of them tries to gently guide me out of the way, but Dr. K shakes her head and I get to stay close, one hand on Jacob's neck, the other on his arm.

"Just a little longer," I tell him. "You're doing great."

In one swift movement, Dr. K and the nurses pull out the breathing tube. Jacob curls toward me, coughing and gagging. He grasps weakly at my cotton T-shirt, and I don't care that the room is filled with people—I curl my fingers into his hair and kiss the top of his head, every bit of me shaky with relief and fear.

"We will need to watch his levels of oxygen closely," Dr. K says. She's turned to talk to someone in the corner. Jacob's mom, I remember with a thud. I risk a glance and find her staring at me, shock and horror written over her face. A second later, the situation is made a hundred times worse by the arrival of Jacob's brother.

"What the hell is going on?" he demands, taking in the sight of the nurses, who are clearing away the plastic tubing they pulled from Jacob's throat, and me, sitting there with my arms wrapped around his little brother, my fingers curled intimately in the hair at the nape of his neck.

"Ah, Monsieur Paul," Dr. K says briskly. "As you can see, we have removed the breathing tube. Very good progress."

"What the hell is this?" Paul repeats, ignoring her. He steps closer, his eyes on me. "What the fuck do you think you're doing?"

Instinctively, I pull Jacob a little closer, as though I can shield him from Paul's anger. But before I can think of anything to say—not that I could've come up with anything, even if I had an hour—Dr. K jumps in.

"Pardon," she says briskly. "We need calm in this room, please."

"Calm?" Paul swivels toward her. "What the fuck do you mean, calm?" He throws a hand toward me and Jacob. "Mom, are you seeing this?"

Jacob's fingers tighten a little around my arm. His grip is so weak, so fragile, it calls me back to myself. I don't give a shit about Paul and his temper tantrum. I'm here for Jacob. And Dr. K, it seems, feels the same way.

"This is not helpful," she says firmly. "I will not have my patient distressed. What keeps him calm, stays. Anything else must go."

Paul's face turns a violent shade of red. "You're trying to throw *us* out?" he spits. "We're his family. Dad—get in here." He gesticulates furiously at his father, who enters the room wearing the same stunned look as his wife. "Did you know about this?" Paul demands.

I flush dark red under Jacob's father's gaze, but before he can say anything, Dr. K saves me again.

"Monsieur Nichols, I have removed your son's breathing tube," she says calmly. "This is an excellent step, but it is very dangerous if he becomes distressed. He must have calm and quiet. If your son cannot be calm, I must ask you all to leave."

"And what about *him*?" Paul points a furious finger at me.

Jacob's father's eyes flick back and forth between me and Jacob and back again. "Paul, Kim, let's just—c'mon." He drops his eyes and hurries from the room, his wife following quietly behind. Paul shoots me one last furious glare.

"We'll be requesting another doctor," he snaps at Dr. K before he storms after his parents.

Dr. K closes her eyes briefly and sighs, while two of the nurses exchange wide-eyed stares.

My face is hot with embarrassment. "Should I—"

"We must keep him very calm," Dr. K interrupts, fixing me with a level gaze. "The nurses will check a blood gas now, and we will get an X-ray of his lungs. Do you have any questions?"

"Er—no, ma'am," I mumble.

"Very good." She nods at the nurses, two of whom hurry out of the room after her. They slide the door shut behind them, leaving me alone with Jacob and the third nurse. She's about five feet tall with frizzy dark hair and a no-nonsense look on her face.

"I will take the blood gas now, oui?" She steps up to the side of the bed, wielding a terrifying-looking needle. "I am needing his wrist, please."

Reluctantly, I guide Jacob's hand away from my shirt. She takes it from me and rests his wrist on the bed. She sticks the needle deep into his skin. I hold him tighter, but he barely even flinches. She draws out some dark red blood and then neatly bandages his wrist and returns his hand politely to me. I shoot her a grateful look, and then she slips out of the room, leaving me and Jacob alone.

I let out a long breath and close my eyes, dropping my forehead to rest against Jacob's hair. His grip is loosening, and his breathing evening out. I hold him until his hand slips off my chest, then carefully lay him back on his pillow.

My heart is beating uncertainly, hope and fear battling it out in my chest. He still looks so fragile, lying there. His skin is pale, and the shadows under his eyes are a deep violet. But at the same time . . . at the same time, his breathing tube is out. I hold his hand and watch his chest rise and fall, hanging on to every small, miraculous movement.

A few minutes later, a tech comes in with a portable X-ray machine. The frizzy-haired nurse gives me a heavy lead vest to wear so I don't have to leave the room, and then pops out for a few minutes and returns with two warm blankets for Jacob and a cup of tea for me. She gives me a small, encouraging smile before she leaves. Another ally in my corner.

For the next eight hours, I sit at Jacob's side. He spends most of it asleep, but sometimes, when the nurses come to check on him, he stirs. His eyes open, cloudy and confused, but I stroke his hair and he settles, slipping back off to sleep. Sometime past midnight, he tries to talk to me, a soft, raspy noise, like a question.

"I'm here," I murmur. "It's okay."

He tries to talk again, but it comes out as a cough.

"Don't try to talk right now." I run a thumb over his cheek. "Go back to sleep."

He stares at me a few minutes more, blinking heavily, and then drifts off again.

The whole night, I wait for his family to reappear. I run it over and over in my mind, every possible attack, every possible argument. But the night passes, and no one shows up. I ask the frizzy-haired nurse, Manon, if they're in the waiting room, but she tells me there's no one out there. Part of me is grateful for it. A much larger part is furious that they can't put aside their obvious problems with me to be by Jacob's side.

As the sky starts to lighten from deep navy to pale purple, my eyelids are so heavy I can't keep them open anymore. I close my eyes for just a second. When I open them again, the room is flooded with light. I blink a few times. My head is throbbing, and there's a monstrous pain shooting up and down my neck.

"Fuck," I mutter, dropping my head and digging my fingers into the tight muscles of my neck. When I look up again, Jacob is watching me. An electric shock runs through me. His eyes are still hazy, but beneath the cloudiness, he's there.

"Fuck," I repeat. "*Jacob.*"

"Hi." His voice is barely a whisper, but the sound of it draws a tight lump to the back of my throat. I reach for him, tucking a strand of hair behind his ear. "What happened?" he rasps.

"You were in a crash," I say, my voice almost as fragile as his. "A bad one."

His gaze moves slowly around the hospital room, taking in the IVs, the heart monitor, the cast on his leg. His brow twitches, like he's having trouble processing everything. My pulse spikes in fear as I remember what Dr. K said—we wouldn't know if he had a brain injury until he woke up.

But he knows me, and he's talking to me. That's got to be something.

I tighten my grip on his hand. "How do you feel?"

Slowly, his eyes move back to my face. He licks his lips and looks around the room again. "Thirsty."

"I'll get you some water," I say hurriedly. "Hang on, okay?"

He gives me a tiny nod, and even that small movement looks like it's taking all his strength. I rise to my feet, only to lean back down and press my lips to his temple.

"Don't die on me, okay?" It's the same thing I said the first day after the crash, and I can't help repeating myself now. I need him to know how terrified I am of losing him. I need him to promise me that he won't die.

But he just stares at me, his brow knitted in faint confusion, and my heart twists painfully. Fuck, I'm so scared of how weak he is.

"I'll go get some water," I say.

"Mm," he mumbles, already half asleep.

I leave the room with my stomach in knots and hunt down his nurse. The night nurse, Manon, has already left, and it takes a few minutes to find his new nurse, an older woman with short blond hair whom I immediately dislike.

"He cannot have *water*," she says, scowling at me like I've suggested giving him poison. "He must pass his swallowing study first."

"When will that be?" I ask, as politely as I can.

Her frown deepens. "Later today," she says curtly. Then she steps around me and strides off. Too busy, I guess, to answer any more questions.

When I get back to Jacob's room, his whole family has invaded.

His mother is sitting at his side, stroking his hair, and his father is standing a few feet back from the bed. His sister, Lily, is sitting by his feet, squeezing his leg, and Paul is thumping him hard on the shoulder.

"Just trying to show off, were you?" he says, in his stupid, loud voice. "Race was getting a little boring for you, was it?"

The rational part of me knows that his obnoxious manner is his own coping mechanism, but the rest of me wants to drag him away from Jacob and beat him into the ground. Jacob looks so confused, so exhausted, and every time Paul thumps him on the shoulder, I see red.

The family turns in unison as I step into the doorway, and my heart pulses nervously in my chest. Beneath my anger, I do want these people to like me. They're Jacob's family, and he loves them.

But, like always, I can't get the right words out in time.

"What the hell do you want?" Paul snaps.

My face burns. I can't think of what to say. I look to Jacob's mother and his sister, thinking they might be more sympathetic, but Lily's risen to her feet, two angry splotches on her cheeks.

"We've been waiting to see him," she says, glaring at me like I'm a piece of trash.

"I—you could've come in," I stammer. I look to Jacob for help, but he looks so blurry and confused, his eyes moving from his family to me and back again.

"I'm sorry," I choke out—to Jacob, more than any of them. "I just thought—"

"You thought what?" Paul demands. "You just thought you'd ruin my brother's career? Turn him into a fucking laughing-stock?"

This is so unfair, I'm rendered speechless, struck dumb by the force of his hatred.

"Paul, enough." Jacob's father steps forward. He won't quite look me in the eye, but he gestures to the door. "A moment, please."

Numb with shock, I follow him out of the room. He leads me all the way out to the waiting room, which is mercifully empty. In the far corner, he gestures for me to sit down across from him. He clears his throat several times before speaking.

"I should apologize for my son's behavior," he says stiffly. "I'm sure you understand, this has been difficult."

I stare at him, though he still won't quite meet my eyes. He's got his hands clasped tightly in his lap, and he's tapping one foot against the floor. I remember Jacob telling me once that his father doesn't like confrontation. A bit of a pushover, he'd called him, though he'd backtracked quickly after he said it. When his father believed in something, he'd stand up for it, like the time some rich family tried to buy out Jacob's seat in F3 for their own son.

Unfortunately, right now it seems the thing Jacob's father believes is that I should stay the hell away from his son.

"The thing is," he says haltingly. "The thing is, this is not about Jacob . . . experimenting. I know kids your age do all sorts of wild things." His lips tighten in disapproval. "But if you keep hanging around here, acting like . . . how you've been acting, someone's going to go to the press. And all of my son's hard work, all of our sacrifices, it'll all be for nothing. This will be his entire narrative. An eccentric chapter in a Formula 1 driver's history. Not to mention all the backlash, all the bigotry he would face from the fans."

"From the fans," I repeat.

He frowns. "You're a famous guy," he says. "You've got plenty of money, plenty of options. You can find someone else."

Blood is thumping in my ears. I can't remember the last time I was this angry. Usually, when I lose my temper, I can't think of what to say, but right now, the words rise straight to my lips.

"I don't want someone else," I say, staring hard at him, trying to force him to meet my gaze. "And Jacob isn't some wild chapter in my history. We've been together for a year."

He flinches backward at that, as if from a blow.

"I'm sorry that he didn't tell you," I say through my teeth, trying to remind myself that beneath all the bullshit he's spewed, he may really believe he has Jacob's best interests at heart. "And I'm sorry that you found out like this. But I'm not going to leave him. He doesn't *want* me to leave him." I throw an impatient hand toward the door to the unit, and he flinches again, like he's remembering the way Jacob clung to me. "I don't want to mess anything up for your family, or for him. I swear I don't. But I'm not going to leave him."

My heart is beating quickly, but I sit back in my chair with a surge of satisfaction. For once in my life, I've said exactly what I wanted to say, right when I needed to say it.

Jacob's father finally looks at me. For what feels like an eternity, he stares at me with a cold expression. I wait for him to yell at me, or to admit defeat, but instead he does something that feels even worse.

Without a word, he stands up and walks away.

13

Intuitive as Hell

I LEAVE JACOB'S FAMILY ALONE FOR ALMOST TWO HOURS. I tell myself I'm being generous, giving them time alone with him, but really I just need the time to regroup. Now that I've had it out with Jacob's father, I expect Paul and Lily will be next. I'm especially frightened of Paul. Not because of what he might try to do to me—I'm in way better shape than him, and if push came to shove, he wouldn't stand a chance—but because I don't want Jacob to know we're fighting. I don't want to make him look the way he did before, when Paul and Lily were snapping at me. So panicked, so confused. Like Dr. K said, he needs calm right now.

I make my way to the hospital cafeteria and buy a coffee and one of the French granola bars Dr. Martin always brings me. I find a table hidden away in a corner and pull out my phone. There are six missed calls and two messages from Brian: Bro, Harper just fucking fired me, WTF!!!! Then, Call me now, you need to sort this shit out!!

I delete both of them, then block his number for good measure. Next is a text from Connor, Harper's travel coordinator: Stefan told me you'll be unavailable for a few days. Please call if you need anything.

Then, the last one, from Matty, who must've noticed my absence at today's team meetings: Shit man, are you sick again?

I stare at it for about ten minutes and then slowly start to type.

> Not sick. Back in France.
> Dating Jacob Nichols.

I stare at my own words for another ten minutes before I hit Send. I'm tempted to add something like *Feel free to delete me from your phone now*, but that would be too pathetic. I probably shouldn't be telling him the truth, but I'm just so sick of lying. Stefan knows. Jacob's family knows. Matty might as well know, too.

I don't expect him to answer straightaway—or at all—so I'm stunned when three dots appear. He's read it. He's typing something. The coffee I drank turns to battery acid in my stomach as I wait for the words to appear. A few seconds later, the dots disappear, and with them, my hope that Matty might react well.

But then my phone rings.

"Dude!" Matty's loud voice echoes through the phone the moment I answer it. "My girlfriend owes me fifty bucks."

"What?" I say hoarsely.

He laughs—actually *laughs*—and the knot in my chest loosens by a fraction. "Last week I bet her fifty bucks you were dating Nichols. She thought I was nuts. But I told her, I said, babe, listen to me, I'm intuitive as hell."

"Matty . . ." I start uncertainly.

"So, how's he doing?" he interrupts.

I swallow hard and try again. "Matty, look—"

"Oh, fuck off, Keeping," he says. "I don't give a shit that you're dating a guy. My older brother is gay. Which you'd know, by the way, if you ever talked to anyone on our team."

A hot feeling spreads through my stomach, something like shame.

"So?" Matty says again. "How's he doing?"

I have to swallow twice before I can get the words out. "He's . . . a little better," I manage. "They took his breathing tube out last night."

"That's awesome," Matty says. "Is his family there, too?"

"Yeah, they are."

I can actually hear Matty grimace through the phone. "Uh-oh. That doesn't sound good."

"Not good, no." I take a breath. "They . . . didn't know we were dating."

Matty whistles. "Shit. That's awkward."

"Yeah. They aren't thrilled."

"Well . . . it's probably a pretty big shock for them," Matty says. "I know my parents freaked when they found out about Eric."

I hesitate. "That's your older brother?"

"Yeah. I think my parents were mostly upset he didn't tell them sooner. Well, that and he was dating this crazy fucking cokehead at the time."

I breathe out a humorless laugh. "I think Jacob's parents would prefer a cokehead."

"Fuck off. You're a super successful F1 driver slash millionaire. What the hell else are they looking for?"

I crack the tiniest smile. "I don't know. I guess they're worried it'll get out in the press."

"Hm." Matty's silent for a moment. "I suppose that's fair. How did your parents take it?"

"They're both dead."

Another beat of silence. "Grandparents, then? Or siblings?"

I shrug, before I remember he can't see me. "Nope."

"You don't have any family?"

I open my mouth to answer, then close it again. The truth sounds stupid, even in my head. But again, Matty surprises me.

"Jacob's your family," he says, answering his own question. He lets out a low whistle. "And now he's in the hospital and his family's furious with you. What the actual fuck, Keeping? Why didn't you tell me any of this shit?"

I don't answer him. I'm not sure what I would say.

"I'm going to get my mom to call you," he says. In the background, I hear someone talking to him. "Ah, fuck, man, I've got to run. But I'll call you later, alright?"

"You don't have to—" I start, but he's already hung up. I put my phone down and stare at it for a while. I feel cold and jittery, like I've had too much coffee.

That didn't go at all like I thought it would.

I put my head in my hands and take several deep breaths. When I look up again, Paul and Lily are standing twenty feet away, holding trays of food and glaring at me. Lily says something to Paul and then they both stalk off to sit at a table far away from me.

I swallow hard and push myself to my feet. I can't stand the idea of skirting around those two for days, but I'm too exhausted to approach them right now. Their narrowed eyes follow me as I slip out of the cafeteria. I head back up to the USI, but when I press the buzzer, the same scowling nurse who snapped at me about the water opens the door. My stomach sinks.

"I'm here to see Jacob Nichols," I say.

The nurse scowls. "Only family may visit."

"I'm . . . his boyfriend," I force out.

I think the look that crosses her face will probably stay with me forever. When I worried about people finding out about me and Jacob, I'd worried about things like the media fallout, the annoying questions at press conferences, the awkward silences at work. I'd never actually thought about things like this. Blatant disgust from a total stranger.

"Only family may visit," she repeats, and then closes the door in my face.

I RETREAT TO my hotel room, struggling not to feel completely defeated. I'm not usually a quitter, but this entire day has worn me down.

When I open the door to my room, I'm enveloped by a warm, homey smell. Heather is cooking in the en suite kitchen, while her laptop plays some TV show I don't recognize. She jumps when she sees me.

"Holy shit, you scared me." She presses a floury hand to her face. "I just came up to use your kitchen. My room is about a tenth the size of yours." She waves a spoon to encompass the vast, modern-looking suite. "Let me just pop this in the oven and I'll get out of your hair."

"No problem," I say quietly. After an awkward beat, I step farther into the kitchen. Every gleaming countertop is covered in plates of food—curried chicken and rice, a lasagna, a plate of Rice Krispies squares.

"I got bored," Heather says, following my gaze. "Please, eat some of it. You look like you had a shitty twenty-four hours."

I scrub a hand over my face. "Fuck. Have we really only been here a day?"

"Mm-hm." Heather kneels down to put a tray of cookies in the oven, then briskly begins cleaning up the kitchen. "How's your boy doing?"

I freeze. *Your boy*, she said.

"Well?" she says impatiently.

I turn to the counter and pick at a Rice Krispies square, just to have something to do with my hands. "He's awake," I say quietly. "But he still looks really bad."

She pulls a face. "That sucks. Do you want a hug? I'm not really a hugger, but I could give it a shot."

My mouth twitches. "I'm fine."

"Thank god," she says. "That would've been awkward as hell."

As I fight a tiny smile, she waves me away from the counter and motions for me to sit down. She loads a plate full of food and sets it in front of me.

"Eat," she orders. "I assume you're running back to the hospital soon?"

"Not for a while, no."

She raises an eyebrow. "What does that mean?"

I take a bite of chicken. I'm not used to talking to people like this, and if I'm honest, talking about it feels a little too much like whining. Still, I actually like Heather, and Matty's words about me not talking to people are ringing in my ears. "His family doesn't want me there. And his nurse right now is definitely not okay with it."

"Fuck that bitch," Heather says vehemently. "And his family . . . well. Have they always been like that?"

"They didn't know until today."

"You told them?"

I hesitate. "Jacob sort of . . . reached for me, I guess, when they were taking his breathing tube out. They all saw."

"Hm." Heather sits down opposite me and takes a thoughtful bite of a Rice Krispies square. "That must've been hard for them."

"I guess," I say skeptically.

"Not just finding out he was dating a guy," she clarifies. "How would you have felt, if he'd woken up and reached for someone else?"

I open my mouth to argue and then shut it again. I let myself picture it—Jacob coughing out his tube, pale and scared, and then reaching out for his mother or father instead of me. Even in my imagination, I feel a pang of distress.

"Yeah, I guess," I repeat. "But his father made it pretty clear they want me away from him. He said something like, it'll be his whole narrative."

Heather pulls a face. "Well . . ."

My chest tightens. "You think he's right?"

She holds her hands up in defense. "Try to think of it from their point of view. Their son worked his ass off through karting and junior racing and F3, then he starts winning races in F2 and getting some serious interest from F1 teams—oh, don't look so surprised, I Googled him after the crash," she adds, seeing my face. "And then he gets in this huge, horrible accident, and it looks like his whole future's been derailed. There's maybe this tiny, minuscule chance he'll ever make it back to where he was, and they're clinging to that idea . . . but then, bam! They find out about you."

I look at my hands. "I don't want to wreck his career."

"Of course you don't. But think about what happens if this story breaks. The media freaks out when you have a migraine, for Christ's sake. You'd be F1's first openly gay driver, and Jacob's name would be dragged into the spotlight right along with yours."

I stab a piece of chicken with my fork. I don't want to admit it, but I'm starting to see what she means.

"That label would follow Jacob everywhere, you know it would. If he got back out racing, the news reports wouldn't say 'Jacob Nichols gets back into racing after tragic crash,' they'd say 'Travis Keeping's boyfriend returns to racing.' And an unfortunate amount of people are dicks, and they'll be ignorant and hateful. And then if he ever gets into F1, what are people going to say?"

I swallow hard. I'd never thought of that. If everyone knows we're dating . . . people might say I pulled strings for him. Never mind the fact that's not at all how F1 works. People will still whisper.

Heather sighs. "I'm just saying, it's fair that they're worried."

"Yeah." I exhale heavily. "I guess. But what am I supposed to do? He's . . . he could die." My chest spasms as the fear resurfaces. "I have to be there."

"Of course you have to be there," Heather says. "But you might want to talk to his parents again. Reassure them that you won't do anything to hurt him or his future."

"I'm not great at talking to people. I'd fuck it up."

"Maybe." Heather shrugs. "But you have to try. Plan out what you want to say to them, and then ask them to hear you out."

I nod once, then again. She makes everything seem so straightforward, somehow. "I guess I could do that."

"You can definitely do it," she corrects. "But not right now. Right now you need to shower and change and sleep a little. Seriously, you look like hell."

I crack a smile. "I can clean up the kitchen after," I offer, as she starts running water to clean the dishes.

"Nonsense," she says briskly. "Get your ass in the shower and don't come out until you've been in there half an hour. I'm sick of looking at your mangy face."

"Thanks," I say quietly.

She shoots me a tiny wink. "Don't worry about it. We're in this together now, babe."

14

I Know

WHEN I GET OUT OF THE SHOWER, HEATHER IS GONE, LEAV-ing the hotel suite spotless and a plate of oven-warm cookies on my bed, next to some flannel pajama pants and a soft gray T-shirt. It's only five, but after eating about ten cookies and downing a glass of milk, I crawl into bed and fall asleep.

I wake to the buzzing of my phone on the nightstand. I fumble for it, still half asleep, and squint at the vaguely familiar-looking number. Something clicks in my brain, and I realize it's the hospital line. It must be Dr. Martin. My heart lodges in my throat as I swipe it open.

"Hello?" I croak.

"It's me."

I sit bolt upright in bed.

"Jacob," I breathe. "Hey."

"My parents just left." His voice is still rough from lack of use, but he doesn't sound quite as hazy anymore.

"I'll be there in ten," I say.

The nasty blond nurse is nowhere to be seen when I get there. Instead, it's my surly friend Jean who lets me into the unit and offers to bring me a cup of coffee.

I pause at the threshold of Jacob's room. He's fallen asleep in the seven and a half minutes it took me to get here. The lights in his room are dimmed, and two of his IVs—the scary one in his neck and the one in his left hand—have been taken out. The tube in his chest is gone, too, and the catheter. With the cast on his leg hidden under the blankets, he's just a little paler and thinner than usual, like he's got a bad flu.

I run my fingertips over the back of his left hand, which is bandaged where the IV used to be. He stirs under my touch, blinking at me groggily.

"Hey," he mumbles.

I sit down on the edge of his bed, my chest painfully tight. "Hey, you." I take his left hand in both of mine. It's impossible not to touch him right now. "How're you feeling?"

His throat moves as he swallows. "Like shit."

"Yeah, you look like shit."

His mouth turns up, like I hoped it would. I can't stop myself anymore—I lean over and brush my mouth over his, careful and soft. His lips are dry, and his skin is still colder than I'd like, but fuck, I never thought I'd get to do that again.

I clear my throat against the lump that's forming in it. "You want me to get you another blanket?"

He shakes his head. "Just gonna close my eyes again."

"Sure thing. I'll be here."

"Mmk." He's already drifting off.

"Hey, Jacob?" I say quietly. With visible effort, he opens his eyes again. I slide my hand over his neck, stroking my thumb over the soft, sensitive skin under his ear. "I love you."

It isn't hard to say this time. I don't have to build up the nerve or push the words out. He's here with me, alive. That's all the push I need.

He stares at me for a moment, then his eyes flutter closed again. "I know," he murmurs.

"Oh yeah?" My voice comes out a little hoarse.

His lips twitch, even as his breathing starts to even out. "Heard you before," he mumbles.

I breathe out a laugh. Of course he heard me, all those months ago. He was probably having a great time, waiting for me to work up the nerve to say it again. It's something he would do. Like the time he ordered Greek food three nights in a row before I finally admitted I don't like it. He grinned and kicked me under the table and said, "About time, idiot."

It was hard for me, sometimes, to tell him what I was feeling. He always said I was too easygoing for my own good, but really, I was just scared that I'd lose him. That he'd learn too much about me and stop thinking I was special.

I lean over and kiss his cheek. "Love you," I whisper again, though I know he's too deeply asleep to hear me. I can't help it. I like the sound of it too much.

Jean comes in a few minutes later to check on him, and rolls his eyes when he sees me holding Jacob's hand. It's a fond sort of eye-roll, though, like what you'd expect from a bratty younger brother.

"I will bring you in a cot," he says grudgingly, and heads out of the room.

I LAST ABOUT four hours at Jacob's side before I give in and crash for a few hours on the cot Jean set up by the window. Jean wakes me at eight by clearing his throat loudly and impatiently.

"Family has just arrived," he says, as I push myself up, my back and neck loudly protesting my sleeping position. "I tell them I am doing rounds. You want to wait at the nursing station while they come in, oui?"

I press the heels of my hands into my eyes. "No," I say firmly. "I want to talk to them."

Jean raises an eyebrow. "Good luck," he says doubtfully.

He leaves briefly and returns with a breakfast tray for Jacob, who's been given the okay to eat, apparently, but only small amounts of soft, bland foods. Jacob's still fast asleep, which Jean tells me is normal after two weeks of being critically ill.

"He will improve quickly," he says. "He is young—you will see."

I thank him, but a nagging voice in the back of my mind reminds me that Antony looked as good as Jacob, and he still died. I make a mental note to ask Dr. K if she knows what Antony died from, and how we can prevent it from happening to Jacob.

While Jean goes to get Jacob's family, I give myself a firm pep talk, though it's mostly Heather's words that I can hear. *Plan out what you want to say to them, and then ask them to hear you out.*

Jacob's mother enters first, followed closely by his father, Paul, and Lily. My pulse doubles, but I grit my teeth. Better to get them all over with at once.

Paul and Jacob's father look unsurprisingly pissed to see me, and Lily, too, but Jacob's mother's face is flat and expressionless, which is somehow even worse. They all pause at the door as I rise to my feet. I force the words out quickly, before Paul can spit out whatever he's about to say.

"If you could just hear me out, please," I say, as calmly as I can. Paul starts to say something, his furious face beet red, but Jacob's father raises a hand and he falls silent. I snatch a breath.

"I know that this has been a huge shock," I say, trying not to stumble over the words I've prepared. "And I understand your concerns about Jacob's future. I know he should have told you sooner—we should have told you sooner—but I can't go back and change that now." I force myself to take another breath. "Jacob and I have been together for over a year now, and I really, really care about him." Heat is rising to my face. I can't believe I'm saying all this out loud. I force the rest out. "I'd never do anything to mess up his career, and I'll do whatever I can to keep this out of the press." I glance at Jacob. He's still asleep, his breathing slow and even. "I don't want to fight with any of you," I finish carefully. "I just . . . I just want to be here and help."

None of them answer me, except Paul, who snorts derisively. The silence stretches out, growing tenser by the second. I look to Jacob's mother, but her face is still expressionless.

"I'd like to visit with my son," she says finally. She walks to Jacob's bedside without looking at me.

Jacob's father clears his throat. "I think you'd better go."

My limbs grow heavy with disappointment. "I'll be back later," I mutter, stepping past him.

"Don't bother," Paul snaps.

I'm waiting for the elevator when the unit door opens again. Jacob's sister, Lily, emerges, clearly looking for me. A fragile thread of hope starts to form in my chest.

It vanishes when she opens her mouth.

"Don't come back," she says. "Jacob doesn't want you here."

I stare at her face, feeling hollow and dull. She's a beautiful girl, but the look in her eyes makes her ugly. The elevator arrives with a ding. I exhale heavily as I step into it. I don't know what to say to her, so I don't bother saying anything at all.

"Don't come back," she says again, as the doors slide shut.

15
Not a Big Deal

HEATHER KEEPS ME BUSY FOR THE REST OF THE DAY, DRAG-ging my sorry ass down to the hotel gym and guiding me through a brutal workout while she drinks an iced coffee and returns e-mails on her phone.

"That article about you and Antony's gone off that site," she tells me as I chug a bottle of water. "And look what's popped up in its place."

She hands me her phone, open to an article with a picture of her and me at the airport and the title 'F1 Driver Travis Keeping Jets to France with Hot New Girlfriend!'

I roll my eyes. "Sorry about that."

She shrugs. "No worries. I do have a boyfriend, though, so don't get any ideas." She winks and hip checks me. "Now c'mon, let's go grab some food."

We have lunch at a restaurant nearby, then she drives us a little ways out of the city to a hike through a national park. We don't talk much, but it feels good to be out and moving. It gives me the illusion of accomplishing something.

Afterward, she books us in for dinner in the city's nicest restaurant. "This is on you, by the way," she tells me as we sit down. The food is good, but I'm getting antsy being away from the hospital so long. I get the feeling Heather is eating slowly on purpose, forcing me to take some time away. After a painstaking hour, she finally asks the waiter for our check.

"You can go to the hospital now," she tells me outside the restaurant. "Remember what we talked about."

"Yeah, yeah."

On the way to the hospital, I force myself to run through the new speech I've prepared for Jacob's parents. I'm going to tell them about the article about Heather and me, and reassure them again that I won't do anything to wreck Jacob's career. Like Heather said, sometimes people need to hear things a few times before they really listen. I'm kind of hoping Jacob might've talked to them, too, though I don't want him stressing himself out about it.

I press the buzzer in the waiting room and wait patiently for a nurse, praying it isn't the older blond woman. When Jean's semi-friendly face appears, I can't help feeling like it's a sign. Maybe this time, I'll make some headway.

This hopeful thinking carries me to his room, where Dr. K is standing at the foot of his bed, talking with his parents. Paul and Lily are nowhere to be seen, which I think is another good sign. Jacob is sitting up further in bed. A warmth spreads through my chest at the sight of him. His skin's got a bit of color in it and his eyes are clearer.

"Ah, Monsieur Travis," Dr. K says pleasantly, turning to greet me.

"Sorry," I say awkwardly. "I didn't mean to interrupt."

I sneak a glance at Jacob's parents but glean very little from their cold expressions.

"We were just speaking about Jacob's transfer," Dr. K says, gesturing for me to sit at Jacob's side, across from his parents. I shoot Jacob the tiniest smile as I sit down, but I'm not sure he sees it. He's staring at his hands, the corners of his mouth pressed together tightly.

"Is he being moved out of the ICU?" I ask.

"Yes, soon," Dr. K says. "But we are also discussing sending him to a different hospital, somewhere a bit more convenient for all of you." She smiles politely at his parents.

"Oh." I sit back in my chair. I hadn't thought of that. Jacob's parents live somewhere in New Mexico. I'm a bit fuzzy on my US geography, but I know it's really far away from here. Jacob always complained about how inconvenient it was to get home for holidays. My stomach clenches. If he goes to a hospital there, it'll be nearly impossible to visit him. After the next few races in Europe, F1 is headed to Singapore.

"There's a hospital in Albuquerque that we've already been in touch with," Jacob's father says. "They have the best doctors in the state. We'd like him moved there as soon as possible."

I glance at Jacob again, but he seems determined not to look at me. He can't be okay with this. He hates going back home. He always says it's too cold in winter and too hot in summer, and that no one sane should live in a place with so many poisonous snakes and spiders.

"I will not clear him for transfer for at least a week," Dr. K says. "Perhaps longer, if there are any complications. I need to see him up and moving with our physiotherapists, and the orthopedic surgeon will need to clear him as well."

"I'm sure he'll be up and at it in no time," Jacob's father says.

"I certainly hope so," Dr. K says pleasantly.

His parents smile at each other, but I can't stop looking at Jacob. He looks absolutely miserable, and I just know he isn't going to stand up for himself.

I clear my throat. "Are you sure that New Mexico's the best place for him?"

Both his parents turn to ice, like I knew they would. Jacob's mother's mouth presses together so tightly that the edges of her lips turn white.

"It's his home," she says tersely. "And he'll need us to take care of him."

"If he were in London—" I start, but his father interrupts.

"If he were in London, he'd be alone," he says sharply. "He doesn't know anyone there."

"He knows me," I shoot back.

Jacob's father lets out a dismissive breath. "You'll be off racing."

"Then I'll take time off," I snap.

"Take time off," he repeats scornfully. "You're an F1 driver. What are you going to do, tell the world you need a personal day?"

My cheeks flush. As much as I hate to admit it, he isn't wrong. F1 drivers can't just take time off. All of my time is booked up months in advance, and I've already missed tons of work since Jacob's crash. I remember the look on Stefan's face when I told him about Jacob. *I need to think about this*, he said.

The last thing I can afford right now is to miss more time.

"I could manage it," I say, but even to my own ears, my voice sounds uncertain.

Jacob flinches a bit when I say it, though he still doesn't lift his eyes. His father scoffs again, but Dr. K holds up her hands.

"As I say, I will not clear him for another week, at *least*. We are getting too far ahead of ourselves. Once he is cleared for transfer, we can discuss this again. Does that sound okay with you, Jacob?"

She waits patiently for him to answer, but he just keeps staring at his hands.

"Jacob," his mother says.

He shrugs one shoulder. "It's fine."

Dr. K's brow creases with concern. "We can talk about it more later. For now, I'll leave you to rest," she says, gently stressing the word "rest."

The minute she's gone, Jacob's father leans forward and snatches an angry breath, but before he can speak, Jacob interrupts.

"Can you guys get me some water?" he asks his parents. "Please?"

His mother's mouth tightens again, but after a moment she and Jacob's father rise to their feet.

"Do you want ice?" she asks Jacob. I fight the urge to scowl at her. Jacob doesn't like ice in his water.

"Whatever," Jacob mumbles.

"Okay, love." She leans over and kisses his forehead, and then they're gone.

I let out a heavy breath and reach for Jacob's hand, but he pulls away. He meets my eye for the first time since I walked in, and his expression makes my blood run cold.

I swallow. "What's wrong?"

His eyes drop down to his hands again. The silence stretches out so long I start to think he's not going to answer. Finally, he shrugs one shoulder. "I think we should cool it for a while."

For a second, I can hear absolutely nothing, not even the thud of my pulse. "What?"

He picks at a loose thread on the bedsheet. "I think we should . . . take a break, or whatever."

I'm too stunned to speak. It's like the whole world's tilted sideways.

"You don't mean that." I reach for his hand again, and this time he doesn't flinch away, but his fingers are cold and rigid beneath mine. "I know it's been a mess with your parents," I say in a rush, "but I can fix that. They just need some time, I can talk to them again—"

"I don't want you to talk to them again." A drop of—something—is creeping into Jacob's voice. I tighten my grip on his hand and his eyes flash. This time, when he speaks, the anger is undeniable. "And it's got nothing to do with them."

There's a painful hollow forming in the center of my chest. "Okay." I try to sound calm, like I'm not about to fall apart. "What is it, then?"

"For fuck's sake." He pulls his hand out of mine and scrubs his fingers over his forehead. "I just don't want to do this anymore, Travis." The curt, dismissive way he says my name feels like a blow. "Look, we always had an expiration date, alright? I know you think this is so fucking serious, but that's just because you've never dated anyone before."

My chest hurts so badly, I can hardly breathe. "We are serious."

He rolls his eyes, and something inside of me fractures. "This isn't that big a deal, alright?"

"Isn't a big deal?" I repeat. "I've been worrying about you for weeks. I've barely slept—I had to lie to the team—"

"No one asked you to do that."

"I almost *lost* you."

Jacob lets out an awful, scornful breath. "Lost me," he repeats. "I'm not your fucking property."

I can't think of anything to say to that. I just stare at him, with my heart bleeding out inside my chest.

In the silence, the door slides open and a nurse comes in, humming cheerfully.

"I have your medicine," she says in a thick French accent, handing Jacob a tiny cup of pills and a glass of water. She watches him take them, smiling at me, unaware of the tension between us. "Can I get you anything?" she asks after Jacob's taken the pills.

"No, thanks," he mutters.

She lingers in the room, fiddling with Jacob's heart monitor and then stepping away to refill the boxes of gloves that hang near the door.

"Why are you doing this?" I ask in a low, strangled voice.

Jacob's cheeks redden, and for a second I think he's upset that he's hurt me. Then his eyes flick to the nurse and I realize he isn't upset. He's *embarrassed*.

Embarrassed of me.

I thought I'd learned what heartbreak was, these last few weeks, but this pain is utterly unbearable.

"I don't understand," I say hoarsely. "If I did something wrong—"

The door slides open again, and Jacob's parents reappear. His mother smiles at him and hands him a glass of water, acting for all the world as though I don't exist.

"We're going to FaceTime your grandmother," his father tells him. Then he scowls at me expectantly.

"He's leaving," Jacob says without looking at me. The way he says it, it's like he's just done with me. A whole year together, then three weeks of hell, and he just dismisses me, easy as that.

I can't even bring myself to say anything, I'm so furious and hurt. I let out a disbelieving breath and then leave him alone with his parents, just like he wants.

16
A Dangerous Word, Fine

I MAKE IT BACK TO THE HOTEL, AND THERE'S THIS WEIRD repetition in my head. I keep thinking, "I'll talk to Heather, I'll talk to Heather," over and over, as if that'll somehow make it okay. As if she can fix this for me. But when I open the door, she isn't there. I fumble for my phone and text her, asking for her hotel number. About five seconds later, she texts back.

> 507, but I'm not there right now. Popped out to get some food. You need me?

I don't text back. I can't bring myself to tell her what's happened, not through a text. And it feels too pathetic to ask her to come back.

I walk circles around my hotel room, Jacob's awful words ringing in my ears.

This isn't that big a deal, alright?

I know you think this is so fucking serious, but that's just because you've never dated anyone before.

I'm not your fucking property.

There's a horrible pain in my chest. Heartbreak, I understand the word now. My heart actually does feel broken. My whole body feels broken.

I'm so consumed with misery, the sharp knock on the door makes me jump. Heather is standing in the hallway with a huge bag of takeout food hanging from one arm, and her forehead slightly sweaty, like she's hurried to get here.

"Is everything okay?" she asks. "Is Jacob alright?"

"He's fine," I say thinly. "He's fine, we just—"

Broke up.

I can't bring myself to say the words, but she must read it in my face, because her eyebrows fly up.

"You're kidding."

I shake my head, not quite trusting myself to speak. She stares at me for one long moment, then drops her takeout bag onto the floor and throws her arms around me. I stand stiffly for a few seconds, then I wrap my arms around her small frame.

"Shit," she says. "Travis, that's *shit*."

"Yeah," I agree in a strangled voice. "Pretty much."

She hugs me tightly for another moment and then releases me. "What happened?"

"I don't know." We crouch at the same time to pick up her abandoned takeout. "He just—he said he wanted to end things."

"That can't be all he said." She crosses to the en suite kitchen to lay the food out on the table.

It isn't all he said, but I don't want to repeat his words to her. But she's looking at me expectantly, and piling Indian food on a plate for me, so I force myself to answer. "He said we were never a big deal," I say. The words taste sour on my tongue.

Heather makes a disbelieving noise. "Weren't you two together for, like, a year?"

"Yes!" I say, frustration spilling into the word. "A year. That's not something casual."

"No," she agrees. "Sit, eat."

I sit down across from her but don't touch the food. I have no appetite at all. "It's his parents," I say angrily. "Or his brother. They must've said something to him."

"Yeah, maybe."

I pick up a piece of naan and tear pieces off without eating them. I remember the way Jacob's eyes flicked to the nurse, and the way he pulled his hand away from me.

"What is it?" Heather asks, watching me.

I tear off another piece of naan. "It's just . . . even if they did say something to him, he's not a kid. He could stand up to them."

Heather winces. "True. But it's hard for some people to go against their parents, no matter how old they are."

"Yeah, I know, but—" I break off abruptly, stumbling over a sudden thought.

"What?"

I shake my head. I was going to say, "But if he really loved me," but Jacob never told me that he loved me. I said it to him, but he never said it back.

And if he heard me say it all those months ago, then he knew all that time how I felt. He would've known that if he said it to me, I'd say it back.

But he never did. He never actually said that he loved me.

Heather is talking again, suggesting I go back to the hospital and talk to Jacob again, saying, "He might not have meant it" and "He might need some time," but I shake my head. I saw the look in his eyes at the hospital. He's done with me. And I'm not going to humiliate myself any further by begging him to change his mind.

"Can you get us a flight out?" I ask, cutting Heather off mid-sentence. "First thing?"

She opens her mouth as though about to disagree, then seems to think better of it. She reaches out and squeezes my arm. "Course I can."

She heads off to her room shortly after. I think she can sense that I want to be alone.

I pace pointlessly around the hotel room after she's gone. I should pack, or get a shower, or do *something*, but my muscles are heavy, dead weight hanging from my bones. I sink down onto the couch, and then I just lie there, staring up at the ceiling, until the sun slips from the sky and the whole room goes black.

THE NEXT F1 race is in the UK—Silverstone, my pseudo-home race. I'm not British, really, but I do have my permanent resident card. I was born in Canada, just outside of Toronto, but I only lived there for six years before my dad moved us to London. I've been to a few Canadian cities for karting and racing, and I've wanted to do a road trip across Canada for the longest time.

Jacob and I used to talk about doing it over F1's summer break.

Heather and I checked out of our hotel in France the day after Jacob ended things, and we've been in London ever since. My place feels barren and empty now that I've boxed up Jacob's things. He didn't ever leave much stuff here, but there were some sweaters and toiletries and pictures on the fridge of places we've been, and stuff I only bought because of him, like the Xbox and the old N64. Heather suggested we burn it all, but I couldn't bring myself to do it. Burning it would be helpful if I was angry, but I'm not angry. I'm just flat and hollow.

"You need to lean into the awfulness at first," Heather advises me, one night at my place. Her boyfriend, Hunter, is with us, too.

He's a muscly, six-foot-tall blond guy who's really into veganism and sustainability. It's sort of weird, given how many burgers I've seen Heather eat, but they fit together. Like I used to think Jacob and I did.

"Not true," Hunter counters. "You need to stay busy. Distract yourself with work. Go out on the rebound, see how many kick-ass gay guys there are out there. What?" he adds, as Heather scoffs. "I know *so* many guys I could hook him up with. My trainer's gay, and my nutritionist—"

"Jesus, please don't start dating a vegan," Heather begs me. "They never fucking shut up about it."

Hunter grins and raises his water glass in a toast. "Damn straight."

"I don't want to date anyone else," I say. "I'll just stay single forever. It's easier."

"That's the spirit," Heather says. "Lean into the awful." Then she hops off the kitchen counter to rummage through my cupboards for something to eat.

She and Hunter have been here almost every day since we got back from France. The first time they knocked on my door with their arms full of takeout containers, I only grudgingly let them in. I wanted to be alone in my misery. But no matter how I acted, no matter how little I spoke, they kept showing up. And since Brian is gone and hasn't yet been replaced, Heather is acting as my trainer and cat-herder (her words, not mine). As the Silverstone GP approaches, she's with me from dawn till dusk, sneaking me coffee during engineering meetings and pinching me on the arm when I get too surly in interviews.

I don't talk to Matty until Friday morning, just before FP1. Heather has been whisked away to do some PR work, and I'm sitting alone in my trailer, throwing a ball against the wall.

Theoretically, this is supposed to be a reflex exercise, but instead I'm just losing myself in each slow, depressing thump.

"Yo, Keeping!" Matty raps on the door and pushes it open in the same movement. He's already in his race gear, holding his helmet loosely in one hand. His broad smile drops when he sees me. "Oh fuck, what's happened?"

"What?"

"You look like shit. Is Jacob alright?"

Hearing his name actually hurts, as if someone's grabbed my heart and squeezed it. "He's fine, I guess."

"You guess?"

I shrug.

Matty tilts his head. "O-kay," he says slowly. "Talk."

I exhale heavily. I wish someone had warned me that breakups were like this. It isn't something that happens to you once. It's something that happens over and over again every time you have to explain it, and it's just as painful every time. "There's nothing to say. It didn't work out, that's all."

"Didn't work out," Matty repeats. "For fuck's sake, Keeping. I told you to call me if anything happened."

"I really don't want to talk about it."

Matty watches me for a long moment. "How long were you two dating?"

I shoot him a flat stare, which he ignores. "A year," I say grudgingly.

"Were you having problems? Before the crash, I mean."

"No." My frustration spills out into the word. It's something I've been thinking about constantly. All the signs I might've missed, the warnings I might not have picked up on. "We were fine."

Matty raises a doubtful eyebrow. "A dangerous word, fine. Every time my girlfriend says something's fine, I know I'm in real trouble."

"It wasn't like that," I say. "Everything was great."

Except he wouldn't tell his parents about you, a nasty voice pipes up. *He wouldn't tell his friends.*

"Hm." Matty pulls a dubious face. Then he stands, holding a hand out to help pull me to my feet. "Tell you what, my parents are in town for the race, and my mom's going to make dinner tonight. Why don't you join us?"

"I really don't—"

"Seven thirty, sounds great," Matty interrupts. "I'll text you the address later."

"I don't think—" My feeble protest dies as Matty scowls at me. "Yeah, alright," I mutter.

He grins and thumps me on the arm. "Attaboy. Now hurry your ass up, practice is starting soon."

17
All Yours

THINGS HADN'T ALWAYS BEEN GREAT BETWEEN JACOB AND me. Or at least, there were times early on when I'd been uncertain. But then one weekend everything had changed, and I'd stopped worrying altogether.

It had been two months since our time together in Scotland. Two months of stolen weekends and intermittent texting and the occasional brief phone call. Then one weekend, the F2 and F1 schedules overlapped in Montreal, and Jacob showed up at my hotel room late Thursday night. It had been two weeks since we'd seen each other, and I barely had time to say hello before he was in my arms, kissing me hard enough to bruise. Eight hours later, I woke up to the smell of coffee and the sight of Jacob getting dressed at the foot of the bed. He grinned when he saw me.

"I didn't want to wake you up. I've got an early practice."

I rose up on my elbows. "Are you around tonight?"

"Nah, I've got a date," he said, tying his shoe on the edge of the bed. "But I'll be around tomorrow."

His words took a second to register. When they did, something cold fluttered in my chest. "You've got a date?"

My tone must not have betrayed my feelings, because Jacob's expression didn't change. "Yeah," he said easily. "This girl I knew in high school lives here now. We're going to hit up some fancy restaurant."

"Oh."

He finished tying his other shoe and straightened. "I'll text you tomorrow, yeah?"

"Tomorrow," I repeated numbly.

He leaned over the bed and pressed a fleeting kiss to my numb lips, and then he was gone.

All that day, my limbs were heavy and cold. I'd thought Jacob and I were . . . I don't know. Not boyfriends, I guess, but together. But he had a date. Some girl he knew in high school. He was taking her out to some restaurant. Some fancy, public restaurant, where anyone could see them together. I wondered what they would talk about. What she might look like. If he would kiss her after dinner. If they would go home together. The thought of it made me sick to my stomach.

I managed to get through FP1 and FP2 without embarrassing myself, but I was even more monosyllabic than usual during the interviews afterward. I made it back to my hotel room around eight, threw my things onto my bed, and then sat heavily on the sofa. My fingers kept twitching toward my phone, even though I knew there weren't any texts there. I'd been checking all day, hoping to see some message from Jacob saying he'd changed his mind, that he wanted to see me tonight instead of her.

But even if he did . . . even if he did, where did that leave me? He obviously didn't think about me the way I thought about him. I couldn't have imagined going on a date with anyone else.

I sat on the sofa for an hour or more before I finally gave in and crawled into bed. When I saw Jacob tomorrow, I decided, I would have to tell him things were done. I didn't want to lose him—the very thought made me feel all hot and panicky—but I couldn't keep sleeping with him if he was going to date other people. And I wasn't stupid enough to believe I could give him any kind of ultimatum. Jacob always did what he wanted. If he didn't want to date me, no amount of arguing would change his mind.

I fell asleep before sunset and woke up in total darkness, bleary and confused. I wasn't sure what had woken me, until someone pounded again on the door.

My first thought was that I'd somehow slept in and was late for qualifying, but the hotel clock read one fifteen in the morning. I stumbled to the door and pulled it open, and there was Jacob, fist raised to knock again. He lurched forward a bit when I swung the door open. He was wearing a thin T-shirt and shivering, even though it wasn't that cold outside.

"Jacob—" I started, then realized I had no idea what I was going to say. "Where's your jacket?" I said finally.

He gave a strange little laugh. "Forgot it," he said, and his words came out a little slurred. "Left it at the restaurant."

"The restaurant," I repeated. "Right." I noticed his hair was messed up, and my stomach sunk. I took an unwilling step backward. "I have to get up early—"

"I'm sorry," he blurted out.

Something flickered in my chest. "What?"

"I'm sorry," he repeated. "I was—I'm so stupid—"

He let out a strange, frustrated noise and then stepped across the threshold and into my arms, burying his face in the crook of my neck. His skin was cool against mine. I stood unmoving against him, frightened his apology was for something I couldn't forgive. If he'd slept with her, if he'd even kissed her—

"I suck," he slurred. "I'm so fucking—so fucking bad at this."

"Bad at what?"

He wrapped his arms around me, and I could smell the alcohol on his breath. "Liking someone," he mumbled into my skin.

All the air slipped out of my lungs. "Jacob . . ."

"Nothing happened," he said. "Nothing happened, don't be mad at me."

I let out a breath. I couldn't have been mad at him if I'd tried. I was so obsessed, so deeply lost in him that his drunken, half-slurred apology completely melted my resolve. My fingers found their way to the back of his neck, and he let out a small, sad noise that just about wrecked me.

"I'm not mad at you," I said. "I can't share you, though."

He shook his head roughly. "No sharing. All yours."

He leaned into me so heavily I had to work to hold him up. He was completely hammered, nearly blacking out.

"Come on," I said, fighting the giddiness that had risen up at his words. "You've got to get to bed."

"Bed," he slurred.

I helped him to the bed and under the comforter, where he lay shivering while I yanked off his shoes. When I crawled in beside him, he just about plastered himself to my skin.

"So warm," he mumbled. About five seconds later, his breathing deepened. Whether he'd blacked out or fallen asleep, I don't know, but I'd never been more awake. I lay there next to him, my heart beating loudly in the darkness. All mine. He was all mine.

From now on, I thought, things were going to be different.

He woke up the next morning bleary-eyed and cranky, bemoaning a splitting headache. He made absolutely no mention of the night before, and for a few awful minutes, I thought I was wrong. But then, after he got out of the shower, he made a cup of coffee and curled up next to me on the sofa. He tucked his head into the crook of my neck and exhaled, all of his muscles relaxing with the breath. It may seem like a small thing, but it was something he'd never really done before. We'd had sex, but we'd never really had intimacy.

"I feel like shit," he said finally, then pressed an unexpected kiss to my shoulder. "How do you feel about qualifying?"

"Um—alright. It's not my favorite track."

He yawned and shifted even closer to me. "I always fuck up the chicane."

"Me too. The whole first sector, I can't get the rhythm of it."

"You'll get it," he said, leaning back to sip on his coffee. "You seemed to have it in practice."

"You were watching?"

He rolled his eyes. "Don't sound so smug."

There was something in the flush of his cheeks that made me bold enough to push a little further. "You were watching," I said, nudging his arm.

His lips twitched. "Shut up."

And from then on, things really were different. His texts became more frequent, until it was almost a daily thing, a constant conversation about our days and our lives. His calls, which had previously been ten-second affairs to ask my hotel room number or double-check a time, grew longer. And when we were together, he was more . . . more present, I guess is the word. He stayed longer in the mornings, talking with me over coffee, and threaded his fingers in mine when we watched movies, once or twice even falling asleep with his head in my lap.

Things got better and better as the season dwindled, until it was the last race of the season, and he was there with me in my hotel room in Abu Dhabi, telling me he only slept well with me, and saying I'd win the championship for sure next year. I went into the race the next day feeling confident, but on the first lap, I got taken out in someone else's crash, and just like that, the season was over.

That night, Jacob showed up at my hotel room again, cursing my bad luck and hugging me so tight I could hardly breathe. Then he asked if it would be okay if he stayed with me in London for a while.

I leaned back to study his face. "Aren't you going home for Christmas?"

He shrugged. "I'd rather be in London."

I hesitated. "Through Christmas?"

"Yeah, if that's okay."

It was pathetic, really, how quickly the idea washed away my disappointment over the race. I hadn't spent Christmas with anyone since my dad died. The thought of spending the holiday with Jacob . . . it was frightening and thrilling, all at once.

"I don't have a tree or anything," I said stupidly.

Jacob laughed. "We'll have to fix that, then. Tree, lights, stockings." He counted the list off on his fingers. "I don't fuck around about Christmas."

I fought a smile. "Yeah, alright."

He went back home to New Mexico for a few days, to appease his parents, and then he showed up at my apartment in London with a massive suitcase stuffed full of clothes. At first, he left his suitcase open on my bedroom floor, living out of it. But in the days leading up to Christmas, his clothes slowly found their way into my dresser. Then one day, the empty suitcase disappeared, shoved into a closet. I felt little bursts of excitement that whole day. I kept thinking, this was more than just a visit. He was practically moving in with me.

The realization gave me an idea for his Christmas present, which was something I'd agonized about. I hadn't been able to think of anything to get him. But when I realized he might spend time at my apartment over the winter, it was suddenly obvious.

I woke up on Christmas morning with his warm weight against me, his head tucked into my shoulder and one leg thrown over mine. I lay there for a while, reveling in his warmth. When he woke up, he was soft and sleepy, and he pressed a row of kisses up my neck. I slid my fingers into his hair and kissed him deeply, and it was several hours before we made it out of bed.

When we did, he made us peppermint hot chocolate ("It's *tradition*, Keeping, I don't care if you don't like it") and insisted we watch some old Christmas cartoon I'd never seen. The whole time, my stomach was in a nervous knot.

When the movie was over, he poked me in the leg with his foot. "What's up? You're acting squirrelly."

I bit my lip. "Want your Christmas present?"

"I thought this morning was my present," he said, smirking.

Flushing, I rolled my eyes. "Do you want it or not?"

He grinned. "Yes, please."

I pulled him to his feet and led him to the spare bedroom, pausing for a moment before I unlocked the door. I gestured for him to go in first. Inside, there was a brand-new racing simulator. It was almost as fancy (and expensive) as the one Harper used in their factory.

My heart was beating quickly as I stepped in after him.

"Wow." He turned his bright smile on me. "This is awesome."

"You like it?"

"Of course." He nudged my ribs. "I'm definitely going to steal some time on it."

I blinked. "It's yours. I got it for you."

His smile flagged a little, then he hitched it back up again and gave a little laugh. "This won't fit in my apartment. And anyway, you need it more than I do."

I shrugged. My stomach had sunk a little. "I usually use the one at Harper, so they can track data or whatever."

Jacob nodded absently. "Right." He turned his smile on me again. It was sort of plasticky, I noticed. "Well, it's really cool. I'll definitely use it sometime."

He nudged my hip again, and then he walked out without really looking at it more. I swallowed down my disappointment. It was my own fault. I should've made it clearer it was for him. Or maybe I should've sent it to his apartment instead.

We ate lunch and messed around for a while on the couch before he went to meet some of his friends who were in London for the holidays. I ate dinner alone, like always, but it felt more hollow than it ever had before. I missed Jacob. And I couldn't help feeling he was slipping through my fingers. Like I was pushing too hard, like I might push him away.

I vowed to back off, to give him more space, but when he came back later that night, slightly tipsy from drinks with his friends, he crawled into my lap and tucked his head into my neck.

"Did you have a good Christmas?" he asked.

I threaded my fingers in his hair. "Of course."

He was silent for a moment, then he exhaled heavily and sat back on his heels. "I didn't get you a present," he said in a rush. "I wanted to, I swear, I just—I couldn't think of anything good enough."

"It's fine," I said. "I don't care."

His expression was guilty, and I felt a swoop of relief. Maybe I hadn't fucked up with the simulator. Maybe he just felt bad he hadn't gotten me anything. "I wanted to get you something good," he said.

"It's okay. Really."

"I'll make it up to you," he said. He flattened his palms on my chest. "Right now, if you want."

My hands were already sliding down his back, pulling him closer to me. "Oh yeah?"

"Yeah," he murmured.

Later—much later—he lay next to me and slid his fingertips over my stomach. I was half asleep already, my muscles warm and heavy. Just before I drifted off, he kissed my neck and murmured in my ear, "Merry Christmas, Keeping."

18
Balance

LOOKING BACK ON IT NOW, IT'S SO OBVIOUS. I WAS SO MUCH
more invested than he was. I was so in love with him, I ignored every single sign, even the glaringly obvious ones. He couldn't have been clearer. He was pushing me away every time I tried to pull him closer. He never used that racing sim, not once. And when Christmas was over, his suitcase and all his things went home with him.

What was it he said in the hospital? *I know you think this is so fucking serious, but that's just because you've never dated anyone before.*

He's right. I did think we were serious. I thought he would be a part of my life forever, and now that he's not, I'm left with this awful, hollow void inside me, this empty space where he used to live.

It's Heather's boyfriend, Hunter, who gives me the best advice after the breakup.

"There's nothing you can do to make things better," he says. "Every week will just get a little less shit, until one day you wake up and you don't remember quite what the pain felt like."

The weeks pass by; race weekends come and go. And it doesn't really get less painful—thinking of Jacob still makes my chest ache, and I still spend hours every night thinking about him, wondering if he's okay, wondering if I could've done something differently—but every week it gets a little easier to pretend that I'm okay.

Racing is helpful. Stefan hasn't said anything since I told him about Jacob, and I'm determined not to give him an excuse to fire me. I throw all my focus and energy into racing and land two second-place finishes in a row, edging out Clayton from Crosswire Racing in the championship. The next two races are wet races, and with a little luck—Mahoney crashes out once, and then he and Clayton both have engine failures—I get two wins in a row.

Then, somehow, there are only three races left, and I have a chance of winning the championship again. But I have to finish ahead of Mahoney every single race. No one really thinks it's possible, not the press, not the fans, not even the team.

No one except Heather, who kisses my cheek before the Brazilian GP and whispers in my ear, "You've got this."

And somehow—*somehow*—she's right. I overtake Mahoney on the second to last lap and cross the line a half second ahead. When I get out of the car, my eyes land on Heather, waiting with the rest of the Harper team behind the barricade. Matty is standing next to her—he retired from the race after an unlucky first lap crash—cheering as loudly as she is, and when I approach, they both pull me into a hug, Heather screaming excitedly into my ear, Matty gripping me hard enough to bruise. For the first time since Jacob broke up with me—the first time since his crash, really—I feel myself smiling a stupid, irrepressible smile.

When I'm done with the podium and the press, Heather pulls me aside and leads me to my trailer.

"Someone wants to congratulate you," she says, and for a stupid moment I really think it'll be Jacob.

Instead, Antony Costa's mother is waiting for me with shiny eyes and a smile.

"Parabéns, darling. Parabéns."

She opens her arms and I go to her, feeling a painful clench inside of my chest. She's just tall enough for her chin to hook over my shoulder, and as I hug her, she breaks into tears, her small frame shaking.

"I'm so sorry," I whisper.

She pulls away after a moment and shakes her head, smiling through her tears. "Don't apologize. I didn't come here to ruin your exciting day."

"You're not ruining it," I say. "Are you doing okay?"

"Keeping!" Matty bursts into the room before she can answer. His smile falters when he sees her. "Oh—shit, sorry—"

"No, no," Mrs. Costa says, stepping away from me to wipe her eyes. "I'll let you boys celebrate."

"My parents are here," Matty tells me. "They want to take us out to dinner." He smiles encouragingly at Mrs. Costa. "Er—I'm sure they'd love it if you'd come, too, ma'am."

"Oh, no," she says.

"Yes," I say, more forcefully than I mean to. "I mean, if you want to," I amend hastily.

Mrs. Costa looks at me, tears shining in her eyes. After a moment, she smiles. "Well . . . alright. If you really don't mind."

AN HOUR LATER, Matty, his parents Alice and Frank, Mrs. Costa, Heather, Hunter, and I are in the back room of a restaurant Matty chose, laughing as Matty and Heather argue with Hunter about whether or not plant-based meat tastes terrible.

Mrs. Costa is sitting next to me, and as the argument shifts to a spirited discussion about some TV show I've never seen, I lean closer to her.

"How are you doing?"

Her smile thins and she sits up a little straighter, a reflex I recognize. It's like what I do whenever Matty asks me about Jacob. An instinct to lie, to pretend everything is alright.

"Oh, we're getting by," she says.

Impulsively, I reach under the table and take her hand. After a moment, she squeezes back hard.

"How is your friend, the other boy?" she asked. "Jacob Nichols."

She says it just as the conversation around the table lulls, and Matty and Heather both glance at me.

I force a smile. "Ah—I don't know. We . . . broke up."

Mrs. Costa's eyebrows lift in surprise. I suddenly remember her talking about church, and I feel a spike of panic. But then her expression relaxes, and a sad smile crosses her face.

"I'm sorry," she says. "I didn't realize you were together."

"It's fine," I lie. "It was weeks ago."

(Nine weeks and two days, if you want to be specific.)

"You need a new guy," Matty says, pointing at me with his drink in hand. "I'm going to get Eric to hook you up with one of his friends."

"You don't want to date any of Eric's friends," his father, Frank, says flatly.

"They're not that bad," Matty says.

Frank snorts. "None of them have jobs."

"Now, that's not true," Matty's mother, Alice, says. "One of them is a DJ. And that other boy, James, he's—what do you call it?—a social media influencer."

"Neither of those are jobs," Frank says.

"Hunter tried to be an influencer once," Heather chimes in.

Hunter groans and covers her mouth with his hand. "She's drunk," he says. "She doesn't know what she's saying."

Everyone laughs, and I sit back a little in my chair. I feel—odd. Sort of off-balance, but not in a bad way. At the end of the dinner, Mrs. Costa asks for my phone number and tells me she's going to call to check in on me, and Alice and Frank tell me they're going to be at the last race and that we need to have dinner again, and Matty squeezes my shoulder and tells me he's going to set me up with some hot guy he knows, and it's all just so—

"You're smiling," Heather says, nudging my arm. Hunter's already gone back to their hotel room, but Heather insisted on walking me back to mine.

I shrug. "That was fun."

"It was," she agrees. She threads her arm in mine as we near the hotel. "I'm proud of you, babe."

"Yeah, well. It's just one race."

"I don't just mean the race. Though you're definitely going to win the next one."

I hesitate. "I don't know."

"Well, I do." She rises on her toes and kisses my cheek. "This year is going to end on a good note. I can feel it."

I crack a smile. "Maybe."

"*Definitely.*" She grins at me. "Now c'mon, let's go."

"You're coming up?"

"Duh. I'm not going to let you sink back into a sulk after we're gone."

"I wasn't going to."

Heather laughs. "Let's go, Keeping. I'm thinking minibar snacks and a movie. Sound good?"

That off-balance feeling comes back, and this time, I recognize it as happiness. "Yeah." I smile at her. "Sounds great."

19
Color

I USED TO THINK THAT, BEFORE JACOB, MY LIFE WAS COLOR-less. When I was with him, everything was brighter, and better, and it never occurred to me that I could find that brightness anywhere else. I put Jacob up on the highest shelf and withdrew even more from the people around me in the process.

Now, Jacob is gone—has been, for almost twelve weeks now—but somehow the world is starting to fill with color again. Mrs. Costa calls me once a week. Matty's mother, Alice, calls every few days; his father, Frank, texts even more often. He works as an investment broker for some multimillion-dollar firm, and he's helping me invest some of the money that's been sitting use-lessly in my bank account. Heather and Matty, though, are my constants. I never had a best friend before. Now, suddenly, I have two of them.

It's a different kind of intimacy than I had with Jacob. I wanted him so badly, and I was so scared of losing him, that I never pushed him when he disappointed me. I hid all my negative feel-ings from him whenever I could, all my worries and doubts and fears. But Heather and Matty have already seen me at my worst.

I trust Heather implicitly, and Matty speaks so frankly about everything, it's impossible to lie to him. He was right when he said he was intuitive as hell. He always seems to know when I'm missing Jacob, or when I'm worrying about things, and he's so relentlessly positive, it's hard to stay down when he's around.

I win the second to last race of the season, putting me only four points behind Mahoney for the championship. If I can beat him by more than four points in the final race, I'll win the title.

Heather and Matty spend every day leading up to it with me.

"You guys do know I don't need babysitters," I tell them the night before qualifying. They both showed up at my hotel room and dragged me to dinner at some ludicrously expensive sushi restaurant in downtown Abu Dhabi.

"We're not your babysitters," Heather says. "We're your keepers. Totally different."

Matty laughs. "Hear, hear."

"We're distracting you," Heather adds. "Keeping you out of your head."

"I'm fine," I tell them. "Seriously."

"You're not nervous," Matty says doubtfully.

I take a sip of water. "Not really. I'll either win or I'll lose."

Matty shakes his head. "You're a robot, Keeping." (And okay, my heart still does tighten just a little at that, thinking of Jacob.)

"I want to win," I admit. "But it's not the end of the world if I don't."

Matty feigns a gasp. "Blasphemy. If you win this year, my contract value is definitely going up. Championship-winning car and all that."

"Yeah, but you're only fourth," Heather points out.

Matty scowls. "Keeping, talk to your woman."

I laugh, but it's partly forced. The media has really run off with this "me dating Heather" thing. Some news site got a picture of her kissing my cheek outside the hotel a few weeks ago, and everyone thinks she's my girlfriend, even in the paddock. I'd set the record straight, if anyone ever asked me about it directly, but no one ever does. They just write about it in articles, making confident statements about things they know nothing about. Heather says to ignore it, and Hunter doesn't seem to care, but it leaves a sour taste in my mouth.

"You'd be second, if you hadn't had such shitty luck," I tell Matty.

His mouth twists, a rare look of unhappiness flickering over his face. "That's generous," he says.

I bite my lip and say nothing, because if I'm being honest, it was a bit generous. Matty's a great driver, but he's had a few less-than-stellar performances this year. I think he gets in his head too much about what the media says.

"You'll get it back," Heather tells him. "This time next year, you two will be at each other's throats fighting over the championship."

Matty manages a grin. "Or I'll be kicking your ass," he says to me, "and you'll have to pretend to be as gracious and wonderful as me."

I chuckle. "Deal."

For a minute or two, we eat in silence, then I look up to find both of them watching me.

"You're going to win tomorrow," Heather says. "I can feel it."

Matty nods. "She's right, man. You've got this."

One corner of my mouth turns up. "Thanks. For everything, I mean. These past few months—"

"We're the best, you wouldn't have gotten through it without us, blah blah blah," Heather says. "We know."

Matty touches his glass to mine. "No need to thank us. We love your strange robot ass."

"We love you," Heather echoes. "And you're going to win."

THE NEXT DAY, I only come seventh in qualifying. Mahoney and Clayton are first and second. I could've been higher, but there was a yellow flag at the worst possible moment in Q3, and I had to abort my last lap. Heather and Matty take me out for dinner again—they really are my keepers—but afterward, I put my foot down and insist on going back to my hotel room alone.

I sit cross-legged on my bed with my phone on the bedspread in front of me, staring at the background. I haven't changed it, not even after everything. It's the same photo from the hike in Scotland, the one that Jacob and I did together all those months ago.

My world has color again, and I have friends, but I still miss Jacob so badly sometimes, I feel sick. Every time something good happens, I want to tell him. And I desperately want to know how he is. If he's okay. If he's happy. I know he's out of the hospital and doing rehab in Albuquerque. Josh Fry told me that much, but that's all I know.

I want to know so much more.

I know I shouldn't. I know I care more about him than he ever cared about me.

But I miss him. And I need to know he's okay.

Swallowing hard, I open a text message to him. The last text he sent me (Just landed. Headed to track now, soo tired lol. Pizza tn?) makes my chest hurt. I push through it and force myself to type.

> Hey, hope your rehab is going okay.

I bite my lip and add the truth.

> Thinking of you.

I hit Send, then I get off the bed and pace the room. I only make it a few steps before my phone dings. I snatch it up, my heart beating somewhere in my throat. There's a message—I swipe to open it—

> Message failed to deliver to recipient.

Everything inside of me goes cold.

He changed his number.

Of course he did.

I think that's the moment when I finally accept it. That he doesn't want me to contact him, that he doesn't want to get back together. That it's really over.

In some ways, it feels like the end all over again. I feel just as crushed, just as devastated. In another way, it's almost a relief. I don't have to keep wondering. I can let it go. I can focus on what's important. My friends, my career, the pseudo-family I've found in Heather and Hunter and Matty and Mrs. Costa and Matty's parents.

Almost on cue, my phone buzzes in my hand. Mrs. Costa is calling me. I lick my dry lips and hit Accept.

"Travis, meu querido," she says. "I hope I'm not disturbing you, I just wanted to wish you luck."

"It's no problem." I smile. "I'm glad you called."

"Are you nervous for tomorrow?"

I look through the blinds. Dark clouds are gathering in the night sky. There hasn't ever been rain in an Abu Dhabi race, not once, but all day, the forecasters were wondering.

"No," I tell her. "I think I've got this."

AND THE NEXT day, in the faintest rain—

I'm right.

Sector Two

Jacob

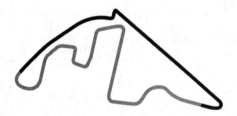

20
Pain

REHAB IS AWFUL.

It's painful. It's boring. It's embarrassing.

Six months ago, I was an athlete. Twenty-three years old, in the best shape of my life. Now, I'm practically useless.

My right leg was broken in two places, and my hip. Four of my ribs were broken. Then there was the surgery to remove my spleen, the liver laceration, the blood transfusions, the days and days spent on a ventilator.

It's like all my stamina has been sapped away. After an hour of physio, I'm breathless and exhausted, when I used to run 5K a day without breaking a sweat. My physiotherapist says I'm making progress, but I can't see it. And every night I go home to my parents' house and sleep in my childhood bedroom, with all of the stupid trophies from my karting days looming over me, mocking me while I try to sleep. My mother fusses over me, my father alternates between being pushy and being distant, Paul is . . . Paul. And Lily's back at home in Lovington, but she won't stop texting, like she thinks hearing about her life is a useful distraction.

I hate it. I hate all of it.

But most of all, I hate the psychotherapy my rehab doctor insists I do. Two sessions a week. Two hours where I sit across from the therapist, Amanda, and try not to roll my eyes too frequently.

It's the middle of December now, usually my favorite time of the year. I walk into her office with the same objectives as always: say as little as possible and get out of there a few minutes early.

"Jacob, welcome," she says with a wide smile. She smiles too much, Amanda. And she fiddles with her braids (she actually wears *braids*, like she's a middle schooler) way too often. "Have a seat."

I sit on the stupid, uncomfortable couch, and wait for her stupid, uncomfortable questions.

"How are you?" she asks.

"Fine."

"I spoke with your physiotherapist," she says. "He says you're doing extremely well."

"I can run for ten minutes," I say flatly. "Hooray."

She frowns. "You're miles ahead of your projected recovery schedule."

I shrug one shoulder and say nothing.

"Are you still in a lot of pain?"

"Not really."

A little silence. "And how has it been living with your parents?"

I stare at her coldly. "You ask me the same questions every single time. Do you realize that?"

"Yes," she says. "And I'll keep asking them, until you answer me honestly."

I let out a harsh breath. "What do you want me to say?"

"The truth." Still in that calm, pleasant voice.

"The truth," I repeat. My temper, always so close to the surface these days, is bubbling over. I let out a harsh breath. "My whole life's been fucked up, how's that for the truth."

"How has your life been fucked up?"

"How hasn't it been," I snap. I should stop talking, but it's been twelve weeks of this shit, and I'm so, so over it. "I was going to get into F1, do you even understand what that means? Do you understand how much effort that takes, how rare it is? Twenty people in the whole fucking world. Twenty people, out of seven fucking billion." I shake my head roughly and look away from her.

"Why do you think that's ruined?" she asks, in that stupid voice. "Your doctor anticipates you'll make a full recovery—"

"In a year," I snap. "Maybe two. In two years, I'll be twenty-five, and there will be a hundred drivers younger than me who haven't been fucked up in an accident." I let out a cold, humorless laugh. "My career is over."

"I see." She nods in a slow, thoughtful way that makes me want to throttle her. "So what are you going to do instead?"

I shrug roughly. "I don't know. My parents think I should apply to business school and go to work with my dad."

"Is that what you want?"

I shrug again. A stupid question deserves a stupid answer.

She taps her pen against her clipboard. "Hm. And have you been dreaming about the crash at all?"

"No."

"Because it's quite common, after a major trauma—"

"I said no," I snap. "I've already told you fifty times, I'm not having dreams about the crash."

Her smile dips, a rare crack in the facade. "Okay. What are you dreaming about, then?"

I roll my eyes. "What is it with you therapists and dreams? They don't all have to mean something, for fuck's sake."

She taps her pen again, slower this time. Her smile is completely gone, now.

"You know, Jacob, we've been at this for three months now," she says.

"I'm well aware."

"I don't think we're making any real progress. Therapy doesn't work if you aren't willing to engage."

"Okay," I say coolly. "What's your point."

"My point is, I think we should take a few weeks off. I want you to take some time and think about what you want. About what you're hoping to get from your recovery."

"Fine." I stand. "Are we done?"

Her expression is impassive. "We're done," she says. "You can book another appointment whenever you think you're ready."

I walk out without looking back.

WHEN I GET home, my mother is in the kitchen making dinner. I head upstairs, holding tight to the stair rail. Going up stairs still feels weird. My physio says my hip flexor is weak. He says that I need to work harder.

But the last few weeks, I just can't see the point.

"Jakey, is that you?" my mother calls. "How was therapy?"

I have to count to five before I can answer her. "Fine," I lie. "I'm getting a shower."

"Do you want to use the shower in our room?"

I grit my teeth so hard, my jaw hurts. "No."

A beat of silence. "Well, be careful of the tub rail—"

I slam my bedroom door behind me and collapse onto my bed, pressing the heels of my hands into my eyes. My heart is pounding with frustration.

Eventually, I drag myself to the shower down the hall and stare at myself in the mirror. It's hard to do. I hate myself so much these days.

It's like—I can *hear* myself being a dick, but I can't stop it. I feel so awful and hateful inside, it spills out into everything I say, everything I do.

I look away from the mirror and strip off my clothes. The doctors all say my scars have healed well, and maybe they're right. But they're still there. A long scar up the outside of my thigh, where they put a rod in my leg and screws in my hip. A dark pink splotch on my side where the chest tube was. Two marks on my right side where they did surgery to repair the cut in my liver. Three short lines where they took out my spleen. A very tiny pale dot in my neck where the central line was.

I step over the tub rail with a grunt of discomfort and stand under the shower's spray, turning it hotter and hotter, until it's almost painful. I wish I could burn the scars from my skin. I looked online and there's some sort of fancy laser therapy that could fade them, but when I mentioned it to my parents, they told me I shouldn't be worried about that right now, and that I should just be grateful to be alive. My father said the scars are a small price to pay for survival. My mother reminded me I'm better off than Antony Costa and Ellis Parrot.

And I know it's terrible—like, bottom-of-the-barrel terrible—but most days, I don't feel that way.

Almost every day, I don't feel that way.

I lie on my bed for a few hours after my shower, staring up at the ceiling, and eventually my mother comes up to check on me. I tell her I have a headache, so she doesn't make me come down to dinner. I hear my dad arrive home, hear snatches of their hushed conversation at the front door. Later, my mom brings me a tray of food, and I feel like such an asshole, I can hardly stand it.

I fall asleep around two a.m.—because although I'm exhausted all the time, I can never get to sleep—and I don't dream of the crash. I wasn't lying when I told Amanda I hadn't dreamt of it.

I only ever have one dream, over and over.

I'm standing on a stage in total darkness, and all I can hear around me is people laughing, laughing, laughing.

21
Champion of the World

I HAVEN'T BEEN ON SOCIAL MEDIA SINCE THE CRASH. I don't want to know how the F2 championship is going without me. I don't want to hear all the new deals my friends are signing, I don't want to find out who my old F2 team, Porteo, has put in my place. It's probably Estefan Ribiero, this seventeen-year-old wunderkind who won F3 last year, but if it is, I don't want to know. I already know I'm never making it back to F2. I don't need it rubbed in my face.

Some of my friends from F2 tried to keep in touch with me at first, but after months of no response, even the most determined of them gave up. Then, in early December, my parents suggested I get a US phone number and join their family plan. Now, no one from my past life has my number, and that suits me just fine.

F1 isn't as big in the US as it is in Europe, so it's not too hard to avoid it, but sometimes I hear snippets when my dad is flipping through sports channels on TV. I walk away every time that happens. I don't want to hear. I don't want to know. I don't care, I don't care, I don't care.

If I keep repeating it, I'm pretty sure it'll become true.

Two weeks before Christmas, I'm sitting in the kitchen with my mother, helping chop vegetables for dinner, when Paul arrives.

"Jakey," he says, thumping me hard on the shoulder. "How's it hanging, little bro?"

I sort of grunt in response, which is better than I usually manage. He kisses our mother on the cheek.

"Smells good, Ma." He pulls open the fridge. "Want a beer?" he asks me.

My mother titters. "You know he can't drink, Paul."

"That's not true," I say through my teeth.

"It's not recommended," she says. "Your doctor says—"

"I know what they said," I snap.

She and Paul exchange a look, like they think I can't see them.

"Of course, darling," my mother says, in placating tones. "It's the holidays, I suppose one beer can't hurt—"

"I don't want one," I say, because I really can't stop being an asshole.

She and Paul look at each other again, then Paul clears his throat.

"Candace's sister is staying with us for the holidays," he tells me. "She's about your age. I'm going to bring her for Christmas dinner. You two can sit next to each other, chat a bit—"

"Paul," my mother says with a nervous laugh. "I hardly think he should be thinking about girls right now."

"That's exactly what he should be thinking about. He needs a distraction. Right?"

"Right," I mutter. Paul grins. He's never been able to pick up on sarcasm. Or maybe he just ignores it, I don't know.

"You'll like her, Ma," he says. "She's a teacher in Highland Meadows, that fancy Catholic school."

"What does she teach?" my mother asks, interest slipping into her tone.

I get up and walk into the living room, just to get away from them. This is about the fiftieth time Paul's tried to set me up with someone. He and my parents have been dealing with the whole Travis situation by pretending it never happened. They're so good at it, sometimes I actually wonder if they've forgotten.

Lily asked me about it once, after I was transferred to the hospital here. We were alone in my hospital room, and she turned to me abruptly and said, "You and that F1 guy . . . you weren't, like, actually *with* him, were you?"

It was so obvious she wanted me to say no. I sort of shrugged, and her expression went all sour, and she never brought it up again. Looking at her, you'd think Lily would be more progressive, with her long curly hair and hipster jewelry, but she went to a Catholic high school, and her awful group of friends really leaned into the idea that being classy meant being ultra-conservative. Now she's dating this Christian block of wood with zero personality and a two-million-dollar trust fund, and she's always harping on about how there's nothing wrong with being traditional, and that a true feminist knows that the greatest joy of being a woman is caring for a good man and bearing his children.

It's always sounded like a lot of horseshit to me, but it used to be easier to ignore. She's five years older than me, and since I traveled so much for karting and racing, I never really spent that much time with her growing up. And although she used to call me every month, it always felt like something she was marking off her checklist: be a good Christian, call your brother once a month.

I sit down heavily on the couch. She and her wooden boyfriend will be here in a week, and I just know they're going to drag us all to church a hundred times and pray before every meal. I know I shouldn't resent her for it—I know she's not trying to ruin my favorite holiday—but I do. And she is.

Not like it was ever going to be good this year, anyway.

I turn on the TV and flick aimlessly through the channels.

"Call now and get forty percent off—"

Click.

"—unrest spreading throughout the country—"

Click.

"—Travis Keeping, champion of the world!"

I freeze in place, my heart rendered motionless in my chest.

I didn't even realize it was a Sunday.

I didn't realize it was the last race.

It's nighttime in Abu Dhabi, and fireworks are exploding over the track. The Harper mechanics are hanging off the fencing beside the finish line, cheering furiously as Travis flies past. Mahoney and Clayton from Crosswire Racing roar by, a second behind him.

The cameras shift to the Harper garage, where the team is in hysterics, jumping up and down and cheering.

I watch, frozen, as Travis pulls his car into parc fermé. He sits for a moment without moving, and my chest feels so tight, I'm not sure that I'm breathing.

He gets out of the car and puts the steering wheel back in. The commentator is laughing about how he still seems so unflappable.

"A man of few words," he says.

"Catching his breath, I'd say," the other commentator laughs. "That was incredible. I really thought Mahoney had him in those last few laps—"

"I think we all did! Ah, there we go—now we're seeing some excitement—"

It's true. Travis' pace is picking up, he's jogging to the crowd of Harper crew waiting for him. With his helmet still on, he pulls two of them into a tight hug.

"Look at that," the commentator says. "That's what we like to see, incredible sportsmanship from Matty—such a shame he didn't finish the race—"

"Ah, and that's Travis' partner, Heather—"

Travis is hugging a gorgeous girl with long dark hair and freckles, and there's something in the way he holds her that just breaks me into a million pieces. She's got tears in her eyes, and Travis' teammate Matty is grinning so hard it looks like his face is going to split open, and I think I might be sick.

I know that Travis is not straight. I know that girl is not his girlfriend.

But I've never seen him hug anyone the way he's hugging those two.

They let him go eventually and he walks back to take off his helmet, but I turn the TV off before it happens. I don't want to see his face.

My chest hurts so badly, and there's the most vicious, painful lump in the back of my throat.

He did it. He won the championship.

And he did it without me.

Paul is shouting something at me from the kitchen, but I can't really hear him. There's a horrible rushing sound in my ears, and it's getting harder and harder to breathe. I stumble up the stairs to my bedroom and lock the door behind me. I curl up on my bed, hug a pillow into my chest, and suck in shallow, wheezy breaths. I've never felt this way before. I can't breathe—I can't *think*. I haven't cried since my crash, not once, but my breath is coming quicker now. Hot tears spill out over my cheeks, and then I'm sobbing, flat-out bawling like a child. The commentator's words are stuck on a loop in my brain, playing over and over and over.

Travis Keeping.

Champion of the world.

22

Five Things

CHRISTMAS IS HORRIBLE. LILY AND HER BOYFRIEND ARE AWful, Paul is obnoxious, my mother is clingy, and my father barely says a word to me beyond asking if I've finished my business school applications.

I have to create an account with the application system when I finally sit down to do them, which means logging into my e-mail for the first time in months. I try to click in and out of my inbox without seeing anything, but my eyes snag on an e-mail from my old F2 team boss, Carl. It's weeks old, and tells me that Estefan Ribiero has signed with them for the next two years. He adds that things might have been different "if I'd kept in closer contact" and that they might be open to re-engaging with me down the road, "depending on the results of my recovery." The tone is polite, but the meaning couldn't be clearer. I've been replaced. They don't want me anymore.

The rest of the holiday passes by in a haze of misery, each day a little more miserable than the last. I don't sleep. I barely eat. There's a constant tightness in my chest, like a string being pulled tighter and tighter, and if I don't talk to someone who isn't in my immediate family, I think I'm going to snap.

At nine a.m. on January fifth, the first business day after the holidays and my fourth day running on two hours of sleep, I pick up the phone and make an appointment with Amanda.

She looks a bit cautious as I sit down on her couch the following day. "I was surprised to get your call," she says.

I nod stiffly. "Thank you for seeing me."

"You don't have to thank me, Jacob. I'm here to help."

I make a vague noise. "Yeah, well. I've been a dick to you."

"Well, yes," she agrees. "But you've been through a lot."

I force a thin smile.

"So?" she says. "What made you book an appointment?"

I pick at my thumbnail. I'm already half regretting the decision. "I don't know. I had a shitty break."

"How so?"

I shift on the couch. "You just want me to jump right into it?"

Amanda leans forward. "Jacob," she says. "Look at me." Reluctantly, I meet her eyes. Her stupid smile is gone, and her gaze is even. "I am not your friend or your family member. We don't need to exchange social niceties. You are here for therapy. You made this appointment for a reason. Didn't you?"

I look away from her, give a tiny nod.

"So?" she says. "What was it?"

I shift again. I feel like I'm sitting under a spotlight. "I don't know."

"Yes, you do."

I glare at her. "I don't know, alright? I couldn't sleep, I guess."

"Why couldn't you sleep?"

"If I knew that, I wouldn't be here, would I?" I snap.

She doesn't say anything in response, just raises an eyebrow like she knows that I'm lying.

Which . . . I guess I am.

"I am not your friend," she says again. "I am not your family. Pardon my language, but I don't give a damn what you tell me. Within these four walls, you can say anything you'd like. But we'll be a lot more productive if you stop arguing and start being honest."

I open my mouth instinctively on another argument, then reluctantly shut it again.

I guess she has a point.

Still, I have to swallow a few times before I can push the words out. "My ex won the F1 championship," I mutter.

"Your ex," she repeats. Then, with a faint air of surprise, "An ex-boyfriend, you mean?"

I shrug. "I don't know. We were . . . together, I guess, last year."

"'Together, I guess,'" she repeats. "What does that mean?"

I shrug again. "I don't know."

"Okay." She leans back in her chair. The silence stretches out, itchy and uncomfortable. "Tell me about him," she says.

"Like what," I say irritably.

"Well, what's his name?"

"Travis."

Travis Keeping. Champion of the world.

"What else?" I ask in a brittle voice, when Amanda just nods.

"Whatever you'd like," she says. "As long as it's the truth."

I look at my hands. The truth. The truth, the truth, the truth.

Fuck. Why is this so hard?

"What's he like?" Amanda prompts me.

"I don't know." I clear my throat. "Nice."

She lets out a surprised snort of laughter, then covers her mouth with her hand. "Sorry."

My mouth turns up a bit. I guess it was sort of a stupid answer. I swallow and try again. "He's . . . kind of quiet, I guess."

She nods. "Okay."

I pick at my thumbnail again. "He's, like, a recluse, practically. I mean, he's supposed to be this huge F1 star, but he'd never even dated anyone before me. And he doesn't have any family or friends or anything."

"Sounds lonely."

I frown. "I guess. I don't know. I think he was fine with it."

She tilts her head. "What made you decide to date him?"

I shrug one shoulder roughly. "I didn't *decide* to date him. We just started hooking up."

She raises an eyebrow. "So it was just sex?"

I grind my jaw together. Fuck, but I want to stop talking about this. "I don't know. At first, yeah."

"And then what happened?"

I look at my hands. Memories I've been trying to ignore since the crash are slipping intrusively into my mind. Travis sitting next to me at the end of that hike in Scotland, taking off his jacket to put around my shoulders. Travis lying next to me in bed, tracing his fingertips over my skin. Travis kissing me in the hospital and asking me not to die.

"I don't know," I say.

"It seems like it's hard for you to talk about him."

I shrug. "What's the point? We broke up."

"When?"

"Right after the crash."

"Did he break up with you?"

I shake my head. "I broke up with him."

The look on his face when I did it flashes in the front of my mind. I'd never seen him look like that, not even when one of the dogs he used to walk from the animal shelter died.

"Why?" Amanda asks.

I pick at a stray thread on my jeans. "I don't know," I say again.

I'm not deflecting this time. I really don't know. When I think back on the breakup, it's all so fucking blurry. All I remember is how mad I was, and how much I hated him. He fucked everything up. Everything.

"What are you thinking, Jacob?"

I open my mouth and the words just slip out. "He had no fucking right to tell my parents about us."

Her eyebrows lift. "He told your parents that you two were together?"

"Yes." My anger spills into the word. "Or—I mean, I don't know if he, like, sat them down and told them, or whatever, but he showed up in the hospital after the accident and made it fucking obvious."

"Your parents didn't know that you were gay?"

"I'm not gay," I snap.

"Bisexual, then? Or pansexual?"

I roll my eyes. "I don't even know what that means. I like women. And I'm not like, *pretending*, before you start getting on me. I'm way more into girls than guys. And I only ever date women."

"So, you weren't dating Travis."

Uncomfortable heat rises to my face. "No. I mean . . . not officially." My chest twists guiltily as I say it, which is stupid. Whatever we were, it's over now.

"Did he think you were dating?" Amanda asks.

"I don't know. Maybe."

Definitely, counters a voice in the back of my mind.

"Hm." Amanda taps her pen thoughtfully against her clipboard. I wonder what she's written on there. *This guy is a total prick*, probably. "You seem very angry with him."

"Yeah, well. He fucking ruined everything," I mumble.

She nods. "It sounds like he was a very selfish person."

I open my mouth to argue with her—I didn't say he was selfish, she isn't listening at all—then I hesitate. She's watching me closely, her expression bland.

I give her a flat look. "You're trying reverse psychology? Really?"

She cracks a smile. "It's a classic for a reason."

I snort. "Yeah, well. Fine. He wasn't selfish."

"No?"

I shake my head. It's probably the last word I would use to describe Travis. "He still shouldn't have told my parents about us," I say. But the words sound more feeble this time.

"Hm." She taps her pen again, watching me. "We have about twenty minutes left," she says. "I'm going to go make myself a cup of tea. I want you to sit here and make a list. Five things you liked about Travis, and five things you didn't."

"Like—write it down?" I say warily.

"No. Just sit here and think about it. Five specific, concrete things that you liked about Travis, and five specific things that you didn't. You don't have to tell me what they are. And you can leave as soon as you're done."

"I'm paying you for the full hour, though, right?"

"Your parents' insurance company is paying me for the full hour, yes," she says sweetly.

It almost makes me laugh. Fair enough.

"You can book another appointment on your way out, if you'd like," she says.

The door closes behind her, and I'm left alone.

I stare around the room. It's nice enough, in a generic sort of way. Light gray walls. Squashy black chairs. A bookshelf on one wall filled with old books I'm sure no one's ever read. Plants in every corner. A single window with an opaque curtain.

I heave a sigh. I should really just leave. This feels like home-work. Really cheesy, stupid homework. Obviously, there was some stuff I liked about Travis. I wouldn't have kept sleeping with him so long if there wasn't. He was, like—

Nice. And hot.

Although I guess those aren't really "specific" or "concrete."

I shift in my chair. My stupid hip is twinging a bit.

It's probably easier to start with the things I don't like. Like that he *told my fucking parents we were dating*, without even asking me first.

I mean . . . I guess I was unconscious, so he couldn't really ask me. But he should've just stayed the fuck away until I was awake. It makes me feel all hot and cringey, just thinking about him at the hospital, sitting by my bed and, like, holding my fucking hand or some shit.

Although I guess he was probably pretty freaked out that I was going to die. I guess it was really bad for the first couple of weeks. The doctors here in Albuquerque kept saying what a miracle it was that I survived. Apparently my lungs were really messed up, and my kidneys.

And like, if I *had* died, I guess it would've been really shit if Travis hadn't been able to see me. I think I'd rather have died with him holding my hand instead of, like, having Lily pray-ing over me and Paul doing his "favorite son holding the family together" act.

But I *didn't* die, did I? And Travis should've . . . known that.

I frown.

Okay, that doesn't quite make sense. Obviously he couldn't have *known* if I was going to die or not.

I sit there frozen for a minute until the obvious solution hits me. He should've told my parents we were just friends. That way, he could have been there in the hospital, but without messing everything up.

Although he probably couldn't have pulled that off. He's completely shit at lying, Travis. Like on my birthday last year, when I asked if he cared if I went out with my friends instead of him. He said it was fine, but he had this hurt-puppy-dog look on his face afterward, and he was so obviously pleased when I came home a bit early.

God, we had the best sex that night. He blew me in the shower, and then we fucked on the carpet in the hall on the way to the bedroom. That's how desperate we were, we literally couldn't make it an extra twenty feet to the bed.

I guess that can go in the "things I liked" list. The sex was amazing. Like, embarrassingly good. I used to dig my fingernails into my palms, just to pull myself out of it a bit.

That's probably why I stayed with him so long, really, even when there was so much about him I obviously didn't like.

Like how he always made me feel guilty for shit. That sim he bought me for Christmas, for example. I got him a present, I'll have you know. I told him I didn't, but that was only because what I got him was so fucking stupid compared to his huge, expensive, basically-asking-me-to-move-in-with-him gift. I don't know what he was thinking, buying it. Did he really think we were going to move in together? It's like he lives on another planet, Travis. Like, F1 races in countries where it's an actual *crime* to be gay. What was he planning to do, just skip half the races so he didn't get stoned to death somewhere?

Probably. That would be just like him, if word had ever gotten out about us. He would've shown up at the F1 press conference with his impassive face and monosyllabic answers and everyone probably just would've accepted it. You can get away with shit, when you're rich and successful and don't have uptight parents and a judgmental sister and an arrogant asshole brother.

The door creaks open and I jump. Amanda looks surprised to see me sitting there.

"Sorry, Jacob. I do need the room for my next appointment."

I glance at the clock. It's been twenty minutes, somehow.

"Right." I rise hastily. "Sorry."

"How did it go?" she asks.

"Oh." My cheeks grow hot. "I don't know. Fine, I guess. The things I didn't like, anyway. Didn't make it to the other list."

"Ah." She smiles. "Well. Something to think about on the way home, then." She steps back so I can get through the door. "Take care, now."

23

Crsswre Ltd

WHEN I GET HOME, I PARK MY MOM'S CAR IN THE GARAGE and then stand pointlessly in the kitchen for five or ten minutes. Both my parents are out, but the house still feels oppressive, like someone is watching me.

It's freezing outside, barely above zero, but I put on a pair of gloves and head out onto the street. My parents live in one of those ridiculously expensive suburbs where every house is large and fancy and almost exactly the same. Everyone who lives here tries to personalize their lawns with these stupid garden flags with cheesy slogans on them like "LIVE LAUGH LOVE" and "MY GARDEN IS MY HAPPY PLACE."

The one on our lawn says "GIVE GOD YOUR WEAKNESS AND HE'LL GIVE YOU HIS STRENGTH." Lily bought it for my mother as a Christmas gift.

The kids at the house next door are playing hockey in their driveway. They wave at me as I pass. I can see in their faces that they want to come talk to me. They love asking me questions about racing. I look away before they can say anything. I just don't have it in me today.

I keep walking, but it seems like every child in the neighborhood is outside, despite the cold. This is the problem with suburbs. You can't get away from people, ever. Even the hikes nearby are always packed.

At the very end of the street, there are three lots for sale. They're ugly but mercifully empty. One of them has a single scraggly tree. I sit down on the frozen ground and lean against it, but the angle makes my hip ache. After a minute, I think, *Fuck it*, and lie down right on the ground, using my scarf as a makeshift pillow.

The sky is a very pale, even gray. I almost wonder if it might snow. I hate being cold, but I do love snow. Especially at Christmas. When I was in London with Travis over Christmas, it snowed almost every night. He lives on one of those quaint, iconic London streets that could be in a movie or something. It had actual cobblestones, and everyone put Christmas lights up, and on the next street over, there were hundreds of lights strung between the houses, crisscrossing over the street. Every night, I'd go to the coffee shop and get a peppermint mocha, and I'd walk back under the lights with snow falling down, like some damn Hallmark Christmas movie come to life. If I'd ever let Travis come with me, it would have been exactly like one.

He always offered to come, and I always felt guilty saying no. But how stupid was he, thinking that wouldn't look suspicious? It's not a friend thing, flying halfway across the world to spend Christmas with someone and then walking under damn twinkly lights with them every night.

I exhale heavily, watching my own breath dissipate into the sky. Thinking about Travis so much is depressing. Is that what therapy is supposed to do? Depress you more?

If Travis and I were still together, I would text him that.

I guess that's something else for the "things I liked" list. It was nice having someone to text all the time. I never was big on texting with old girlfriends. It always felt like a production with them, like it had to be a whole conversation, with a start and middle and end. But it never felt like that with Travis. I could send him off a random text after a race, and a few hours later, he would text back. Sometimes it was a response to what I'd said, or just something else random. Our schedules were so different, he never expected me to text back right away, and I never expected him to text me back right away. But it was nice to have someone to send my random thoughts to. And most nights, when we weren't in the same place, we would end up texting for a while. Nothing deep or groundbreaking, just talking about our days, or whatever.

Sometimes it felt pretty cool, though. Almost like talking to a celebrity. I would watch F1's press conference and he would give some bullshit non-answer to the reporters, then later he would tell me that yes, he was pissed off at Mahoney for causing that crash. Or yes, he did think he deserved that five-second penalty for the incident with Josh Fry.

Nobody else knew how he really felt. Nobody but me.

I sort of felt . . . I don't know. Special, or whatever, when I was with him. Like, all the other F2 drivers were trying to get to F1, and wondering what it would be like, and sometimes I wanted to tell them, no, they were wrong about this or that. I knew what it was really like, because Travis told me everything.

It's weird to realize now, but Antony Costa was one of the only F2 drivers I ever talked to about Travis. I didn't tell him anything about us dating, obviously, but he knew that we were friends. I'm not even sure how it happened. I think I just mentioned Travis' name one time, and then later Antony asked me a question about him. Antony was one of those nice guys who remembered little things about people. And it was kind of fun, talking about Travis to him. It was kind of nice that someone knew that we were friends.

I wonder, if Antony had lived, if we would have become better friends. We were chatting more and more the last year or so. He told me when he broke up with his girlfriend, and he was the second person I told when I got a call from Crosswire Racing about coming in for a "chat."

The first was Travis. To be fair, he was sitting right beside me when it happened. It was one of the rare weekends we both had off, and I was at his place in London, sitting cross-legged on his bed while he made coffee in the kitchen. My phone went off as he came back into the room. I groaned as he sat down beside me.

"Who's calling?" I complained. "It's, like, five a.m. on a Saturday."

"It's eleven thirty on a Sunday," Travis said. "You want your phone?"

"Mm."

He handed it to me, and the caller ID said CRSSWRE LTD.

"Fuck." I put my coffee aside, spilling a quarter of it on myself and another half on the bedside table. "It's Crosswire. *Fuck.*"

"Don't say that when you answer," Travis said.

My fingers were shaking as I pressed Accept. Getting a call from Crosswire as an F2 driver was like—I don't know, getting a call from the queen, or something. I wish I remembered the details, but it all sort of happened in a blur. The man on the phone was one of the higher-ups at Crosswire Racing, and I remember him saying they were impressed with the season I'd had, and asking if I wanted to come in for a chat about my future. I remember Travis shoving a piece of paper and pen into my hands so I could write down the time and date. I remember saying "Holy shit" about a hundred times after I hung up. I remember Travis grinning as he watched me pace the room.

"They're going to ask you to be their reserve driver," he said.

I raked my hands through my hair. "No, they aren't!"

"They are," he said. "Why wouldn't they?"

"Because I'm only third in the championship."

"You're only third because you've had appalling luck all season. Everyone knows that. Otherwise, you'd be leading by a mile."

"No, it's probably nothing," I said. "They're probably meeting with hundreds of drivers."

He looked amused. "They're going to ask you to be their reserve driver," he said again.

I fell onto the bed, grinning stupidly. I remember being so, so happy in that moment.

"This is awesome," Travis said.

I turned my grin toward him. "You won't be saying that when Mahoney retires and I take his place. I'm going to kick your ass every weekend."

Travis smiled. "You probably will."

I rolled my eyes, still smiling. "You're so cheesy."

"Mm." His fingers curled around my wrist. "It would be cool if you were in F1."

I shifted onto my side so I could face him. "Yeah?"

"Yeah." His arm snaked around my waist, pulling me closer. "We could see each other more."

Normally, I would've ignored a comment like that. Pretended not to hear or changed the subject. But right then, it didn't bother me quite as much. If we were both in F1, it would be different. I could see him more, and it wouldn't be suspicious. Plenty of F1 drivers hung out outside of racing. And Crosswire Racing was the biggest team in the sport. They would have a huge press team to make sure that nothing got out about me that they hadn't approved.

And then, once I won a few races, and maybe a championship or two . . . once I had a long, successful career full of concrete accomplishments, who knows? Maybe I could be with Travis properly, years and years down the road, after we both retired from racing. It would still be a scandal if it got out, but no one would be able to take away anything we'd done. And no one would really be interested in two retired drivers for that long. It would be a flash in a pan, a brief flurry of media attention that would settle down quickly, and then Travis and I could travel around or something, doing whatever we wanted. We could get a place somewhere awesome and remote, like in the mountains somewhere, and every night, it would be just like this. Lying in bed with his arm pulling me closer, and his fingers digging into my skin.

They're going to ask you to be their reserve driver. He sounded so sure of it.

But the meeting ended up getting pushed a few weeks, and then I got in the crash. So I guess I'll never know if he was right.

I take a shaky breath. A year ago, I was in bed with Travis, thinking I was going to be Crosswire Racing's reserve driver. Now, I'm lying on the ground in an empty lot in the middle of winter, alone and almost crying, practically.

Slowly, I climb to my feet. I definitely feel worse than when I started this stupid little thought experiment.

I'm going to tell Amanda that at my next session.

24
Plans

"IT WASN'T SUPPOSED TO MAKE YOU FEEL BETTER,"
Amanda says.

She sounds amused. This session is actually going a little better so far. She asked me about my family when I first sat down, and it was much easier to complain about them than to talk about Travis. But now we're back on the topic. Travis, and racing, and how I *feel* about it all.

"What was it supposed to do, then?" I say tetchily.

"It was supposed to make you reflect on your relationship with him, and how you feel seeing him win the championship without you."

"Well, mission accomplished," I say. "I've reflected, and I feel shitty. What's next?"

She chuckles. "This isn't a checklist, Jacob. Therapy isn't like a video game, where you beat all the levels until you win."

"Good lord." I roll my eyes. "Did you make that shit up yourself?"

"Oh, no," she says. "I got it from my *Therapy For Dummies* textbook."

I snort out a surprised laugh. Amanda's eyes crinkle in amusement.

"Now, then," she says. "Let's do another thought experiment. Tell me, in a perfect world, what would you want your life to look like?"

"What do you mean?"

"I mean, if you had a magic wand, and you could have anything you wanted, what would your life look like? Give it a try. There are no wrong answers."

I roll my eyes again. "Okay. I'm a billionaire, and an F1 driver, and I've won, like, ten championships in a row. And teleportation is a thing, I guess. Because flying is stupid."

She laughs. "What else?"

I shrug. "I don't know." I cast my mind around. "It's never cold except at Christmas. But it's not crazy hot, either. It's just, like, fall all the time."

"Okay."

"Oh, and I have a dog."

"Alright." She taps her pen. "Anything else? Maybe sticking closer to the realms of reality, this time?"

"You should've said that in the first place."

She chuckles. "Go on."

"I don't know." I look at my hands. "I wouldn't have been in that crash, I guess."

"That's not within the realms of reality," she points out.

"Ah. Right."

She studies me. "Keep trying. Think about what you want, Jacob. That's all I'm really asking."

I hesitate. It should be such an easy question. I'm not sure why it's so hard to answer.

"I don't want to live with my parents anymore," I say finally. That's true.

"Okay."

"I want a dog." Also true.

"As you should."

"And I do want to be in F1." I let out a humorless breath. "But I guess that's outside of the realms of reality."

She frowns. "Why?"

I fight a stab of frustration. "Look, I know you mean well—believe in my dreams and all that—but that's not how F1 works. My old F2 team already replaced me with a seventeen-year-old."

"Then find another team."

"It's not—that's not how it works. They're the only team that can take me back. I had a contract with them. I still do, technically. It doesn't expire until next year."

"So, ask them to release you from your contract. Hire a lawyer if you need to."

"I can't."

"Why not?" Impatience creeps into her voice. She leans forward, putting her notepad onto her knees. "I deal with two types of people in this work, Jacob. People who are unhappy because they don't know what they want, and people who are unhappy because they do know what they want but they won't let themselves go after it. You know where you want to be. You're just making excuses because you're afraid of failing."

I hesitate. She's never spoken to me like this before, firm and direct. I feel like I've been thrown off balance. "Aren't you supposed to, like, make me realize that on my own through your weird thought experiments and annoying questions?"

"If we had years to do this, yes. But you just told me yourself—your sport moves on quickly. You can't afford to spend a year wallowing in misery, afraid to try, afraid of failing. Get through your rehab. Find a new team. Go to a lower league if you need to. There must be something below F2. F2-and-a-half, perhaps."

I crack a grudging smile. "F3."

"F3," she agrees. "Go there if you need to. Hell, go to F10 if you need to. Work your way back up."

"There's no such thing as F10."

She holds my gaze. "Look, Jacob. Last time, we did reverse psychology. This week, it's time for another classic. Tough love. The biggest obstacle between you and the things you want isn't your injuries, or your parents, or a contract. It's your own attitude and lack of motivation."

I let out a harsh, disbelieving breath. "You think I'm not motivated?"

"Yes," she says evenly. "I do."

I stare at her for a minute, fury and defiance burning hot in my chest. But when I open my mouth to argue, she interrupts.

"Am I wrong?" No longer impatient. Just a question.

I hesitate. Then, slowly, I shake my head.

She's not wrong.

"If you want something," she says, "and it's within the realms of reality that you can get it, then you need to do something about it. Right?"

I swallow and say, in a small voice, "Yes."

"Yes?"

I clear my throat and try again. "Yes."

"Good." She leans back, and it feels like the tension has snapped, as if she was holding me on a string and suddenly cut it.

I let out a shaky breath. "That was impressive," I admit. "Much better than the video game line."

She smiles. "It was good, wasn't it?"

I would laugh, if I didn't feel so off-balance. "So . . . what do I do next?"

She shrugs. "How would I know? I don't know anything about motorsport. I told you to go back to F10."

I snort. "Fair enough."

"You've got about fifteen minutes, this time," she says, rising to her feet. "I'm going to make a cup of tea while you think on your next steps."

"You're really milking this tea break thing," I say.

She smiles, and the door swings shut behind her. I'm left alone with her words circling around and around my mind, like a horse on one of those carousel rides.

If you want something, and it's within the realms of reality that you can get it, then you need to do something about it.

"WANT SOME MORE coffee, love?" my mom asks.

I look up from my computer. "Sure. Thanks."

She puts her hand on the back of my head. I don't pull away, even though I want to. I hate it when she does that, like she thinks I'm five years old. It didn't use to bother me, before the crash. Or maybe I just didn't notice, because I saw her so infrequently.

"What are you working on so early?" she asks.

"Just . . . writing an e-mail to Porteo." That's the name of my old team.

She looks alarmed. "Why? Did they reach out to you?"

"No. I just thought I would let them know I was getting better. They wanted me to stay in touch."

"Didn't they hire someone to replace you already?"

"Yes," I say stiffly.

"Well, okay," she says warily. "I just don't want you getting your hopes up."

"It's just an e-mail," I mutter.

She touches my head again, and this time I do lean away. Her words are like poison, seeping into my skin and making me rethink this whole idea. Maybe she's right. Maybe this e-mail idea is stupid.

But then I hear Amanda's voice in my head, talking about my attitude and motivation.

"Thanks for the coffee," I say through my teeth. "I'm just going to get back to this."

It's about as polite a dismissal as I can manage. My mother sighs heavily, but after a moment, she wanders off. I take a sip of coffee and refocus on my e-mail. I'm trying to find the right tone, somewhere between apology and self-defense. I stare at it for about ten minutes and then delete all the self-defense. The team boss, Carl, is a bit of a hard-ass. He won't want to hear my excuses.

A few hours and a hundred drafts later, I hit Send, then I slam my computer shut and drive to the gym. I get on the treadmill and tell myself I'm not going to look at my e-mail again until after dinner.

I last about an hour before I open my e-mail on my phone. I'm not expecting anything. Carl is a busy guy, he's not going to be sitting around checking his e-mail.

But there is something.

My fingers go numb as I click on it. As I read it, my stomach sinks lower and lower.

To be fair, he isn't a dick about it. He says he appreciates my reaching out. He admires my dedication to motorsport. He hopes my recovery continues to go well. But, no. There isn't a place for me on the team right now.

I'd offered to come back in any capacity, even as a reserve, but he doesn't even acknowledge that. And at the end is the worst part—a polite note that he'll connect me with the team lawyer to arrange a release from my contract.

My heart twists painfully. If he thought I had a chance of getting back in F2, he wouldn't be offering to release me. The fact that he is . . . it means he knows I don't have a chance at any other team.

My hand drops heavily to my side. I'm trying to stay positive, but there's a painful lump in my throat.

Fuck.

Somehow I get back on the treadmill, just to have something to do, and I end up walking another five miles, staring off at the wall, trying to feel nothing. My physiotherapist is going to tell me I pushed myself too hard, but I'll deal with that tomorrow.

I go home and shower and stare at my reflection in the mirror, and I say it out loud. "Porteo doesn't want me back."

Then I crawl into bed and have a stupid cry in the dark.

In the morning, I make a list of all the other F2 teams, and start hunting for contact information.

25

A New Classic

I NEVER THOUGHT I'D SAY IT, BUT IT'S A GOOD THING I HAVE a therapist now.

For weeks, I've done nothing but send e-mails and make phone calls. I have a list in my phone of all the F2 teams, and every few days, I delete a few more names off of it. Everyone sings a different version of the same song. They're so happy I survived the crash. They're so glad I'm working on my recovery. They're so sorry they don't have a place to offer me, but maybe I should check back again next year.

I feel like I'm living in a cycle. Send an e-mail. Get my hopes up. Get rejected. Feel like shit. Find another team. Send another e-mail. Get my hopes up. Get rejected. Feel like shit.

Over and over and over.

My parents don't know anything about it, which is just as well. My mom's been making comments lately about how relieved she is that I'm not driving anymore. She says she doesn't know how she'd survive it, seeing me get into another "metal deathtrap," and all my dad ever asks me is if I've heard back from my business school applications.

I have, actually. I got into two of them. I could start in the fall, if I wanted to.

Which I don't.

Amanda has become sort of a pillar in my life, as much as I hate to admit it. I see her three times a week now, which is beyond pathetic and yet somehow feels like too little, and I tell her about every single rejection. Part of me almost hopes that she'll give up and admit I was right. But she never does. And on the third week of February, when I delete the final two F2 teams from my list and have a total fucking breakdown in her office, she listens to me curse and cry and then tells me to make a new list, for F3.

"I was also reading about Formula E," she adds. "It's all electric, which I expect some drivers won't be interested in. That's got to be easier to get into, surely."

A few months ago, I would've snapped at her ignorance, but now it cheers me up a little.

"It's not easier," I say. "But thanks."

She smiles. "How are you doing with your other homework?"

I grimace. "Do we have to talk about this today?"

"Yes," she says evenly.

With effort, I resist the urge to sink down into the couch like a sulking child. A few weeks ago, after she spent twenty minutes asking probing questions about my relationship with Travis, which I did my level best not to answer, Amanda frowned and said, "You seem to have a complicated relationship with queerness."

I grimaced at the word, then rolled my eyes and told her no, I didn't. She proceeded to spend the next three sessions proving why, exactly, I was wrong.

Since then, she's insisted on devoting a great deal of time to conversations that, more often than not, make me want to claw my own skin off. Like when I first remember being attracted to a guy, and how I *felt* about it, and why I never considered dating a guy before Travis. That was my homework from last week's session, and if I'm honest, I haven't tried to think about it at all.

"Well?" Amanda prompts me.

I sigh. "I don't know. He's not, like, some average guy, I guess. I mean, he's famous and everything."

"And you think that outweighed your internal resistance? That it's 'okay'"—she frames the word with her fingertips—"to date a guy, as long as he's rich and famous?"

"I didn't say rich," I say dryly. "And yeah. I guess so."

"Hm."

That's her disagreeing sound. "What?" I complain. "It's the truth."

"Part of the truth, maybe. Dig deeper."

I make a frustrated noise. "I don't have anything 'deeper.'"

She gives me a flat look. "Yes, you do. Think, Jacob. What was it about Travis that made you willing to break your self-imposed rules?"

I look away from her. I cast my mind around for some bullshit answer to give her, because the real answer has risen up to my mind from out of nowhere, and I don't like it. I don't like it at all.

"Jacob," Amanda says.

I lick my lips and spit it out. "I was always in control."

The words hang in the silence that follows, which stretches out long enough that my palms start to itch. I wait for Amanda to press me for more, but instead she puts down her notepad and nods.

"Good," she says quietly. "Very good."

AT THE END of the session, instead of heading home, I drive to a nearby park and go for a hike. It's way too cold out, and I'm not dressed for it at all, but going back to my house right now would be impossible. My mind is too full of spinning thoughts.

I walk quickly to try to stay warm, keeping my eyes on the frozen ground. I know all the poisonous snakes in New Mexico hibernate in winter, but I'm still convinced I'll step on one every time I hike here.

That's what my mind feels like right now, actually. A huge pit full of snakes I don't want to step on. I snort at the image, and the tense muscles in my shoulders relax just a little.

I let out a long breath. Despite what Amanda must think, I'm not actually an idiot. I know I have issues with being bi. And I've always known, in a distant sort of way, that someday I'd have to face up to them. But the truth is, the thought of dating a guy doesn't scare me nearly as much as the thought of dating *anyone* seriously. The thought of . . . opening up to someone.

Even thinking the words makes me cringe. I've never been—to use Amanda's stupid therapy words—"emotionally vulnerable" with anyone. My high school girlfriend and I dated for three years and had a great time together, but she was an easygoing, pragmatic kind of girl, and I was away a lot of the time for racing. I liked her a lot, but I never felt like I lived or died on our relationship. More than anything, we felt like good friends who just happened to have sex.

Since her, I've never dated any girl longer than a few months, and I've never had anything but one-night stands with guys. And if I look back on the girls I've dated . . . honestly, I knew going in that I wasn't in any danger of falling for any of them. That's probably a large part of why I went out with them in the first place. I was always nice to them, always respectful and attentive and all that, but I never really *cared*. I never let things get serious. I never wanted anything serious.

Then Travis Keeping walked into that TV interview at the Austrian Grand Prix, with his insane answers to that reporter's game (what kind of psychopath likes rain more than sun?) and his empty Photos folder and his weird spa music. He was so obviously interested in me, and so shockingly different from the stoic figure he cut in the press, and from our very first moments together, I felt in control.

It's a shitty thing to admit, but it's true. I had all the power, and all the experience. Because it wasn't just that he was a huge F1 star. He was a huge F1 star who'd never kissed anyone, never slept with anyone, never even had a close friend before me. And for some reason, he was ridiculously into me, and not even remotely able to hide it. I had all the control, and I knew it.

I think that feeling of control lured me into a false sense of security. I was so confident I had Travis on a string, I didn't notice the warning signs. Thinking about him all the time. Texting him more and more frequently. Finding any excuse to go to London to spend time with him. I told myself it didn't mean anything, that it was just a fun, casual thing, but the truth crept up on me, as it so inevitably does.

The first time I realized I was in trouble was in Montreal. It was always one of my favorite Grand Prix weekends. I liked the city, the track, the restaurants. A girl I knew from high school, Talia, worked as a chef there. She and I had kept in touch a bit over the years, and I sent her a message a few days before to see if there were any new restaurants I should check out.

My message wasn't meant to be suggestive—if anything, I had a half-baked plan of taking Travis to whatever place she recommended—but she sent back a winky face and said she'd love to go with me to check out a new place.

My first thought when I read her message was, *I can't, I'm not single.*

My next thought was *Fuck*.

It was coupled with an enormous wave of panic, and if I'd been an emotionally mature, self-actualized person, I would have realized where the panic stemmed from and told Talia no, I couldn't go out with her, because I was already dating somebody else.

Instead, I said yes to prove to myself that I could, and tried to convince myself that Travis wouldn't care. Or that even if he did care, it didn't matter, because I had to make it clear to him that whatever we had between us wasn't a serious thing. That he didn't have any power over me, didn't have any hold on my heart.

But that damn look on his face when I told him. Like I'd slapped him, or pulled the rug out from under his feet.

I pretended not to notice, not to care, but then it was ten o'clock that night, and I was sitting across from this pretty, interesting, perfectly dateable girl, and all I could think of was Travis. Alone in his hotel room, being sad about me. I had all the power in our relationship, and I was using it to hurt him.

A mature person would have politely excused himself from dinner and headed straight to Travis to have a serious talk. Instead, I got plastered to silence my fears, and made a slurred, barely coherent admission in his doorway. *All yours*, I told him. *All yours*.

I don't remember the trip to his hotel, or what I said to Talia when I left the restaurant, but I do remember the look on his face after I told him that. And I remember the look on his face the next morning, when I sat down next to him on the couch and hooked my chin over his shoulder. I had made him happy, really happy, and damn it if it wasn't like a drug. I got addicted to it, that feeling of making him happy. I let myself open up to him, because I liked how much he liked it.

And then, six months after our first night together, he stood in his kitchen in London and told me he loved me.

I remember exactly how it felt. It was just like the start of my first race in Formula 2. I started in sixth, but I got an amazing run off the line and was in second place by the end of turn one. There was one moment of huge, leaping joy—then someone slammed into the side of my car, and I went cold all over with terror. I wasn't scared of being injured, but of crashing out of my very first race. In that split second, I had a vision of being dumped by my team, laughed at in the press, my whole racing career crumbling into nothingness.

Maybe that vision was a prophecy, now that I think about it.

Anyway. That brilliant, leaping joy followed by a wave of utter terror, that's how I felt when Travis told me that he loved me.

I pretended not to hear him, pulling out my earbud and saying, "Sorry?" and hoping to hell he wouldn't have the confidence to say it again. I saw him panic, watched him falter, and then I walked out of his house with my whole body trembling.

I went for a run with my friend Nate, who was visiting London, and tried to listen while he told me about his new girlfriend, a flight attendant.

"She has the wildest stories about people on planes," he said. "I swear they should make a TV show out of it. She's crazy good at calming people down. She could be, like, a hostage negotiator for the FBI, or something."

I made a vague noise of agreement, and he kept on talking, his affection for her spilling out in every story. I was tempted to ask him if he loved her, and if so, how he knew.

I convinced him to go for dinner afterward, as an excuse to stay out a little longer, but by nine o'clock he was eager to get back to his girlfriend. I was not eager to get back to Travis. I was cold and jittery and anxious, and sorely tempted to do something incredibly stupid, like go to a bar and get trashed.

I was just sensible enough to know what a bad idea that would be. Instead, I sat on the front steps of Travis' house for an hour or more, shivering and trying to think about nothing. I would have happily stayed out there all night, but the cold finally drove me inside. I opened the door quietly, hoping Travis would be asleep. It wasn't that late, but he went to bed early most nights.

The kitchen and living room were dark, but yellow light spilled from Travis' open bedroom door. I went completely still at the sight of it. If turning around and bolting had been a viable option, I would have done it.

Somehow, I forced myself to walk forward. Travis was reading a book in bed, his legs stretched out in front of him. He looked up when I entered and said, "Hey."

I didn't answer him. I was caught in his warm, easy smile, my heart pounding like it was trying to escape my chest. I don't know how I'd ever tried to convince myself this was a casual thing. It wasn't casual, the way that he looked at me. It wasn't casual, the way I felt when he looked at me.

I cleared my throat and turned away. "I'm gonna grab a shower."

He made a noise of acknowledgment, and I escaped to the bathroom. I stood under the shower's spray for way longer than necessary, trying to figure out what the hell I was going to do if Travis told me he loved me again. I couldn't pretend I didn't hear it if he said it straight to my face. And he'd expect some sort of answer.

"You have fun with Nate?" he asked, when I finally returned to the bedroom.

"Yep." A little silence fell as I pulled on a T-shirt and boxers. When I looked up again, he was looking at me. Meaningfully, I thought. Like he might try to say those words again. "What're you reading?" I blurted out.

He glanced down at the book in his hands. "*1984.*"

"I think I read that in high school. Or I was supposed to, anyway. I don't remember if I actually did." I was only vaguely aware of what I was saying. I climbed into bed, keeping a careful foot of distance between us. "'Kay, well. Night."

"Night." He sounded faintly amused.

I rolled onto my side so my back was to him, yanked the covers up to my chin, and closed my eyes. He couldn't tell me anything if I was asleep.

But a second later, he said, "Hey, Jacob?"

My heart thudded anxiously. "Yeah?"

"I'm gonna go to the store early tomorrow. D'you want anything?"

"Oh." A flood of relief ran through me. Relief, and the tiniest bit of disappointment. "No. I'm good."

"'Kay."

I waited, with my heart in my throat, for him to say something else, but the minutes ticked by and the silence remained unbroken. After ten or fifteen minutes, I heard him put his book down and turn off his bedside lamp. He shifted down into bed, not touching me. We rarely fell asleep touching, but more often than not, I woke up with his arm around me, or my fingers tangled with his under my pillow.

His breathing evened out into sleep, but I don't think I'd ever been more awake. When I was sure he was asleep, I rolled over to face him. There was just enough light filtering in around the edge of the closed curtains for me to make out his features. The strong angle of his jaw, the soft curve of his lips. Travis Keeping, the man who was in love with me.

I knew what I should do if he tried to say it again. I should tell him I wasn't looking for something serious, and put an end to things.

But I also knew I couldn't do that. The very thought made me feel anxious and sick. I didn't want to break up with him. I wanted to be the guy he was in love with. I wanted him to love me, and I wanted to never have to say it back.

It was selfish, but that's how I felt. All the power I thought I had in our relationship had slipped through my fingertips, and now that it was gone, I realized it had never really existed. Travis was a rich Formula 1 star who read books and donated money to animal shelters and looked like a statue of some Greek god come to life. Who was I, but the first bisexual guy he'd happened to stumble upon? It was absurd that he loved me. Absurd that he looked at me like he couldn't believe his own good luck.

Fear bubbled up in my chest. Someday, he would realize that, and the thought was almost as terrifying as the idea of telling him I loved him.

Which I did. Of course I did. I didn't need to ask Nate how he knew he loved his girlfriend. I knew the answer, because I knew I loved Travis. I just didn't know what the hell I was supposed to do with that information.

I shifted closer to him, suddenly desperate to be touching him, and he pulled me close without waking. With my head on his chest, I listened to his heartbeat, one strong beat for every three rapid beats of my own.

I would tell him, I decided, with a surge of reckless bravery. When he said it again, I would say it back. I mouthed the words against his T-shirt, practicing. *I love you. I'm in love with you.*

For the next few days, every time a silence fell between us, my stomach would tighten in anticipation. But the days turned to weeks turned to months, and he never said it again. And now—

I pull myself out of my memories. I've reached the end of the hike. The view ahead is brown and gray and drab, and my face and hands are numb from cold.

I sit down heavily on the bench nearby, and for a minute, I let myself imagine what would have happened if I hadn't been such a coward. If I'd woken Travis up that night and asked him to say it again. The look on his face if I'd said it back. He would have been so, so happy. And I would have kept chasing that feeling, I know I would have. Moving in with him, telling my friends about him, maybe even telling my parents, for whatever that shitshow would have been worth.

Maybe I wouldn't have been in the crash, if I'd told him I loved him. Maybe I'd have been distracted thinking about him during qualifying, and started behind McDougall or Theriot. Or maybe he would've given me some tip about the track, and I would've started farther up the grid, with Ellis Parrot behind me.

Or maybe the crash would have been even worse, for some reason, and I would have died on track. I don't know. I don't know what would have happened, really.

I know I still love him. I do know that.

But I guess it doesn't matter, now.

26
The Realms of Possibility

THE FEBRUARY WEATHER GETS EVEN MORE MISERABLE, AND I start making my way through my list of F3 teams. I add some teams from the F4 leagues in the US and UK as well. That would be . . . a huge step down. But I figure it can't hurt. Plus, I'm kind of hoping for some easy yeses, to make myself feel better. I was running third in last year's F2 championship before the crash, and I finished second the year before. Surely some team will want me.

Spoiler alert: they don't.

I start to have nightmares about e-mails. Every time I go to therapy, I get this weird terror that Amanda is going to sit me down and tell me it's finally time to give up. And when I'm at home, I get these random bursts of panic, my heart rate suddenly taking off at the thought of wasting another day in Albuquerque. I need to get back into racing. I need to get out of my parents' house.

"Get an apartment now, then," Amanda says, when I tell her this.

I shake my head. "I'll need every dollar I've saved if I want to race in F3 or F4. Unless I can find a sponsor, which I can't." Trying to get sponsors has been even worse than trying to find a new team. At least the teams tell me no. Sponsors—the big money ones, anyway—don't answer e-mails, and they definitely don't answer cold calls.

"Who was your sponsor before?"

I make a frustrated noise. "They were all through Porteo. I got into their young driver program in karting, then I was with them all through F3 and F2."

My manager was through Porteo, too. I reached out to him weeks ago, and he sent back a polite e-mail saying he thought it would be best if we parted ways. On his website, he has Estefan Ribiero listed as a new client.

Amanda opens her mouth and then closes it again, and something wobbles inside of my chest.

"I should give up now, right?" I hate the way my voice shakes. "I know you're thinking it."

"No," she says slowly. "But you might end up having to try again next year."

I press the heels of my hands into my eyes. "*Fuck.*"

"Is that the worst thing?" she asks. "Your physiotherapist's only just cleared you to race again. Is waiting another year really all that bad?"

"Yes." I swipe angry tears from my face. "It is the worst thing. I need to race this year."

"Why?" she asks. "And don't tell me about the younger drivers again. I've done my research, you know. There are plenty of twenty-three and twenty-four-year-olds in F2. I know it's not what you wanted, but in the grand scheme of your life—"

"I have to race again this year," I interrupt. "I have to. I can't piss away another year. I can't go another year feeling like *this*. I want my old life back."

She looks up from her notepad. "Your old life?" she asks. "Or Travis?"

My stomach lurches forward, as if I've come to the end of a set of stairs and thought there was another step at the bottom.

"What do you mean?" I ask warily.

"I know you want to get back to racing," she says, sounding like she's choosing her words carefully. "But is this also about Travis? Being part of his life again, maybe, or being 'good' enough to be with him?" She frames the word "good" with her fingertips.

My face is on fire. "No."

"Are you sure?"

"Yes." I look down at my hands. "No. I don't know."

She nods slowly. "I see."

I scowl at her. She knows I hate when she says that. Just like she knows when I'm being full of shit.

Because, yeah. I have been thinking about Travis lately. Almost constantly, really, since my hike in the park. It's, like, part of the cycle of feeling shitty. Send an e-mail. Get my hopes up. Think about what Travis will do when I show up at the track again. Play out the first conversation we'll have. Think about having sex with him again.

Get rejected. Feel like shit. Repeat.

"If you want to see him again," Amanda says, "then go see him."

My cheeks burn hotter. "I can't."

"Why not?"

"Because," I stammer. "I don't have a seat for next year. I can't even get the worst teams in F4 to take me."

"So?"

"So, it's pathetic."

"Is that what he liked about you? Your racing credentials?"

I scowl. "Don't say it like that, like it doesn't matter."

"Does it?"

"Yes," I snap. "It does. I wouldn't be into Travis anymore if he turned into a shit driver. I wouldn't be attracted to him if he got really lazy and stopped caring about winning. And that's not being a bad person, okay, that's just being honest."

"Okay," she says slowly. "But we're not talking about you being lazy, or being a 'shit driver.' You've had some terrible luck, and yes, you don't have a new team yet. But you're working incredibly hard. Your rehab team cleared you two months earlier than they thought they would. And you haven't given up, even after all these rejections."

I make a dismissive noise. "Yeah, and I have nothing to show for it."

"I disagree," she says. "You are a completely different person compared to when I met you. Do you know how rare it is, for people to change?" She gives me a small smile. "You're very impressive, Jacob. Truly."

I look away from her, discomfited.

"Look," she says. "Do you know why a lot of people struggle with diets? It's because they keep waiting for the ideal circumstances to start. They'll start working out when their new gym equipment arrives. They'll stop eating sugar after that office party next week. They slipped up at breakfast, so now there's no point eating well the rest of the day." She shrugs. "If you wait for everything in your life to be perfect before you take action, then you'll be waiting forever. If you want something, and it's within the realms of reality that you can get it . . ."

"You need to do something," I mutter. "You're really proud of that one, aren't you?"

"Definitely." She smiles. "I think it's a new classic."

I manage a small smile in return. "I guess . . . you're not wrong."

"High praise."

I look at my hands. "But, like . . . even if I wanted to see him, I don't have his number anymore. I got rid of my old phone." I don't tell her about the time a week ago, when Paul and his girlfriend—fiancée, now—came over for dinner and I was playing a drinking game with myself, where I drank every time I wanted to smack him, and I accidentally got drunk and stayed up till two a.m. trying to remember Travis' number. That's the problem with cell phones, you don't ever see anyone's number. I thought it ended in 4697, but the old woman who answered that number was definitely not Travis and definitely didn't appreciate being bothered on a Sunday morning.

Amanda raises a wry eyebrow. "If only there were some other way of communicating with people these days . . ."

"Travis doesn't have any social media. I mean, he must have an e-mail address, I guess, but I don't know what it is."

Amanda frowns. "I thought he had Instagram." She reaches into her pocket and takes out her phone. "I would never look up a patient's partner online, mind you, but when I was reading about F1 I could've sworn I saw a post from his Instagram."

I shake my head. "His team has an account, it was probably from there."

Amanda is still frowning at her phone. "Isn't this him?"

She hands me her phone, and my stomach drops. It's an Instagram account, @traviskeeping94, with a little blue check by his name and 4.6 million followers. There are only three pictures. The first is a picture of him, Matty, and Heather. It must have been taken right after he won the championship. They're all smiling, and bits of golden confetti are caught on their hair and clothes. Travis has one arm around Matty's shoulders and the other around Heather's waist. There isn't any caption.

The next picture is of a dog with black fur and a white patch over one eye. It's one of the dogs from the shelter near his house. It's sitting on his kitchen floor—I recognize the tiles—wearing a bright blue collar that looks new.

The last picture is another one of him and Matty and Heather. It looks like they're camping somewhere. Heather is sitting in a camp chair with a beer in her hand, looking effortlessly pretty with her long hair tucked under a ball cap, and Matty is laughing at something, and Travis is only half in the frame, putting a log on the fire. There's a big lake in the background, and a mountain.

"I'm sorry," Amanda says. "I didn't realize you didn't know. I shouldn't have sprung it on you."

I try to answer her, but there's a painful lump in my throat. I swallow hard until it goes away. "It's fine. Looks like he's doing great."

She frowns at me. "Right. Because everything that's posted on Instagram is a completely realistic reflection of a person's life."

I give her a hollow smile. "Travis doesn't play games like that."

"Okay," she says. "Maybe he is happy. Or maybe he's miserable. Or maybe he's happy some of the time, and miserable some of the time, and in-between some of the time, like most human beings are. Maybe he misses you and wants you back, or maybe he's moved on." She gives me a gentle smile and a shrug. "You'll never know unless you reach out."

IT TAKES ME a day to work up the nerve to log in to my Instagram account. I haven't been in it for months. I have to download the app on my phone again and reset my forgotten password. The moment I log in, I'm hit with that stupid little red number on the top right-hand corner telling me I have sixty-six new messages. I stare at the number with my gut twisted into knots for ten minutes before I finally click on it.

All the messages are months old, every last one of them. I click through them slowly. Most of them are from other drivers or people involved in F2, polite messages saying they hope my recovery is going well. One of my exes sent me a weird, rambling message about how the crash "made her realize how much she needed me," and how she always thought fate would bring us back together, and to message her so we could meet up. I click on her profile and see about fifty pictures of her with some muscular guy I vaguely recognize as an Olympic skier. I snort. I guess fate took her in a different direction when I didn't message her back.

I get to the end of the messages, trying not to be disappointed that none of them are from Travis. Slowly, I type in his handle and click on his profile. There are still only three pictures, and he's only following about fifty people. I go through every single one of them, because I'm just that pathetic, but they're all pretty standard, other F1 drivers and engineers and team accounts. The only one that gives me pause is a private account, @notrlyahunter, but when I zoom in on the profile pic, I could swear that's Heather with her arm around a handsome blond guy. My spirits lift a little bit when I find the same blond guy in a few pictures on Heather's account. I bet that's her real boyfriend.

I go downstairs and get two beers from the fridge, trying to be quiet so my parents don't hear, like I'm a teenager again. I know it's childish, but I can't answer another question about business school. I cracked and told my parents I got into a few, and now they won't stop asking which one I've chosen.

I down the first beer in about five minutes. I think this will be easier if I'm slightly tipsy, and ever since my accident I have the alcohol tolerance of a tiny child. Amanda and I have had several lengthy, exhausting talks about my previous tendency to use alcohol to stifle unwanted emotions, but I'm hoping she'll let it slide just this once. I crack open the second beer, log in to Instagram on my laptop, and open up my messages. I type in Travis' handle, open a direct message, and then I just sit there, staring at the screen.

Honestly, he probably won't even see whatever I send. He isn't following me, and he's got 4.6 million followers and a verified account. I'm sure whatever I send will go straight into the "creepy unsolicited fan mail" folder.

But it's not like I have any other options.

I start typing, then immediately delete what I've written. One hour passes, then two. I check my e-mail. Another rejection from an F3 team. They're so flattered I thought of them, but no. They don't have a spot for a washed-up loser. I drink a third beer. Draft another ten messages to Travis.

Hey. You finally caved and got Instagram?

How's it going?

Congrats on the championship.
How's the break going?

> Did you really get Instagram? Or did
> the team set this up for you? lol

> I AM A FUCKING IDIOT.

I bang my head against my desk. All of these are terrible, though at least the last one is true.

I open my phone and type in the first six digits of Travis' phone number. I'm sure those are right. It's the last four numbers I can't figure out. 4796? 4776? There was definitely a four and a seven.

And a nine, I think.

Fuck, fuck, fuck.

I slam my laptop closed. I don't want to send him an Instagram message that he'll never see. It's too hard, and I'm too bad with words. If I could see him, I probably wouldn't even need to say anything. He would just look at me and then let out a long, heavy breath and pull me into his arms. I can imagine it so clearly, I can practically feel his warmth against me. I can remember what his skin smelled like, that British brand of soap I can't remember the name of.

I open my laptop again and type "Travis Keeping manager London" into Google. Maybe I can find a number for his manager's office, and somehow get his number from them.

I don't have any luck. The only thing that comes up are press articles. "Keeping's Manager Colt Drops Hints About Extended Harper Contract" and "Aaron Colt, Manager of Formula 1 Racers Such as Travis Keeping and Peyton Small, Signs New IndyCar Talent."

I click through the articles aimlessly, until my finger freezes over one from some scammy-looking tabloid site called *Star-*

Watch. It was posted a day ago. The headline reads "Formula 1 Star Travis Keeping Walks Dog Near London Home."

There's a picture of him walking the black dog from his Instagram. He has a gray sweater on, and black jeans I've never seen him wear, and he's got a coffee in one hand and his dog's leash in the other.

Jesus, he looks so fucking good.

I stare at the picture longer than I'm proud of. I keep noticing little details. He's got a thin rope bracelet on his right wrist that I've never seen before. His sneakers are different, too. And his hair is a little bit longer than the last time I saw him. It suits him really well like that.

His body is insane. It must be freezing in London—everyone in the back of the picture is wearing jackets and gloves—but he only has a sweater on, and his right sleeve is shoved up past his elbow, revealing the strong lines of his forearm. And I don't know if it's because I know what he looks like naked, but I swear I can see the outline of his abs through his sweater.

Fuck. My eyes travel up and down his frame. He really could be a model. And he has no idea how hot he is, which of course makes him a hundred times hotter.

I run my thumb absently over my beer and shift on my chair. I don't want to send Travis an Instagram message. I want to see him. I want to feel his skin on mine.

My eyes move to the photo's timestamp. It was taken two days ago.

Two days ago, Travis was in London.

My heart starts beating faster. I'm half hard and three-quarters drunk, and I open Expedia without letting myself stop to think about it. Albuquerque is stupidly inconvenient. The shortest last-minute trip to London costs two thousand dollars and takes eighteen hours, with two stops.

But for two grand, I could be in London the day after tomorrow. The day after tomorrow, I could be standing at Travis' front door.

I stare at his picture a little while longer. I think about what it would feel like to be in his arms.

Then I drain the last of my beer and click Book.

27

A Huge Deal

MY FLIGHT DOESN'T LEAVE UNTIL FIVE P.M. THE NEXT DAY, which gives me about eight hours to make up a lie to tell my parents. I'm pretty proud of what I came up with. My old high school girlfriend Kelsie lives in London now. I tell my parents she reached out, and that we've been messaging a bit, and that I'm going to go visit her for a while.

"A while?" my mother says anxiously. "What does that mean?"

I shrug. "I don't know. A week. Maybe two."

"You didn't book a flight back?"

I shrug again. "Not yet."

My parents exchange a look. "Are you sure you're well enough?" my mother asks.

I make myself count to three before I answer. "My rehab team's cleared me to race again. I think I can handle sitting in a plane for a few hours."

More than a few hours, actually. I'm flying from Albuquerque to Chicago to Dublin to London, with two-hour layovers at each stop.

My mother hesitates. "What does your therapist say?"

I count to three again and force a smile. "She thinks it's a great idea."

That part is actually true. I left a message with Amanda's secretary telling her I wouldn't make my sessions for a while, because I was going to London to see Travis. An hour later, Amanda called and told me she was proud of me.

I'm kind of proud of myself, too. I mean, yes, I was a little drunk when I did it, but it was definitely the right thing to do. I keep getting these little bursts of fizzy excitement every time I think about it. In less than twenty-four hours, I'll see Travis again.

"What does Kelsie do in London?" my mother asks.

"She's going to school there, doing her masters in anthropology." I know this, because I looked at her Instagram.

"Is she married?"

I roll my eyes. "Mom."

"What?" She holds her hands up. "I'm allowed to ask." She's quiet for a second, then her mouth turns up a little. "I always liked her."

Of course she did. On paper, Kelsie was her idea of a perfect girlfriend. Shiny blond hair, pretty pastel clothes, always smiling, always polite.

When our parents weren't around, though, she was kind of a badass. She was the first person I ever got drunk with, and the first person I smoked weed with, and the first girl I ever slept with. We were together all through high school and broke up completely amicably after graduation. I remember her grinning and saying something like, "This isn't *High School Musical*, babe. High school sweethearts who stay together forever wind up as bitter alcoholics with no imagination and fifteen kids."

We kept in touch for a while—we even hooked up a few times when we both happened to be in Albuquerque—but I haven't talked to her in ages. I have half a mind to actually message her once I'm in London, after I've sorted things out with Travis, to see if she wants to grab coffee or something.

I can kind of see telling her about me and Travis. I don't think she'd judge me. She would probably be like, "That's hot, babe," and ask me to text her a sex tape of me and him or something.

"Are you going to stay with her the whole time?" my mother asks. "You don't want to impose."

"I'll get an Airbnb or something."

Her eyes widen. "You haven't booked anything yet?"

"You should book a hotel," my father says. "Most of those Airbnb places are scams. You show up and it's a shack, or there's nothing there."

"That happened to Janice and Bob!" my mother says. "And they never got their money back, you know. The foreign police wouldn't even investigate."

I can guarantee that's not what happened to Janice and Bob, whoever they are, but I can't be bothered to argue.

"Fine." I rise to my feet. "I'll go book a hotel."

I've actually already booked one. For the first night, anyway. I want to have somewhere to shower and throw my things before I go to see Travis. But I'm hoping I won't need it after one night.

"Do you need help packing?" my mother calls after me.

I roll my eyes as I climb the stairs. "Nope. Thanks."

"What time should we leave for the airport?"

I almost say that I'll get a taxi, but I count to five and think better of it. "Three o'clock," I call back.

WE GET THERE at two o'clock, because my mother was worried three hours wasn't enough time to get through security.

"Call as soon as you land," she says, kissing my cheek. She looks anxious, like she's sending a five-year-old off to their first day at school. I had to count to five about a million times in the car, but I do feel a twinge of guilt as she walks away. I know she means well, deep down. And I really think I'll be able to tolerate it better once I'm out of the house. People just aren't meant to live with their parents after high school.

I kill an hour grabbing dinner in the Albuquerque airport and then another watching old episodes of *The Office* on Netflix. I've got Travis' Instagram open in another tab, and I hear a little ding as a message comes in. My heart leaps. For a second, I forget that I never sent Travis a message, and I wonder if he's messaging me.

Obviously, he isn't. The message is from @london.kel247.

Shit.

I click on it nervously.

> Hey babe! Your mom called mine a little while ago. Really looking forward to our London trip this week. Can't believe it slipped my mind ;);)

I let out a strangled laugh.

There's a green dot by her name—she's online now. I type quickly. Shit. Sorry. Should've messaged. Kind of used you as an excuse . . .

She answers right away. Don't apologize, I love it. Hope you're doing something scandalous.

> I think you'd approve.

;);) Bet I would. If your mom asks, though, make sure you tell her about the London Portrait Gallery. And the Tower of London. And Stonehenge. My mom kept asking about our plans. Had to make up a bunch of shit.

I laugh out loud. Thanks.

No worries, babe. How are you? I heard about the crash. Really glad you didn't die. Has everything been total shit since?

Thanks. And yes. Been living with my parents again.

!?!?!?!!?!?!? Are you kidding?

Nope.

BABE. Come and stay with me in London! I'll kick my flatmate out tomorrow.

I laugh again. You don't have to do that.

Meh. I was planning on doing it anyway. She's the worst. For real, though. You need to get out of your parents' place!!

Tell me about it. Working on it, though. I hesitate and then add, That's why I'm headed to London, actually.

Oh yeah??

I hesitate again and glance around the airport. People are milling about, minding their own business. I still have a half hour to kill. I lick my lips and look back at my phone. It's so easy to talk to Kelsie again. It was always like that, every time we met up. We just fall back into step with each other.

Slowly, I start typing again. Yup. Meeting up with an ex.

If it's that dumbass model from two years ago, Jacob, I swear to god . . .

Lol. She wasn't that bad.

She was EXACTLY that bad. She uses the hashtag #skinnygirlproblems on ALL OF HER POSTS. ALL OF THEM.

I snort. Okay, fine. She was that bad.

So who's the new girl?

I hesitate. My heart is doing gymnastics in my chest, and I'm biting my lip so hard, I'm going to draw blood.

I don't know what to type, so finally I just go to the screenshot that I saved of the picture of Travis walking his dog, say a prayer to a god I don't believe in, and send it to her.

The next five seconds are some of the longest in my life. I wait, clutching my phone, then—

SHUT THE FUCK UP.

ARE YOU KIDDING ME RIGHT NOW!?!?!

HE

IS

GORGEOUS!!!!!!!!!!!

The words are followed by a GIF of a girl fainting.

My cheeks go bright red. Omg, lol, chill out, I type. It's not a big deal.

(It's a huge fucking deal.)

IT'S A HUGE FUCKING DEAL!!! You have blown my mind right now, for real. Travis fucking KEEPING!

?? Do you follow F1 now?

No, but I don't live under a rock. He just won the championship, didn't he? It was in all the papers here. And he's BANANAS hot.

I bite into my lip, fighting a stupid smile. I feel sort of shaky with relief and adrenaline, like after you get off of a really crazy roller coaster. I *knew* Kelsie wouldn't care.

And she's right. Travis is bananas hot.

Are you two dating?!!?!? she asks.

> We were, yeah, before the crash.

> What happened?

Parents found out, I type.

> THOSE STONE AGE FUCKERS. Did
> they make you break up with him???

I wince. Ahh. Not really. Sort of fucked it up on my own. I pause, then add, Trying to fix it now, though.

> Hence the London trip?

Hence the London trip. A crackly announcement overhead draws my attention. The seats around me have emptied out, and people are lining up by the gate. Speaking of which—flight's about to board.

> You're really just going to drop this
> bomb on me and then LEAVE!?

> Haha. Sorry. I have another two-hour
> layover in Chicago. I could message then.

> YOU'D BETTER!!! Text me immediately
> upon landing. I mean the MINUTE the
> wheels hit the tarmac. Don't wait for the
> pilot to say it's okay. Everyone knows
> that shit about cell phones interfering
> with planes is made up anyway.

Umm I don't think that's true.
But I'll text when I can.

Amazing. Talk soon, babe. Safe flight.

There's a heavy warmth in my chest as I stare at the screen.
Talk soon, I agree.

28

Too Late

TWENTY-SIX HOURS LATER, I ARRIVE AT MY HOTEL IN LON-
don. My last flight was delayed for hours, and I'm so exhausted
and jetlagged I can barely see straight. It's late afternoon in London, so I crash for a few hours on my hotel bed and set my alarm
for eight p.m. When I wake up, I feel jittery and anxious, like I'm
getting ready to take a test.

I shower and throw on a hoodie and a pair of jeans. Travis'
place is only two tube stops away, and I spend the whole time staring at my reflection in the train windows, ordering myself to calm
down. I consider messaging Kelsie again, to distract myself, but
I've been chatting with her on and off for almost a day now. I don't
want to bother her too much.

Plus, this feels like something I have to do on my own.

My chest is filled with hot, twisty knots as I climb the stairs out
of the station and make my way onto the street. Everything about
this is familiar. I know all the restaurants around here. I know all
the shops. I bought the Christmas present I never gave Travis at
that store there on the corner. The guy that owns it makes all these
weird sculptures out of wood and metal, but he also makes normal

stuff, if you ask him. He made me this custom iPhone case with a tracing of a log cabin. I gave him a picture of the place Travis and I stayed in Harris, and it looked just like that, with the mountains in the background and everything.

It was kind of stupid and cheesy. I don't know, though. Travis probably would've liked it.

God, my heart is beating hard now. Travis' place is only a block away. The fancy private parking garage he uses is just up ahead. There's a car turning into it now.

Oh, fuck.

That's *his* car.

It hits me, all of a sudden, how insane this is. It's been—what? Nine, almost ten months since I saw him? I haven't given him any warning. I'm just showing up, unannounced, without any idea what I'm going to do or say.

It's insane, but my feet are still carrying me forward, like I'm being pulled by a magnet. I could go ahead to his house and wait for him to show up there, but I can't wait. I need to see him again, right now. I think I might even be more excited than scared.

I wonder if he'll kiss me.

I'm pretty sure he will.

The parking garage has security, obviously, but they haven't changed the codes since I left, and my fingers move automatically over the keypad, 7161*. The doors click open and then I'm jogging up the staircase to level three, where Travis' parking spot is.

I'm about to push open the glass door to level three when I spot him.

I lurch backward automatically, cursing under my breath. He isn't alone. Both car doors are open, and some guy is getting out of the passenger seat. Fuck, fuck, *fuck*.

It's probably his manager or trainer. Or it might even be Matty, they're such good friends now. I sneak another look, really quickly. They're heading this way, but neither of them sees me. I don't recognize the guy, but he looks like he could be Travis' trainer. He's around our age, and he looks pretty fit. I curse again as I scramble up the stairs. I don't want to talk to Travis for the first time in months in front of some random stranger. And now what am I going to do, hover outside of Travis' house until he's gone? If it's his new trainer, they might be off to do a workout or something.

I go up one flight of stairs to hide, swearing viciously in my head. The door on level three swings open, and their voices carry through the staircase.

"You said there's a subway station nearby, yeah?" The guy's voice is American and pleasant. "Or y'all call it a tube station, don't you?"

I hear Travis' laugh, and my chest tightens. Fuck, I missed that laugh.

"Yeah, it's a few blocks away," he says. "You want me to walk you?"

The American guy chuckles. "Mm, what a gentleman."

I go completely still, as if my body's turned to ice.

That . . . didn't sound like something a trainer would say.

Their footsteps are getting quieter as they head downstairs. Numb and slightly dazed, I follow them. Travis says something I don't quite catch, and the guy laughs again.

"Are you going to be at Hunter's party this weekend?"

"Yeah, should be," Travis answers.

"Perfect. Ah, hang on—" There's a faint beep, like Travis has opened the security door. "Wait a sec." Some scuffling, a quiet laugh. "We won't be able to say goodbye at the tube station."

No.

No, no, no, no.

They're kissing.

Travis and this guy—this fucking random American asshole—they're making out, right below me. I can hear them. A soft noise, the rustle of clothing.

I feel like my ribs are splintering apart. I feel *sick*.

I honestly feel like I might throw up.

I don't know how long it goes on. Finally, the guy sighs and says, "Alright, you can walk me to the damn tube now. Unless you want me to come back to your place . . ."

Travis laughs. "I told you, I have to get up really early."

"Yeah, yeah. But you know—"

The door swings shut behind them and I don't hear anything else. The stairwell is completely silent now. I sit down on the stairs with my heart torn open in my chest, and the word "no" running circles in my mind.

No, no, no.

Sector Three

Travis and Jacob

29
Party

MY BIRTHDAY FALLS ON MARCH THIRD, TWO DAYS BEFORE
Hunter's, so Heather insists on having a party on March fourth
for both of us. It's a small, laid-back thing, twenty or thirty people
drinking beer and eating barbecue in Heather's backyard. She's
baked two cakes for us. Mine is in the shape of an F1 car, as if I'm
about six years old, and Hunter's is in the shape of a man talking
too much about veganism. (That's what Heather says, anyway. It
just looks like a man waving, to me.)

I don't know everyone here, but I know enough of them that
I don't feel awkward. Matty shows up a bit late with presents
that he pretends he bought himself, though we all know his
girlfriend, Erin, did it for him. He definitely bought the cards
himself, though. Mine says "Our deepest condolences" on
the front, but he's scratched a line through that and written
"HAPPY BIRTHDAY ROBOT" instead. Typical Matty. After I
won the championship, he gave me one that said "Sorry for your
loss," but he'd scratched out "sorry" and "loss" to change it to
"HAPPY for your WIN."

"Thank Erin for me," I say as I unwrap the gift. It's a case for the new iPhone Heather and Hunter gave me yesterday, fancy black leather with my racing number stitched on in black thread. "Where is she today?"

"Some swanky shoot in South Africa," Matty says. Erin is a wildlife photographer. A pretty successful one, too, I think. There are prints in their house of photos she took for big magazines like *National Geographic* and *BBC Wildlife*. "I'm headed there tomorrow for the rest of the break."

"Nice."

"What about you? Going anywhere?"

"Ah, I'll probably just stick around here. Have to train Morocco more." Morocco is the name Heather gave to my new dog. They called her Sprinkles in the shelter, which Heather said was the stupidest dog name she'd ever heard.

I kind of agree, to be honest.

"Riiight," Matty says, stretching the word out. "You're staying 'cause of *Morocco*."

He gives me an exaggerated wink afterward, and I realize he's talking about Thomas. My eyes stray toward him automatically. He's sitting in a lawn chair a little ways away, chatting with Hunter. Heather and Hunter set us up a couple of weeks ago, and we've been out a few times now. He's in school to become a veterinarian, and he's really funny and handsome and clever. He's exactly the type of guy I should be dating—and I'm going to end things with him after this party.

I feel really awkward about it, although Hunter and Heather have both assured me it'll be okay. Among Thomas' many redeeming qualities is how understanding he is. He understood when we couldn't go anywhere public on our dates, and when I asked him not to post any photos of us online, and I'm sure he'll understand when I end things.

But, still. It's awkward.

I have a drink to try to settle my nerves, but my palms are still prickling when I ask him if we can talk privately. Some people are starting to head home, while others are talking about moving the party to a pub down the street.

"Are you okay?" he asks, as we step into Heather's bedroom. "You seem a bit squirrelly."

I hesitate, and he immediately seems to realize what's going on.

"Ah." His mouth twists into a wry sort of smile. "This is the talk."

My cheeks redden. "It has nothing to do with you," I say hurriedly.

He snorts. "That's a bit of a cliché. It's not you, it's me."

I manage a thin laugh. "I know. It's true, though."

He tilts his head and studies me thoughtfully. "Have you developed some sort of allergy to super cool people?"

I crack a smile. "No. I'm just . . . not over my ex."

"Ahh." Thomas nods wisely. "The mysterious ex I've heard so little about. That bastard."

"I really thought I was over it." (And okay, that's sort of a lie.) "I'm sorry."

"You should be," he says. "Honestly, I don't think I'll ever love again."

I chuckle. "Of course. Sorry about that."

"It's okay. I imagine I'll slowly waste away from grief and consumption, and then someone will write a depressing novel about me, and I'll die famous. So that's a plus."

"I'll make sure to buy a copy of it."

"You'd better." He smiles again, but this time I see a trace of genuine sadness in his eyes. I feel a stab of regret. He really is a great guy.

"You really are a great guy," I say out loud. "I'll probably be kicking myself for this in a month."

"Nah." Thomas squeezes my shoulder. "We just weren't meant to be. And hey, we can still be friends. And not in that fake 'let's say we'll be friends but in reality never speak again' way. Actual friends."

My mouth curves up. "I'd like that."

"And in forty years, when my kids are watching some boring documentary about F1, and they talk about the really hot guy who won a hundred championships, I'm going to say to them, Kids, you know what? I very nearly fucked that guy."

I let out a startled snort of laughter. "You're going to say that to your kids?"

"Obviously." He steps forward and hugs me, kissing my cheek before he pulls away. "Let's go get drunk now, yes? I assume Heather and Hunter knew this was going to go down?"

"Um . . . maybe," I admit.

He groans. "Wonderful. Tell you what, I'll forgive you if you cheat with me so that Hunter loses all the drinking games."

I smile at him. In forty years, wherever I am, I'm definitely going to remember him as the nicest guy I ever broke up with.

"Deal," I agree.

A FEW HOURS later, Matty and I stumble through the door to my apartment. Morocco comes sprinting out of the living room, trying to jump on us and lick our faces. She's about five years old, the shelter thinks, but she still acts like a puppy. I rub the top of her head, and Matty sits down on the kitchen floor and lets her climb onto his lap.

"What a good puppy," he slurs. "Do I smell like tequila, Morocco? Hm?"

"She's going to get drunk off your breath," I tell him. Although honestly, I can't talk. Thomas and I didn't have any luck conspiring against Hunter, and we kind of got plastered in the process. The room spins as I lean down to untie my shoes. "What time's your flight leave tomorrow?"

Matty is now lying on the floor with his arms spread out wide while Morocco paws at his face. "Not till four, thank god."

"I'll set an alarm. See you in the morning."

"Late morning," Matty stipulates with a groan.

I go to my bedroom and change into sweatpants and a T-shirt. I leave my bedroom door open until I hear Matty stumble to the spare room. He's crashed there a few times over the past months. I hear his telltale curse as he hits his head on the lamp near the bed.

"Every time!" he complains.

"Every time," I agree. "Night. Drink water."

Morocco comes padding into my room a few minutes later. I close the door behind her and crawl onto the bed. She hops up beside me and we both lie down. The ceiling is swimming over my head. I watch it for a while, my thoughts skipping around pointlessly.

They settle, as they always do, on Jacob. And yes, I know it's pathetic to be hung up on someone I haven't heard from in months. And I know Heather and Hunter think I'm slightly insane for breaking up with Thomas. But it is what it is. I'm still hung up on Jacob. If anything, dating Thomas just made me more sure of it. He was a really awesome guy. There wasn't anything about him I didn't like.

He just wasn't Jacob.

I grab my phone and open Instagram, which is the only app I have on my new phone, other than a clever language app that Matty showed me that helps translate road signs and menus and things in foreign countries. I only have to type in "j" and Jacob's profile pops up, @jacob.tn01. Every time I open it, I kind of hope there will be a new post. At the same time, I'm terrified there will be. I don't know how I'd feel if he posted something normal and happy, like a picture of him and his friends, or with a new girlfriend.

I'd like to say I set up my own Instagram account because Harper's press team made me, but that's not really true. They suggested it a few times, especially in the lead-up to the last race, but I only agreed because of Jacob. I thought that maybe, if he saw it, he might reach out.

Which was stupid. But yeah.

I throw my phone away and sigh heavily, raking a hand over my face. Morocco whips her head up to glare at me. I'm keeping her awake. I pet her obediently until she falls asleep again.

Even though it's well past three a.m., and even though I drank what felt like a hundred drinks, I can't fall asleep. The F1 season will start up in a few weeks, and for some reason, it feels like there's a clock ticking down. I don't want to go into the new season with this hanging over me. My brain knows that Jacob doesn't want me, but it's like my heart still doesn't believe it. I need to hear him say it out loud. Heather and Hunter have both said I need "closure," whatever that means. And Matty once told me that he hopes Jacob ends up in F2 again, so I can tell him off to his face the first time I see him.

I don't want to tell him off, but I do want to tell him how crappy he made me feel. And how mad I am at him. And how sorry I am for not fighting for him harder. And how much I miss him.

He's changed his phone number, but I could send him a message on Instagram, I guess. He doesn't follow me, but there's a chance he would see a message. I don't want to do that, though. I've never been good at putting my thoughts into words, and I don't want to send something off into the ether and then wait days or weeks or months for an answer.

I don't want to send him a message. I want to see him, in person, and talk to him.

I grab my laptop from my nightstand and open Expedia. As I wait for it to search for flights, I wonder how much Expedia makes off drunk people booking last-minute flights to visit exes.

A lot, probably.

After a few minutes of scrolling, though, my stomach is churning with frustration. How can it take eighteen hours to get from London to Albuquerque? The quickest journey has three separate stops, and none of the flights have any seats left in business class. The press and fan attention have gotten pretty intense over the past year, and the last thing I want to do is sit on a plane with a bunch of people staring at me.

Sighing, I do what I always do when I run into a problem I can't solve. I text Heather.

You up?

She texts back a few seconds later. Yeah, but I'm not interested in a booty call.

?

"You up" is a booty call text.

Ah. Good to know. This is not
a booty call text, though.

Darn. What's up?

Can you get me a private flight somewhere?

Depends. Is that "somewhere"
Albuquerque, New Mexico?

. . . Maybe.

There's a pause, then a ding.

Give me thirty minutes.

I REALLY DON'T know how I functioned before Heather. She arrives the next day at noon to pick up Morocco and send me off to the private flight she's arranged.

"I am literally your *mother*," she complains as she repacks my bag. Apparently, everything I packed was wrong.

"You love it," Matty grumbles from his position on the couch.

Heather grins. She sort of does. She buys all my clothes now, too. I didn't ask her to, she just started doing it one day. She says it's like having a full-sized Ken doll, which is extremely weird. But I like the stuff she buys, so I don't argue with her.

"Wear this shirt when you go see Jacob, yeah?" She waves a gray T-shirt at me. "And that black jacket I got you."

"What are you going to say to him?" Matty asks me.

"I don't know."

"You need a strong opening line," he says. "Like, 'Yo, asshole, what has two thumbs, an F1 championship, and doesn't give a shit what you think of him? *This guy.*'" He points both his thumbs at his chest. "Then just drop a mic and drive away."

Heather rolls her eyes. "So, in this scenario, he's brought his own mic with him?"

"Obviously."

"What if he wants the mic back afterward, though?" Heather asks. "Like if it's an expensive mic, should he ask Jacob to post it in the mail afterward, or—?"

"What's your suggestion, then?" Matty says.

She shrugs. "Just tell him how you feel." She hesitates. "But don't let him brush you off. And make sure you hold him accountable for all the stupid shit he did."

Okay, I seriously regret telling Heather so much about our relationship. She pointed out that a lot of the time, when I thought Jacob was just being normal, and that the issue was that I wasn't used to relationships or that I was being too demanding, Jacob was sort of being . . . intentionally dismissive. *He should have thanked you for that racing sim*, she said once. *And he should have gotten you a damn Christmas present.*

Personally, I think it was more complicated than that. But I guess I'll find out soon enough.

The private plane is so expensive and fancy, I feel guilty, but it is nice to know I'll get to Albuquerque in way less than eighteen hours. The flight attendant is a nice guy who asks me to sign his

Harper T-shirt and then brings me some food and leaves me alone to watch movies on my laptop. An hour in, I ask if he wants to watch with me, because it seems pointless for him to just stand there waiting to see if I need anything.

We make it through *Die Hard* (Matty's recommendation) and *Moana* (Hunter's recommendation) before we land. The pilot asks me when I think I'll want to head back.

"I don't know," I say honestly. "Might only be a couple hours."

"No problem. We'll refuel now, and you just text whenever you want to go."

"Thanks," I say. "You can pick the movies on the way back," I add to Joey, the flight attendant.

The car Heather rented for me is waiting. She also managed to get me Jacob's address, and I'm honestly not sure how. She just said "Ways and means" when I asked. I swear she has secret connections in every team in motorsport.

I put the address into the GPS and head off. I should get a hotel room to shower in, but I can't be bothered. Jacob has seen me looking way worse than this. And now that I'm here, I just want to get it over with. Rip the Band-Aid off.

My stomach is a cold, anxious knot the whole way there. It's an hour from the airport, which gives me just enough time to envision every possible worst-case scenario.

It's late morning when I finally get there. Jacob's parents live in a really fancy, really creepy-looking suburb. All of the houses look almost identical, and all the streets have basically the same name. Grace Haven Road, Grace Haven Crescent, Grace Haven Lane . . . the postal service workers must need a drink delivering mail here. Even the GPS seems confused once we pass through the gates.

I finally track down the right house and step out into the cold, dry air. I'm not wearing the gray shirt Heather told me to wear, but I do pull on the black jacket. The temperature isn't that low, but it's the kind of cold that cuts right through you. I can't imagine how Jacob stands it.

I walk past a garden flag that says "GIVE GOD YOUR WEAKNESS AND HE'LL GIVE YOU HIS STRENGTH," rub my palms on my jacket, and ring the doorbell. After a few agonizing moments, the door swings open.

My heart sinks. It's Jacob's mother.

I probably should have realized that might happen, considering it's his parents' house.

I swallow nervously. "Hi, ma'am. I don't know if you remember me—"

"I do." Her voice is clipped and cool.

"Right. Sorry. I was just wondering—"

"Jacob's not here."

My heart sinks a little further. "Oh. Is he . . . will he be back soon?"

"He's in London," she says. "Visiting his old girlfriend."

It feels like she's kicked me in the chest. The old girlfriend part would be bad enough, but he's in *London*.

He's in London and he didn't even tell me.

His mother moves to close the door, but I take a half step forward. "Are you able to give me his address there? I need to speak with him."

She stares at me for a moment, then lets out a disbelieving breath and looks to the side. "This isn't appropriate."

I narrow my eyes. I really don't like this woman. "Okay," I say flatly. "Sorry to bother you."

I turn and walk away, but I only make it a few steps before she speaks again. "He's finally happy again," she says. "After everything that horrible sport did to him—after everything *you* did"—her voice is tight with anger—"he's finally himself again. How dare you show up here and try to take that all away?"

I keep walking. A year ago, I might've cared about her disapproval. But if Matty and Heather and Hunter have taught me anything, it's that some people are great, and other people are shit. And Jacob's mother is one of the shit ones. I'm not going to waste my time arguing with her.

"How dare you," she repeats, her voice wavering. "You show up here, trying to—to intimidate me—"

I glance over my shoulder. There are two red spots on her cheeks and tears in her eyes, and she's fanning herself rapidly with one hand like the stress of dealing with me—the intimidating thug who knocked politely on her door and asked her two reasonable questions—is too much for her to handle.

I roll my eyes. "Who is this performance for? Stop behaving like a child."

Her mouth drops open in furious shock. I get in my car and drive away before she can recover the power of speech. When I look back in my rearview, she's still standing in the exact same spot. I feel a little surge of satisfaction. Matty would want me to drop a mic right around now.

The adrenaline rush wears off pretty quickly, though. I text the pilot to see how soon we can leave, and wind up grabbing food at a diner to kill time while they finish refueling. All of my muscles feel heavy and dull.

I am glad Jacob is doing better. I'm glad he's well enough to be visiting London.

It just really hurts that he went to London without telling me. Really, really hurts.

In a way, it's the sign I've been looking for. I don't have to wonder anymore. He's better now, and he's in London, and he's visiting an ex-girlfriend instead of me. I came here looking for an answer from him, and now I've got it.

Time to move on.

30

Grow Up

I FORGOT HOW MUCH I LOVE LONDON. THERE'S SOMETHING about it that makes everything better. It's cold out, but there are coffee shops on every other corner where you can sit by the window and watch strangers wander by. It rains a lot, but I kind of like aimlessly wandering the streets under an umbrella. It's crowded, but not in the way my parents' neighborhood in Albuquerque is crowded. No one here knows every little detail of everyone else's life, and even better, no one cares. Every day, I get up and wander the city, and every day, I breathe a little easier.

It doesn't make the whole Travis situation better, though.

That's still total shit.

Kelsie is helping a lot. When I told her what happened, she insisted I come crash with her. The first night, we stayed up till four a.m., drinking and catching up. I've been sleeping on her couch ever since. Her roommate, Amelia, absolutely hates me, but Kelsie doesn't care.

"Maybe it'll convince her to move out," she says, stabbing her fork into a piece of curry chicken. It's eight p.m. on a Tuesday, and we're sitting in a booth at her favorite Indian restaurant. That's another thing about London. Amazing restaurants, everywhere.

"She's not . . . that bad," I say. Kelsie snorts. "Okay, she sucks," I admit. "How did you get stuck with her?"

Kelsie shrugs. "She paid six months' rent up front."

"Fair enough."

"I'd kick her out in a heartbeat, if I had a new roommate."

"Your apartment's amazing," I say, ripping apart a piece of naan. "You could find a new roommate in, like, five minutes."

She chews thoughtfully. "I don't know. I'm very particular."

"Mm?"

"Yeah. I thought about posting an ad, actually. Wanted: twenty-three-year-old racing driver, recently heartbroken over sexy F1 champion, great at making coffee, terrible at doing dishes . . ."

"Come on." I put my fork down. "Are you kidding?"

"No."

I really can't tell if she's joking. I force a laugh. "You don't want to live with me."

"Hell yeah, I do!"

I lick my lips. She doesn't look like she's joking. "I mean—you'd have to give Amelia some warning . . ."

"Please. She's already going on about moving in with her awful boyfriend, and the end of the month is coming up. It's perfect. You can keep crashing on our couch until she leaves."

My heart is fluttering anxiously in my chest. It's kind of insane, but at the same time . . .

It feels right.

Like, a hundred and fifty percent right.

"You're smiling," Kelsie says.

I grin wider. "Hell yeah, I am."

Kelsie slaps the table in excitement, loud enough that people at the other tables frown at her. "Fuck, yes!" The people frown harder, and I cover my head.

"Can you lower your voice, please?"

"Fuck, no!" Kelsie says, even louder.

I snort. "You're ridiculous."

"Duh." She takes a sip of her soda. "So, you'll move in? For real?"

"For real." I'm smiling so hard, my cheeks hurt.

"I'll kick Amelia out tomorrow."

We grin at each other for a minute, then my smile fades a bit.

"I don't know what I'll do here, though."

Kelsie shrugs. "So, take a little while to figure it out. I'll tell my parents Amelia moved out. They'll front the rent."

"I can't do that."

"Why not? They can afford it."

I grimace, although it's true. Kelsie's parents own a chain of walk-in clinics. I'm pretty sure they're millionaires.

"I have enough money for a few months," I say.

"Eh, don't bother. Last week my dad said he hoped I wasn't dating anyone too 'ethnic' here, so let's just consider it a racism tax."

I smile thinly. "Still. I'll find a job soon."

"A job you love," she stipulates.

I make a noncommittal sound. I've been trying to think of other things I can do with my life. But all I can think about is racing.

"Any word back from other teams?" Kelsie asks, watching me.

I shake my head. I got an e-mail from one F4 team, offering me a seat. I got excited for about two seconds, before I saw their casual note that they were a new team, with limited funds, and I would have to pay the entry and travel fees—which would be about two hundred thousand dollars. I couldn't afford that, unless I begged my parents for the money, which I won't.

"Are any of the teams left based out of the UK?"

I open my mouth to say no, then I pause.

There is one UK-based team that I haven't e-mailed yet.

"What is it?" Kelsie asks.

I push a piece of food aimlessly around my plate. I'd never even considered them, because why would I?

"There is this Formula 1 team," I say slowly. "Crosswire Racing. I was supposed to have a meeting with them before the crash."

"That's amazing!"

"Yeah, not really. They're the best team in F1. I can't even get a seat with the worst team in F4."

"That's because you don't have a connection with them. And because it's, like, five minutes before the season is starting. But if they wanted you beforehand . . ."

"I don't know for sure that they did. It was just a meeting." I hesitate. "Travis thought they were going to ask me to be their reserve driver."

"Ooh, they *definitely* were."

I roll my eyes. "You don't know anything about it."

"I know there's no harm in trying. Just e-mail them and see if they'll meet with you. What's the worst thing that could happen? They say no, it sucks, we move on."

I hesitate. Despite everything—despite all the rejections—I can feel myself being pulled into the cycle again. Find new team. Get hopes up.

And Kelsie's right. What's the harm in trying one last time?

I take another bite of food. Living in London with Kelsie, working for Crosswire . . . life would be damn near perfect.

"What now?" Kelsie says, as my smile fades again.

"I was just thinking my parents are going to flip when I tell them I'm staying here."

"Good thing you're an adult who can make his own decisions."

"I know. It's just so hard to talk to them."

Kelsie takes a thoughtful sip of her wine. "It's not your job to make your parents happy," she says. "But they are your parents, and they do love you, and they, like, kept you from starving as a kid and taught you how to talk and read and all that. So, it *is* your job to acknowledge and respect their reasonable concerns."

"Have you been bingeing Oprah or something?"

She snorts. "No. Well, yes, actually, but that's not relevant. It's something my sister and I figured out after years and years of fighting with our parents. I used to sit with her when she called them with these little Post-it notes that said 'Reasonable' and 'Unreasonable,' and she was only allowed to push back against Unreasonable things."

"Did it help you stop fighting with them?"

Kelsie laughs. "Fuck, no. But it stopped us from feeling like shit when we got into arguments. Because it's not our job to make them happy, or to live our lives to please them. It's only our job to acknowledge and respect their reasonable concerns."

I nod, and for a moment we eat in silence.

"You want me to be there with you when you call them?" she asks.

"Oh, you don't need to . . ."

"Jacob," Kelsie says.

"Yeah, I absolutely want you there. Thanks."

She grins. "I don't know how you managed without me."

I clink my glass against hers. "Me neither."

TWO DAYS LATER, I sit in front of my laptop, listening to my mother go on about the new wedding venue Lily's found—for her own wedding, this time, not one of her horrible clients. Kelsie is sitting behind the screen, out of sight, drinking a cup of coffee and painting her nails.

"It won't be available for a year because it's so popular, but at least that gives us more time to plan. Lily still has to narrow down her bridesmaids—she has twelve so far, but Caleb only has ten groomsmen. Although Lily did tell me that if she can't narrow it down, you should expect a call!"

I grimace. "To be a groomsman?"

"Of course! You're her brother. And you like Caleb."

When did I ever say that? I glance at Kelsie, but she just holds up the "Reasonable" Post-it she made without even glancing up from her nails. Damn it.

"I guess if they really need someone," I say grudgingly. "If I'm around."

"It's going to be next summer, so you shouldn't be in school," my mother says.

"Unless you do an accelerated program," my father adds. "But I'm sure you can take a weekend off to go to your sister's wedding."

I swallow and sit up a little straighter. Kelsie looks up from her nails. Here we go.

"Well, actually," I say, "I wanted to talk to you guys about that." I take a deep breath and dive right in. "I'm not going to go to school in Albuquerque. I've decided I'm going to stay here in London, with Kelsie."

My parents go still, as if the screen's frozen.

My mother gives a strange little laugh. "What do you mean? You don't know anyone in London."

"I know Kelsie. And her roommate is moving out, so it works out perfectly."

She gives another forced laugh. "Darling, I think you should give this some thought. I'm so glad you've reconnected with Kelsie, but you don't want to rush things. Moving in together is a big step."

I bristle. "Kelsie and I aren't dating. We're just friends."

My mother gives my father a doubtful little glance, like she doesn't believe me. "Either way," she says, "you don't want to rush into such a big decision. I think you'd find it's quite hard being away from home."

"And you won't be able to get into any schools in London this late in the game," my father adds. "You don't want to waste a whole year."

"I'm not going to go to school at all," I say irritably. "And I've already turned down the ones I got into. I'm going to stay here in London."

"And do what, exactly?" my father demands. "You can't get a good job these days without any education."

"I'm trying to get back into racing," I say. "I've . . . got a meeting with Crosswire Racing next week."

I feel a familiar rush of excitement and terror as I say it. I e-mailed them when Kelsie and I got home from dinner at that Indian place, telling them how I've recovered and am cleared for racing again, and asking if they might still want to meet with me. Kelsie and I had this whole plan of going out to a club and drinking all night to distract me after I sent it, but before she'd even finished doing her makeup, they e-mailed back.

And they offered to meet with me, next Tuesday.

"What?" my mother says thinly.

My father looks shocked. "They've offered you a job?"

"Well—no." My cheeks color. "I just reached out to see if they would meet with me."

"Oh." My mother settles back in her chair. "Well, darling, that's very nice of them, but that doesn't mean they have a job for you."

"I know that," I say tightly.

"You should've reached out to Porteo, if you wanted to race again," my father says. "But now they've signed that Brazilian kid, they won't have a seat for you. I spoke with Carl a while ago, he says he's the best racer they've ever had."

Kelsie's head snaps up, her expression indignant. She holds up the "Unreasonable" note and taps it furiously.

"Why are you talking to Carl?" I snap. Carl is the team boss at Porteo.

My father frowns. "Carl is an old friend. He reached out to see how you were doing."

Oh he did, did he? I grind my teeth together. I guess he didn't bother mentioning they'd turned me down.

"I'm just saying, you shouldn't get your hopes up," my father says.

"And are you really well enough to race?" my mother adds. "I think you'd find it a lot harder than you realize, getting back in a car after what happened to you."

"I'm not scared of racing. The crash was shitty luck—"

"Please don't swear."

"—but what do you want me to do, go around being scared the rest of my life? I could get hit by a bus walking out of the apartment tomorrow, or get cancer or something. I *want* to race."

"Yes, well, so do a lot of people," my father says. "Sometimes you have to adjust your expectations in life."

I press my knuckles into my forehead. There's an awful pressure in my head, like someone's put a tight elastic band around it. "Great advice," I say shortly. "Thanks. Either way, even if the Crosswire meeting goes nowhere, I'm staying in London."

"Darling—"

"I'm twenty-three, mom," I snap. "What do you think I'm going to do, live at home forever?"

"You've been injured . . ."

"Yeah, and I'm better now."

"You need someone to take care of you."

I don't need Kelsie waving the "Unreasonable" note around. I know it is. "No, I don't," I say firmly. "I'm an adult. I'll be fine."

"You're an adult," my father repeats acerbically. "An *adult* would recognize how hard it is for your mother to watch you try to put your life at risk again, just to chase after an impossible dream."

I throw my hands up. "So, what? You want me to make all my life decisions based on how you two feel about them?"

"No. That's not what I said." Two angry patches of color have appeared on my father's cheeks. "But I do expect you to be considerate of your mother and me, especially after all the money and time we've poured into your career."

My mother is looking away from the camera, shaking her head slightly and waving her hand in front of her face, as if she's bravely holding back tears. I'm trying to remember if she's always been so theatrical. My anger wanes, replaced by impatience. I want to tell her to grow up.

"I do appreciate everything you two have done for me," I say in a voice of tight, forced calm. "But I'm staying in London, and I'm going to try to get back into racing." I take a steadying breath. "I'm sorry if you're upset, but I'm not going to argue about it anymore."

Kelsie gives me two thumbs up across the table. My father is red-faced. My mother is still shaking her head in disbelief.

"What about your things?" she says finally. "All of the things in your room."

I put on a very thin smile. Kelsie and I made a plan for this. "I thought you and dad could come visit. There's probably only one or two suitcases of stuff in my room, you could bring it over with you. And that way you can see the apartment and everything."

I initially wanted to ask them to mail all my stuff, but Kelsie suggested this instead. And she promised to be there for moral support the entire time they visit.

"You won't even come home to get your things?" My mother's voice wobbles.

"I just thought, it'd be more convenient—"

"More convenient for *you*," my father says.

"And what about Paul?" my mother asks. "He and Candace are coming for dinner this weekend. I already told them you'd be here."

It takes a lot of effort not to roll my eyes, because why exactly would she tell them that? I never said anything about going home this weekend.

"I have my meeting with Crosswire on Tuesday."

"If you came home tomorrow, you could spend five or six days here and still make it back in time."

I glance up helplessly at Kelsie. I'm desperately hoping she'll hold up the "Unreasonable" note, but instead she shoots me an apologetic grimace and lifts the "Reasonable" one.

I take a deep breath and briefly close my eyes.

"Fine," I say through my teeth. "I'll book a flight now."

31

Autograph

THE EIGHTEEN-HOUR TRIP BETWEEN LONDON AND ALBU-
querque is no more fun the second time. Actually, it's about a
thousand times less fun, because at least last time, I had the delu-
sion of getting back together with Travis to distract me. Now, all
I have to look forward to is three and a half awkward days with
my parents. My mom is still mad that I'm not staying longer, but
I wasn't about to risk missing my meeting with Crosswire.

I spend the whole trip studying. I've been intentionally avoiding
F1 since my crash, and now I've only got eight days to get up-to-
date. Not that I'm expecting them to suddenly pitch questions at
me during the meeting, but I'm determined to go into this as well-
informed as possible. I need to know all the new regulations and
tech developments, I need to know which teams failed or succeeded
last season and why.

I start from the beginning of the season and watch every race, one
by one. I jot notes down in the notebook Kelsie gave me (it has this
creepy drawing of an evil unicorn on the front, and I don't know if
I love it or hate it), making notes about technical developments and
regulation changes and track updates. It's actually sort of fun.

Or it would be, if it didn't mean thinking about Travis all the time.

It's impossible to avoid. From the very first race, it's clear the championship battle is between Crosswire and Harper. At first, Matty holds on with Travis and the two Crosswire drivers, Mahoney and Clayton, but then he has a string of bad luck with engine failures and crashes, and then it's just Travis, fighting alone against the best team in F1.

The first half of the season is the hardest to watch, because I was with him then. I wasn't actually at every race, but I watched them all. I remember everything that happened. I remember talking to Travis about all of them. I know more than the commentators do. I know he had brake issues the whole Melbourne race, and that he almost had to retire in Monaco because he had a really bad flu and his vision was starting to go spotty. He was so annoyed afterward, it was kind of cute. Like he couldn't believe a fever of 104 could actually affect him.

I make it to the French GP while I'm waiting for my last connection. I feel strangely disconnected and numb, watching it. The commentators are subdued, and the whole pre-race show is about the crash. My crash. They do a tribute to Ellis Parrot, and a moment of silence before the race where everyone stands around his helmet. The camera mostly focuses on Ellis' team and his family, but they show the F1 drivers a few times. I swipe at my eyes impatiently and click back in the video to stare at Travis' face.

He looks tired. Really, really tired.

I must be feeling masochistic, because I end up watching all the press conferences and interviews and everything. I listen to Travis say he didn't know any of the drivers in the crash that well. I watch his face while the others answer questions.

I hear my own awful voice in my head.

I know you think this is so fucking serious, but that's just because you've never dated anyone before.

This isn't that big a deal, alright?

God, I was such a piece of shit.

I spend the last flight going over every shitty thing I ever did to him, and arrive in Albuquerque in a bleak mood. Paul and his fiancée, Candace, pick me up at the airport, and for once I'm glad for Paul's complete self-absorption. It's sort of distracting, listening to him ramble on about his business and his new car and how well everything's going for him. He tells all the same stories at dinner, which is also helpful, since it leaves no time for my parents to fuss at me about moving to London.

Paul and Candace decide to stay over, after they both polish off their fourth glass of wine, which is also surprisingly helpful. Candace doesn't really have a personality, which means my mother adores her, and the two of them are still chatting happily when I escape to my room. I'm exhausted, but I stay up till three a.m. watching races. Even though I know Travis ends up winning the championship, I still curse at the ceiling when that dumbass Cole Milton turns in on him and ruins his race in Hungary, and I freak out when Travis passes Clayton on the second to last lap at Monza.

God, I'm so fucking proud of him.

He really earned this championship. He had way worse luck than Mahoney and Clayton, and an objectively slower car, and he still ended up winning.

I'm too tired to make it past Monza, but over the next three days, sneaking hours here and there between awkward family dinners and obligations, I finish the season. I don't know if it's because it's five a.m. when I watch it, but I actually cry when Travis wins. I'm so proud of him, and happy for him. And I'm so, so sorry I wasn't there.

On impulse—and because I realize it's an amazing excuse to get out of the house for a few hours—I call Amanda and book an appointment. My mother tells me to make sure I get Amanda's professional opinion on my London move and the idea of going back to racing. I wait till she looks away to roll my eyes, imagining Kelsie's "Reasonable" Post-it note in my mind.

It's strange, coming back to Amanda's office. I know it's only been a couple of weeks, but it looks different, somehow. It sort of feels like walking through an old school building. It's nostalgic, and I'm not unhappy to be here, but it's not like I actually want to go back to high school. I think I'm ready to move on.

"I think you are, too," Amanda says, smiling at me. "I'm so happy for you."

I can tell she really means it. Her eyes lit up when I told her about the meeting with Crosswire. I think she's gotten her hopes up just as much as I have.

"It's going to be weird, not talking to you about things."

Her eyes crinkle. "That's what your friends are for. And you can always find a therapist in London, if you feel you're starting to struggle again."

"If the Crosswire meeting goes badly, I probably will," I joke.

Really, though, I don't think I'll need to. I want to race again so badly, but I also know I'll survive if I can't. Like Kelsie says, I'll just find another job that I can love. It's weird, how she can say the same things my parents do, but I don't hate her for it. Maybe it's because I know she wants what's best for me, whereas my parents . . . I'm no longer sure.

Amanda is quiet for a moment when I tell her this. I can tell she's weighing her words carefully. "Relationships between parents and adult children can be incredibly complex. And I do believe that we have to acknowledge all the hard work our parents did in raising us, and be grateful for it. But as an adult, you have to make your own decisions, and live the life you want to lead. All you can do is try to be as kind and understanding as you can, without giving up too much of yourself."

"My friend Kelsie says it isn't our job to make them happy, but it is our job to 'acknowledge and respect their reasonable concerns.'"

"Ooh, I love that." Amanda's pen dances across her notebook. "I'm definitely going to steal it."

I laugh. "Go ahead."

"She sounds like a good friend, this Kelsie."

"Yeah, she's the best. And I told her . . . you know." I lick my lips. "That I'm bi."

The corners of her mouth turn up. "That's good."

"Yeah." A beat of silence falls. I clear my throat. "It's weird how easy it is to be around her. Like, we hadn't seen each other in ages, but we just fell right back into step."

"Just as friends, you think? Or something more?"

"Just friends. I'm still . . . not over Travis."

"Have you tried to see him again, since the parking garage?"

I shake my head. "No. I mean, it wouldn't be fair, right? If I show up it'd just mess with his head. He's moved on."

Amanda makes a little "hm" noise that I know means I've said something wrong.

"What?" I ask.

"Well, are you really thinking about what's fair?"

I snort. "Clearly I'm not, or you wouldn't be asking."

She laughs. "If Travis doesn't want to date you again, he won't. But he deserves to know all his options. At the very least, he deserves an apology."

I shift in my seat. "But don't you think he would've reached out, if he wanted to talk to me?"

"I don't know," she says. "I've never met him. Does that seem like something he would do?"

My cheeks color. It definitely doesn't. Travis was never the one to make the first move. Even after we'd been together for months, he was rarely the first one to text, and almost never the one to initiate any plans.

Probably because every time he made a gesture, like buying me that sim, I brushed him off.

"I guess I could try again." My palms prickle at the thought of it. What if I show up at his house and that guy answers the door?

"I think you should," she says firmly.

She usually never tells me what to do, which means she feels strongly about it. I nod.

"I will," I say. "I promise."

"And you should think carefully about what you want to say," she adds.

I raise an eyebrow. "Are you going to go make yourself tea while I do?"

She grins. "You read my mind."

SOMEHOW, I MAKE it to the end of the trip without exploding at my parents, but it's a very near thing. My mother tries at least six times to convince me to stay, and my father makes about a thousand passive-aggressive comments about racing and "realistic expectations." I force myself to stay calm and speak politely, which seems to be working. On my mother, especially. It's like she doesn't know what to do when I don't rise to her tears and pleas.

I pack up the stuff I want to take to London into two suitcases, and the day of my flight finally arrives. My mother has been twisting her hands together and pacing all morning, like she's trying to find a last-minute reason for me to stay. It's easier to be patient with her today, knowing I only have twenty-two minutes to go.

Scratch that—it's twenty-one minutes, now.

"I'm going to throw my suitcases in the car," I say pleasantly. "And I thought maybe we could get coffee on the way?"

This is a bit sneaky, since I know it means we'll have to leave a bit earlier. My mother manages a watery smile in response.

Her car is parked in our driveway. As I heave the second suitcase into the trunk, I see the neighbor's kids approaching on their bikes. I wave at them politely. This should kill a few more minutes.

"Nice bikes," I say.

"We got them for Christmas," says the older kid, Oliver.

"Very cool," I say. Oliver's younger brother, Mason, smiles at me shyly.

"Are you leaving?" Oliver asks.

"Yep. Heading back to London. I'm going to be living there now."

They both look suitably impressed, which is nice. "Are you on a race team again?" Mason asks.

"Not yet, but I'm working on it."

"That's so cool," Mason says.

I smile. "It is cool," I agree.

"Is Travis Keeping going to come back here again?" Oliver asks.

I blink. "Is—what?"

"Travis Keeping," Oliver says. "We saw him talking to your mom. We were wondering . . ." He glances at Mason. "If he comes back, could you get him to sign our bike helmets?"

My whole body's gone cold. Mason and Oliver are both staring at me eagerly. I force a rictus smile to my face. "When did you see Travis Keeping here?"

"A little while ago," Oliver says.

"It was a snow day!" Mason adds.

A little while ago.

I try to sound casual. "Do you remember the date?"

They look at each other uncertainly, shaking their heads. Of course they don't know the date. They're kids.

But then Mason brightens. "Oh! I know! It was March fifth. 'Cause Steven's birthday party was s'posed to be that day, but it got canceled 'cause of the snow. 'Member, Oliver?"

Oliver nods vigorously.

March fifth.

I flew to London on the last day of February. I saw Travis with that guy on March first. Which means he came to see me *after* that.

My heart is pounding hard in my chest. "You guys said you saw him talking to my mom?"

They both nod eagerly. "He didn't stay very long," Oliver says. "I was gonna get my helmet and ask him to sign it, but by the time I got it he was already gone."

"Do you think he'll come back soon?" Mason adds.

I force a thin smile, trying to hide the fury bubbling in my chest. "I don't think so. But I'll tell you what, if I see him again, I'll ask him to sign something for both of you, okay?"

They both beam and thank me, then their mom appears on their front step, yelling at them to stop bothering me. I manage to smile and wave as they head inside, but I'm so mad, I can hear my pulse thudding in my ears.

I walk back into the house. My parents are both in the living room watching the news. I pick up the remote and turn the TV off.

"We don't have to leave for another ten minutes—" my mother starts.

"Did Travis come here?" I interrupt.

She looks startled. "What?"

"The Hilton kids just said they saw you talking to Travis on March fifth," I snap. "Are they lying? Or was he here?"

She glances at my father, visibly discomfited. "Well—I'm not sure—"

"He was here," my father cuts in. "And he was extremely rude to your mother. He's lucky I wasn't here when it happened."

I let out a cold laugh. "Why? What would you have done? Beat him up?"

"You think it's okay that he yelled at your mother?"

My narrowed gaze moves to my mother. I can't picture Travis yelling. Not unless the situation called for it. "Did he?" I demand. "Did *actually* yell at you?"

"He made your mother cry," my father snaps.

"Everything makes her cry," I snap back. "I asked you a question. Did he actually yell at you?"

My mother's mouth is pressed together tightly. "He called me childish," she says.

I almost laugh. I can hear him saying it, in his flattest, most cutthroat media voice. My heart is racing, and my skin is thrumming with adrenaline.

"You *are* childish," I say. "Both of you are."

My father's mouth opens furiously, but I speak over him.

"Neither of you have even *mentioned* Travis since the crash. Not once." My hands curl into fists as I realize how ridiculous it is. I lived here for months, and not *once* did they say anything. "What do you think would happen? If you pretended it didn't happen, I'd just miraculously become straight?"

My father's face goes dark red. "You are straight."

"And that *horrible* boy nearly ruined your life," my mother says.

"How?" I demand. "How did he *ruin my life*? By being really nice to me all the time? Helping me be a better driver? Always believing in me, even when I was a total shit to him?"

"He would've ruined your career," my father says coldly.

"The career you don't even want me to have, you mean?"

His expression is ugly. "He would have made you a laughing-stock."

"Oh, fuck you." The words burst out, cold and impatient. My mother gasps. I ignore her. "Fuck you for saying that. And fuck you for thinking that it's true."

My father looks so angry, I honestly think he might hit me. Part of me hopes he does. My hands are fisted at my sides.

"How dare you speak to your mother and me like this?" he demands. "After everything we did for you. You got to race because of us, in case you've forgotten. We sacrificed everything—"

"That's not reasonable!" I snap. "I was six years old when I started karting. Do you think a fucking six-year-old understands the concept of time and money? I don't even *remember* most of it. If you didn't want me to do it, or if we couldn't have afforded it, you were adults, you could have said no."

"You think I could say no to—to my little boy—" My mother's voice breaks, but it does nothing to move me. This is all just a show she's putting on for herself.

"Yes, I think you could have said no. And I would've been mad for, like, a day, and then I would've watched fucking *Teenage Mutant Ninja Turtles* or something and forgotten about it. Because I was *six*."

"Ridiculous," my father snaps.

"It is ridiculous!" I let out a strangled laugh. "It is ridiculous. You two did a lot of things for me. But you didn't do them because I *forced* you to. And it's completely unreasonable to hold everything you did for me as a kid over my head, like some sort of lifelong ransom!"

"We just want you to be *happy*," my mother cries.

I throw my hands up and laugh again. "Well, living in London makes me happy. And trying to get back into racing makes me happy. And being with Travis made me happy. So, are you sure you still want to stick with that line?"

My mother looks away from me, shaking her head in that stupid, heartbroken way, like she thinks there's a sympathetic audience watching somewhere.

"That's enough," my father says. "You need to apologize to your mother, right now."

"No."

His face is ruddy with anger. "I mean it. You need to climb down off this high horse you've created and apologize to your mother. We are trying to stop you from ruining your life and making a fool out of yourself. You really think people are going to support two drivers dating each other?" His voice is scornful. "The world's not changed that much. F1 fans would tear you apart."

He's practically spitting with anger, but as he's speaking, my own fury vanishes, as though someone's slapped me across the face and woken me up. A voice is speaking in my ear, and I'm not sure if it's Amanda's voice or Kelsie's or my own.

This is not reasonable. And I don't have to stand here and listen to it.

"This is a waste of time," I say quietly, almost to myself. My voice sounds eerily calm after all the shouting. I let out a breath and look my father in the eye. "And you know what, even if you're right about F1 fans, I don't care. I don't live my life to please igno-rant people. And I don't care about the opinions of small-minded idiots. And on that note"—I look at my watch—"I've got a flight to catch. Good luck with your lives. Feel free to reach out if you ever realize how despicably you've just behaved."

And with that, I turn my back on them and walk out of the house.

32

Foolproof

"HOLY SHIT," KELSIE SAYS. "YOU REALLY SAID ALL THAT?"

It's six a.m. in London. I landed about an hour ago and immediately dragged Kelsie out of bed to give her a word-for-word recap of what happened.

"Yep." My voice comes out a little shaky. I've been oscillating rapidly between "totally proud of myself and high on adrenaline" and "one wrong move away from a total breakdown." "It was insane."

"I'm so proud of you." Kelsie reaches across the table to grab my hand. "Seriously."

"Yeah." I look at my hands for a moment.

"Hey." Kelsie squeezes my fingers. "It's going to be okay."

I nod once, then again. There's a painful lump in the back of my throat. "I'm going to be fucked if I can't get a job."

"Jacob."

A thin panic rises in my chest. "I can only stay here six months without some kind of visa."

"That's plenty of time. If things don't work out with Crosswire, we'll find something else. And if that doesn't work, we'll just arrange a sham marriage."

I manage a laugh. "Right."

We smile at each other for a second, then she kicks me under the table. "Come on. You wake me up this early, I demand you take me out for breakfast."

"Yeah, alright." I rise to my feet. "Hey—thanks, yeah? For letting me stay and everything."

She shrugs. "I'm not doing it to be nice. I'm doing it so that you'll buy me a bunch of fancy shit when you become a millionaire F1 star. Obviously."

My lips twist into a smile. "Obviously."

ON TUESDAY MORNING, twenty-two minutes after eight, I walk into Crosswire Racing's factory, thirty minutes outside of London. I rented a car for the day to get here, and I was so nervous about getting lost or delayed that I got here twenty minutes early. After agonizing about it for a while, I decided that showing up eight minutes early shows initiative and courtesy. I was originally going to do twelve minutes early, but that seemed a bit *too* early, almost rude.

I've overthought this way too much, obviously.

The Crosswire factory is scary impressive. Even the parking lot is amazing. There are these two crazy metal statues of F1 cars when you turn in, and every parking spot is marked with a glossy wooden sign. There are five labeled "Guest" and twenty labeled "Visitor," and I agonized about that choice for about five minutes before I decided on Visitor.

I smooth down my T-shirt as I walk toward the building. I decided on casual clothes, a dark gray jacket, black shirt, and dark jeans, and I've got a black messenger bag that I bought yesterday over my shoulder, with my race stats and stuff printed out in a folder.

I pull open the frosted glass door and step into the lobby. The ceiling is so high it feels like a church and the walls are covered in really huge, artsy black-and-white photos of historic F1 cars and drivers. Farther ahead, to the left, there's a vast marble-floored room with a long line of old Crosswire cars. I gape at them for a moment, feeling like a little kid visiting a cool museum.

The sudden clicking of heels makes me jump. "Can I help you?" asks a pleasant voice.

The speaker is a woman about my age with a friendly smile.

"I'm here to meet Tom Kellen," I say nervously. "I'm—"

"Jacob Nichols, of course. Mr. Kellen is expecting you. Right this way."

She leads me past the incredible row of cars and up a flight of stairs to a hallway lined with doors. The door labeled "TOM KEL-LEN" is already open. I swallow hard. Tom was the team principal of Crosswire for about ten years. He took over when Crosswire was a crap team and turned it into three-time championship winner. He trained his replacement for a few years, a woman named Sofia Conyers, and then he bought out the previous team owners and took over the whole team. On TV he always seems friendly enough, but you can tell he's one of those people who's scary smart and expects everyone else to keep up with them.

Naturally, I'm terrified of him. But Amanda suggested what she calls a "foolproof" interview strategy. No matter what they ask, she said, be completely honest. That way, if you get the job, you know it's because they really want you. And if you don't, you can find a little comfort knowing you wouldn't want to work with someone who doesn't want you for your true self.

It seems kind of basic, but at the same time, it does make me feel a bit calmer. I don't have to try to think of fancy, impressive answers. I'm just going to tell the truth.

"Ah, Jacob." Tom rises and shakes my hand, firm and brisk. He's a tall, thin white man with pale hair and glasses. "Thanks for coming in."

"Of course." My voice is thin and nervous. "Thanks for having me."

"Have a seat, please." The woman melts away, shutting the door behind her, and I sit in the chair Tom points me to, on one side of a glossy wooden desk. He sits in the chair opposite me. The window behind him overlooks the parking lot with the two car statues. "Did you find the place okay?"

"Yes, sir."

"Where are you living these days? I hope you didn't have to come too far."

"No, sir. I'm living in London. I moved in with an old friend from high school."

"You like it here?"

I nod earnestly. "Yeah, so much. I love London. And I was living with my parents in Albuquerque before that for a while, during rehab, which was . . . not ideal."

That might be a bit too honest, but luckily Tom laughs, revealing very white, straight teeth. I looked up his net worth on Google, and it said he's worth six hundred *million* dollars.

"I can certainly relate to that," he says. "I lived with my parents for five years when I was trying to get my first company off the ground. 'Not ideal' is a mild way to put it." He pushes his chair back. "Would you like an espresso? I've only had four so far today, so I'm struggling."

"Oh—sure, thanks."

There's a Nespresso machine on the other side of the office, and I watch as he makes two espressos.

"How did your rehab go?" he asks. "You must have been in physio for quite some time."

I nod. "It was good. I mean, it was hard, and it took a while. But it went well. The rehab team cleared me to race again about a month and a half ago."

"Have you done any racing since?"

I swallow. "No, sir. I reached out to a few F2 teams . . ." Nope, that's not true. "All of them, actually."

"Porteo didn't want you back?"

I wince slightly at his bluntness. "No," I answer honestly. "Which . . . you know, I get it. I was really injured, and I was off for so long—"

"They're idiots," Tom says.

I stare at him. "Sorry?"

"They're idiots," he repeats, handing me an espresso. He sits down across from me and takes a sip of espresso, watching me through sharp blue eyes. "You were by far the best driver in F2 last year. They should have taken you back."

My cheeks are warm. "Oh. I mean, it was mostly my fault, though. I didn't keep in touch with them at all after the crash—"

"That's not your job," Tom says dismissively. "Clayton's younger sister died very suddenly three seasons ago. Terrible tragedy. It wasn't his *job* to tell us he needed time off. It was our job to support him through his grief and recovery." He takes another sip of espresso. "The same thing goes for the rest of our staff. Drivers are valued in this company, but not more so than everyone else."

I smile faintly. "I like that."

Tom nods briskly. "Good. Now, there are still things we'll have to work through. You'll need to be cleared by our team here—the physios and doctors, and our psychotherapists—"

"I—sorry, cleared for what?" My heart is skittering.

"To join the team," he says, as though it's obvious. "We already have a reserve driver for this season, Farin Leblanc, but we can bring you in as a test driver. And I'll tell you in confidence, it's likely our reserve spot will be open next season."

I feel kind of jittery and unstable, like I've drunk my espresso too quickly. Also sort of like I might cry, which would be humiliating. "Is Farin . . . going somewhere?" I manage.

"He is likely to receive a very exciting opportunity," Tom says vaguely. "One we would fully support him in."

"That's nice," I say stupidly.

Tom watches me for a moment. "I've surprised you."

"Uh—yeah, a little." I let out a nervous laugh. "I guess I'm just . . . I mean, don't you need to, like, interview me, or something?"

"Interviews," Tom says, "are a useless social construct. Anyone with half a brain is going to give the right answers and say the right things. Do you know how I like to select employees?"

"Um—no, sir."

"I find people I think are qualified, then I talk to the people who've worked below them. Everyone is nice to their boss. They have to be. I want to know how people treat their admin staff, their interns, their rivals. That's the only true way to measure a person." He drains the last of his espresso. "In your case, it was Billy Gaines, Ella Fairchild, Tony Carson, Maria Coutreau, and Sam Austin. I always speak to at least five people, to ensure a fair sample."

I sit silently, feeling sort of stunned. Billy Gaines was a sixteen-year-old kid who was going through karting, who spent a month with Porteo a few years ago. Ella was the team manager's assistant. Tony was a physiotherapist. Sam was one of the mechanics. And Maria . . . it takes me a minute to place her. I think she was my teammate's girlfriend.

"You are an extremely talented driver," Tom says. "But so are a lot of people. You treat people well. You work hard. And you've overcome a hell of a lot over the past months. I can imagine what it's taken for you to get to this point."

"Uh—yeah." I clear my throat. "It's been . . . a lot."

He nods. "Well, I'm not going to lie to you, you've still got a lot of hard work ahead of you. And if you slack off, or start acting like a jackass, you'll be held accountable."

"Yes, sir."

"Very good. Now, come." He stands. "I'll give you a tour of the place and walk you through our expectations of you."

I stand automatically, then abruptly sit down again.

"Sir," I say, in a voice that sounds distant.

"Yes?"

I swallow on a dry throat. "I want to be part of this team," I say. "You have no idea how much I want that."

Tom frowns as he sits back down. "Okay."

I dig my fingernails into my palms. "There's something you should know."

Be completely honest, Amanda said. That way, if you get the job, you know it's because they really want you.

Tom inclines his head. "Go on."

I have to swallow a few more times before I can speak. "The year leading up to the crash . . . I was dating someone." My heart is hammering. *Spit it out*, I order myself. "Another driver."

Tom's eyebrows lift, just for a moment, then he stares at me so intensely I can feel myself start to sweat.

"Travis Keeping," he says.

Holy shit.

"Um." My hands are shaking. I wasn't going to tell him it was Travis. "I don't know if I should say . . ."

Tom is still staring at me. "It will not leave this room."

I swallow hard. It's just occurred to me that I don't know this guy—this straight multimillionaire—at all.

And yet, something about him makes me trust him.

I rake a hand over my head. Have I gone completely insane?

I must have, because I find myself nodding jerkily. "How did you know?" My pulse spikes in sudden panic. Was it completely obvious to everyone, all that time?

"Travis is our team's greatest competition. He is almost fault-less as a driver. We were interested in signing him four years ago when he was coming out of F2, but Harper-Torrent got to him first." My eyebrows lift. I didn't know that. "His performance was incredibly poor in the race after your crash, and he was distracted for several races afterward, which is uncharacteristic of him. And he has always seemed withdrawn, as people who perceive them-selves as outsiders often are."

"Oh," I say stupidly.

He studies me again for a moment. "I won't pretend this doesn't make things . . . complex."

My stomach sinks. "Right."

"All of our staff sign strict nondisclosure agreements, however I am not fool enough to think that those agreements stop them from speaking to their partners and spouses about our work. But none of those partners or spouses are drivers who've just beat us in the championship. And if you were ever to drive against him . . ." He trails off and drums his fingers on his desk, looking so serious my heart rate triples.

It suddenly occurs to me what a huge problem this could be. The rivalry between Crosswire and Harper is notoriously contentious. Why on earth would Crosswire hire a test driver who's literally slept with their enemy?

"We're not together anymore," I blurt out. "We broke up months ago."

"Do you think you'll get back together?" he asks bluntly.

I hesitate. "I don't think so. We don't talk anymore, or anything."

I don't add that I wish we would get back together. Amanda told me to tell the truth, not to shoot myself directly in the foot.

My knuckles are white on the edge of my chair. Please don't take this away, I think desperately. Please, please.

"Hm." Tom drums his fingers on the desk again.

"I really want to be a part of this team," I say again, in a thin voice.

Tom tilts his head from side to side, as though he's weighing something in his mind. I can't help but feel he's running through a list of other drivers in his mind, weighing my skill and work ethic against their convenient lack of a relationship with Travis Keeping.

"Yes," he says finally. "We want you to be a part of this team, too."

My shoulders sag in relief, even as a little voice in my head whispers, *But Travis.* I shake it away. I'll cross that bridge if I have to.

"Was that all?" Tom asks.

I hesitate. I should probably just shut my mouth, but my father's angry words are running through my mind. "What if . . ." I lick my lips. "What if word got out? If I dated someone else. Not Travis, I mean, but another . . . guy."

Tom snorts. "That would be quite the media circus, wouldn't it?" He sounds amused by the idea, rather than horrified. "The press could feast for months on a story like that."

I swallow nervously. "I'm not saying I'm going to run around making it obvious, or anything. I just meant, if it got out accidentally—"

He shrugs. "If it does, we'll sort it out. This is a massive operation, Jacob. We know how to deal with the media."

I peer uncertainly into his face, but he seems genuinely unperturbed. I don't think he cares if I date a guy, as long as that guy isn't Crosswire's number one rival. My stomach twists a bit unhappily at the thought, but I force myself to ignore it. There's, like, a one-in-a-million chance Travis will take me back. He's probably still dating that American guy, so it would be stupid to ruin my chances with Crosswire on the slim possibility we'll get back together.

I nod once, then again. A nervous laugh escapes my throat. "I guess that's all, then."

"Very good." Tom rises to his feet, as though we've been talking about something totally mundane and normal. "Let me show you around."

33
Breathing

I HAVE A *CONTRACT*.

I keep saying it over and over in my head, but it still doesn't feel real.

A messenger biked it over the day after I met with Tom (because Crosswire is too fancy for e-mail, I guess), and Kelsie and I just stared at the dark blue envelope for a while. She hooked me up with some high-powered lawyer she knows who spent a few days poring over it and making recommendations. A week later, after a few back-and-forths and minor adjustments, I signed it.

I'm officially a test driver for Crosswire Racing.

I'm so happy, it's honestly hard to sleep. I just grin up at the ceiling of my new room (Kelsie's roommate finally moved the last of her stuff out) and whisper it out loud. I'm a test driver for *Crosswire Racing.*

I call Amanda's office to tell her. She sounds like she's crying when she calls me back, which nearly makes me cry, too. And when Crosswire releases a press piece online about signing me, I get a flood of messages from people congratulating me. Carl from Porteo even sends me a sort of passive-aggressive congratulations, saying something like, I must be glad he released me from my contract.

I spend a full day responding to e-mails and Instagram messages. I owe some big apologies to my close friends for disappearing for so long. It makes me feel awful, seeing how many times some of them tried to reach out and check in. None of them call me on it, though, and I set a plan to meet up with Nate in a couple of weeks. The girlfriend he told me about all those months ago is now his fiancée, and they're in and out of London quite a bit.

There's radio silence from my parents and Paul and Lily, which shouldn't surprise me, but somehow still does. Sometimes I'll be walking along and suddenly remember some happy childhood memory, and I'll feel sort of sick inside.

But then I remember my dad saying I'd be a laughingstock, and my mother looking away from me, and I move past it.

The only other downside, which I'm trying not to think about, is how this could affect things with Travis. Not that there's anything to affect.

"He's probably still with that guy from the parking lot," I tell Kelsie for the fiftieth time. "So, it's probably just as well."

She gives me a skeptical look over the rim of her coffee mug. It's midmorning on a Saturday, and I've been rambling at her for about ten minutes now.

"Even if he's not," I continue, "he probably doesn't want to get back together. I was such an asshole to him. Plus he's, like, a world champion now. He could date anyone he wants."

Kelsie opens her laptop. "Mm-hm."

"Plus, I still think it'd be kind of rude to just show up out of nowhere at his door. If he wanted to see me, he could. So, I should just . . . respect that. Right?"

Kelsie doesn't look up from her typing.

"Right?" I say again. "Kels?"

"Huh? Oh—sorry, babe. I was just Googling synonyms for 'coward.'"

I give her a flat look. "Ha, ha."

"'Chicken,'" she reads. "'Scaredy-cat.' 'Wimp.' 'Milksop.' Ooh, I like that one. Stop being a fucking milksop, Nichols."

"Hilarious."

She grins. "I thought so. For real, though. You want to be with him, so just stop making stupid excuses and go talk to him."

I fiddle with my coffee mug. "They're not stupid excuses. Okay, they're not *all* stupid excuses," I clarify, reading her expression. "It could ruin things with Crosswire if I got back together with Travis."

"They can't fire you for dating him, that's discrimination."

"If they fired me for dating guys in general, yes. Not for dating their main competition."

She shrugs. "So don't tell them."

I shift uneasily, remembering Tom's penetrating stare. "I don't think I could do that."

"Okay, so then don't try to date Travis again. Give up on him completely. Forget him and move on."

I look down at my hands. "I don't think I can do that, either."

She gives me a fond, exasperated look. "Duh. Look, babe, not that I don't enjoy our heart-to-hearts, but you've been saying the same things for, like, days now." She kicks me under the table. "You know what you need to do, so just stop whining and go *do* it."

I fall silent for a while, chewing the inside of my lip.

She's right. Obviously, she's right. I'm just latching on to the Crosswire thing as an excuse.

I don't really think that Crosswire would fire me for dating Travis, but if they did . . . if they did, I would survive it. It would mean going back to the drawing board, maybe waiting another year or two to claw my way back into F3 or F2 . . . but I would do it. If Crosswire couldn't trust me to date Travis and still be loyal to their team, then I would suck it up and find another way back into racing.

But I can't see any way forward without at least trying to get back together with Travis. If he doesn't want me anymore, that's one thing. But as long as there's hope, even if it's a one-in-a-million chance . . .

"I'll go and see him," I say.

Kelsie grins. "Finally."

I CONVINCE MYSELF it's better to wait to talk to Travis during F1 testing in Barcelona. If he's still dating someone (and he probably is, even though he *did* come to see me after I saw him and that guy together), there's no way he'll bring them to testing. Or if he does, they won't be following him around all the time. Surely I'll be able to talk to him alone.

Testing is a bit later than usual this year, the very last weekend in March. I'm flying over with the Crosswire team, although I won't be doing any driving. They're really putting me through the ringer with fitness and psychological testing, and I've been sitting in on tons of engineering meetings.

Yesterday, though, I got to drive an F1 car for the first time. It was Crosswire's car from two seasons ago, before the regulations changed, and Tom arranged to let me drive it as a sort of welcome to the team. It was crazy, really. This entire team of people bringing a monstrously expensive car out on track just so I could drive around in it awhile. When I first got there, I felt like I was having an out-of-body experience, like I was floating off the ground, watching someone who looked like me walking around the car in a race suit and answering the team's questions.

When I got in the car, though, everything changed. I felt inexplicably calm, and present. Like all the colors around me had gotten brighter, and the smells of hot tarmac and race fuel had gotten stronger. I had the strongest sense of déjà vu, too. A girl I dated briefly a few years ago said that if you have déjà vu, it's a sign that you're following the right path in life, the path that fate set out for you. Total bullshit, obviously, but in that moment, pulling an F1 car out on track for the first time, I really hoped it was true.

Then I reached the end of the pit lane, and I stopped thinking at all and just *drove*.

And fuck, I'd forgotten how fun it was. People used to ask me all the time what it felt like to drive my F2 car, but I'd never found a good way to describe it. I could say something about the g-forces and the noise and the acceleration, but really, it was just a lot of fucking *fun*. And driving an F1 car was even better. Like my F2 car on steroids.

The team let me drive all morning, pushing the limits of the car until my neck muscles were absolutely aching. When I finally pulled back into the garage, the muscles in my cheeks were sore, too, from grinning inside my helmet. In all my desperation to get back to racing, I hadn't let myself remember how it felt, and how much I loved it. The team probably thought I was a bit weird with how hard I was grinning, but I couldn't have stopped smiling if I tried.

I didn't think about my crash at all, not even when I almost lost the car running a bit too fast into a corner. If my mother were there, she would have cried and fussed and asked me how racing a car didn't trigger bad memories. I would have told her she was looking at it the wrong way. If you almost drown, you don't give up breathing afterward because it's too triggering.

It'll probably be a while before I'm allowed to drive Crosswire's current car—though the team principal, Sofia, promised me a free practice drive later on in the season—but I don't feel impatient anymore. Things will happen when they're meant to happen. All I can do is work hard and stay positive.

It helps that the team is so cool. Everyone is so friendly and helpful. They all work hard, and they all take their jobs seriously, but no one takes *themselves* too seriously, like the people at Porteo used to. I cheered against Crosswire last year, because I wanted Travis to win, but now that I work for them, I can see why they're always so good. They work for it. And they don't take their own success for granted.

"Can you shut up about Crosswire, please?" Kelsie asks. We've been on the phone for a while now, and okay, maybe I have been going on a bit. "Have you seen Travis yet?"

I glance at the hotel room window, which looks out over the city of Barcelona. "I've been here, like, two hours. Testing doesn't start until tomorrow. We're all just hanging out in our rooms tonight."

"Hm," Kelsie hums doubtfully. "You'd better not chicken out."

"I won't. I promise."

We hang up shortly after, and I lie back on my hotel bed and stare up at the ceiling, stretching my arms out as far as I can reach. I'm not going to chicken out. I miss Travis too much. And knowing that he went to my house, that he confronted my mother . . . I can't help but feel like there's hope.

I just have to get him alone, and get the words out.

34

:-)

OKAY, I MAY HAVE SERIOUSLY UNDERESTIMATED HOW HARD it would be to get last year's championship winner alone.

Testing starts the next morning, and I show up at the Circuit de Barcelona-Catalunya bright and early with the Crosswire team. I'm determined to work harder than anyone, and learn absolutely everyone's names and jobs, so I don't have any free time to look for Travis until lunch. There's one moment when I spot a guy in a Harper racing suit in the distance and my heart jumps into my throat, but then he pulls off his helmet and I realize it's Matty, not Travis.

At lunch, I eat with the team and force myself to pay attention to what everyone's saying, but the minute I finish eating I get to my feet and excuse myself. I've only got about ten minutes before I have to get back to work, which is not nearly enough time to actually talk to Travis, but I still feel compelled to try. I jog toward the Harper motorhome, a monstrous construction of black and white and gold. My heart is thrumming with nerves. As I grow nearer, my feet slow to a stop.

Fuck.

There he is.

He's sitting outside at a table with Heather and Matty, eating lunch. Matty's still got his racing suit on, but Travis hasn't done any driving yet. I've been watching the time screens obsessively all morning and I haven't seen his name pop up. He's got a white T-shirt on, and black jeans, and he's laughing at something Matty is saying. He looks so fucking gorgeous and happy, I could die.

He's also completely surrounded by press. There's a camera trained on him and Matty, and a group of people in media gear clearly setting up for an interview. As I watch, a few of them approach him, blocking him from my view.

I back away before he can see me. I'll just have to try again later.

And I do, every chance I get, but beyond that first lunchtime sighting, the closest I get to him is watching his lap times show up on the monitors. Harper folk stream in and out of their motorhome all day and mill around the paddock, but never Travis. I kind of forgot what a recluse he is at work. I might be able to track him down if I were brave enough to actually go inside Harper's garage, but I'm way too chicken to do that. And I don't want it getting back to Tom Kellen that I was sneaking around Harper's turf.

I might be able to track Travis down after work, but every night, someone from Crosswire invites me to join them for dinner. The first night, it's the engineers and Sofia, the team principal. The next night, it's Eric Clayton, one of Crosswire's current drivers. He's a few years older than I am and insanely nice and helpful, and we end up staying out at a restaurant till midnight, talking about racing.

On Sunday, I manage to make it to the end of the day without getting any dinner invitations, but tracking down Harper's hotel information turns out to be as impossible as breaking into the White House. Kelsie tells me to just message Travis on Instagram and ask him, but after I spend about forty minutes drafting a message, I can't bring myself to hit Send. I don't think he'd see it even if I did send it, and anyway, I want to do this in person.

Still, when I wake up on Monday, the last day of testing, I'm feeling a bit desperate.

The team works furiously all day—our car has some flaws, but it's still looking really good, definitely the best in the field—and I don't end up getting more than five minutes to bolt down lunch. By three p.m., all the driving is long done, and the team is packing up everything to leave. When Clayton and Mahoney head out at four thirty, I start to panic. Travis is probably going to be leaving soon, too. Flying back to London on some private plane.

Still, I can't just leave. I have to look like a team player. I help pack things up until Sofia touches me on the shoulder.

"You should get to the airport," she says. "Aren't you booked on an eight o'clock flight?"

I nod. I swear, Sofia is a genius just like Tom. She remembers absolutely *everything*. I heard her tell an engineer earlier not to forget to call his son to see how his orthodontist appointment went, and then when we were talking about last year's testing, she didn't just remember the order of the drivers, she remembered their *exact lap times*. All twenty of them.

Crazy.

"Go on and head out," she says. "The team's got it from here."

I thank her, shout a goodbye to the others, and then all but sprint out of there. I brought all my stuff from my hotel already, so I can just head to the airport straight from here. It's five fifty-seven p.m., which means I have at best an hour before I have to leave.

The paddock is quieter now, with only a few people milling around. It was warm earlier today, but it's cooled down quite a bit. I'm shivering slightly in only a T-shirt as I hurry toward the Harper motorhome.

A guy with a Harper T-shirt on is coming out as I approach.

"Hey, man," I say, trying to sound as normal and non-spy-ish as I can, "do you know if Travis Keeping has left yet?"

"Not sure, sorry," he says.

The door swings closed behind him and he heads off. I lurch forward and pull on the handle, but it's already locked. There's a keypad that beeps angrily at me when I press Open.

I spin around, but the guy's already vanished. I could go in through the main doors, where their cafeteria is, but when I passed it just now, their team principal was sitting outside talking with one of their engineers. I can't exactly sneak by in my very obvious Crosswire T-shirt.

"Fuck," I mutter under my breath.

Someone clears their throat behind me. "Can I help you?"

I turn. Heather is standing there, watching me. She's got a black Harper shirt on, and her long, dark brown hair falls in loose curls over her shoulder. Her expression isn't unpleasant, exactly, but I think this must be how a mouse feels when it runs into a snake.

I'm also almost completely sure she knows about me and Travis. Like, not just that we dated, but that I dumped him and was mostly a total bastard.

I swallow hard. "I was just . . . wondering if Travis left already."

Her eyes narrow slightly. "Oh."

She doesn't say anything else. I clear my throat awkwardly. "Do you . . . know if he has?"

"Yes."

Another silence. "Yes, he's left?" I say. "Or yes, you know if he has or not?"

I think she's not going to answer me, but finally she says, "He's still here."

A rush of relief runs through me. "Oh. Well—can I talk to him?"

She tilts her head. "Depends. Are you going to be a dick?"

Yeah, she definitely knows everything.

And damn it, I really like her.

"No," I say honestly. "I'm not."

She scrutinizes my face for another minute and then nods. "Alright, then." She leans past me and punches in the keycode. The door clicks open. "His room's at the very end of the hall, on the left."

"Thank you." I shoot her a thin smile and head inside. She doesn't follow me in, which I'm grateful for. Inside, there's a long narrow hallway lined with doors. I pause for a moment to rub my palms against my shirt and try to slow my racing heart.

I'm about to start walking again when a door clicks open and Matty steps out into the hall.

He does a double take when he sees me standing there, and then something shifts in his usually cheerful face. And seriously, does *everyone* know about me and Travis? Because Matty definitely does. He looks me up and down and then gives me this really sharp, predatory smile. I wait for him to speak, but he just leans against the wall with his arms crossed, staring at me.

The tips of my ears are on fire. I clear my throat and move to step around him. "Excuse me—"

"Oh, I'm sorry," he says, holding up his hands. "Was I making you uncomfortable? Because if I'd known I was making you feel bad, I would've realized it and stopped."

Okay, that felt pointed.

"It's fine," I mutter awkwardly.

"No, really," he says. "If I'd realized I was being a huge asshole, and making someone feel really badly for months and months and months, I would've thought to myself, Hey, maybe I *shouldn't* be such an asshole—"

"Yeah, I got it," I say, walking past him.

"What do I know, though?" he calls after me. "I'm just a dumb ol' racing driver, only got two brain cells to rub together—"

"I said I got it!" I snap.

I hear him laughing as he heads the other way. What an ass.

I mean, he's totally right, and that was kind of funny. But he's still an ass.

I reach the end of the hall, and then it's just me alone, standing in front of a closed door labeled "T. KEEPING."

Fuck. Here we go.

I knock loudly, in case he's got headphones on or something, then I stand there freaking out until the door swings open. And then I'm just standing there in front of him, suddenly feeling like I might burst into tears.

For one second, he looks completely shocked to see me, then whatever emotions he's feeling vanish under a blank mask.

"Hey," I blurt out.

Too loud. That was too loud.

I clear my throat and try again. "I mean, hey. Can I come in?"

His throat moves as he swallows. God, I'd like to put my mouth there. "Uh . . . yeah," he says. "Sure."

He moves aside, and I step past him. I swear I can feel the warmth radiating off his skin, and I can definitely smell his soap, a faint peppermint scent.

I clear my throat and turn to face him. With the door closed behind him, there's not much room for two people. It's a small space, with a closet for his racing stuff, a padded bench, and a desk with a chair. I stand a few feet away from him, shifting from one foot to the other. I don't know what to do with my arms. He's looking right at me, but he's got his media face on, completely unreadable.

I clear my throat again. "Congratulations on the championship," I say. "I watched the last race the other week. I mean, I watched it before then, too. Or—well, not the whole thing, actually. I mean, I saw the end of it, so I knew you won, but I didn't watch the whole race until the other week. That last pass on Mahoney was crazy. I thought the two of you were going to touch, like, five times. I was freaking out. But you didn't touch. Obviously."

Okay, I need to shut up about this now.

Travis nods slowly. "It was a good race."

He's using his most neutral voice, and it breaks my heart a little. I don't want him to talk to me like this.

I swallow hard. "I wish I could've been there."

He looks a little surprised by that, but still wary. "Mm." It's not really an answer, more like an acknowledgment that I spoke. He nods at my T-shirt. "Congrats on the Crosswire gig."

"Oh. Yeah." I look down at my shirt, as if I don't know what it looks like. "Crazy, right?"

He shrugs one shoulder. "You deserve it."

I feel a sudden surge of desperation and impatience. I don't want us to stand here like this, being polite to each other. I curl my hands into fists at my sides and dig my nails into my palms. Enough of this. It's hardcore honesty time.

"I really miss you," I blurt out. "Like—really, really miss you."

He blinks. "What?"

My cheeks go hot. "I fucked up," I say unsteadily. "I was a shit boyfriend, and then I broke up with you for some stupid reason that didn't even make sense, and everything was completely awful for months, and my parents just, like, pretended you didn't exist, and physio was awful, and I didn't think I'd ever be able to race again." I can't look at him when I'm talking. I don't think I've ever been this scared in my life. "And then I flew to London to see you, but you were with some guy in the parking lot, which is—I don't know, like, it's fine if you've moved on, you totally should move on. You deserve someone who hasn't been a total asshole to you—"

"Hey." Travis touches my wrist, and I stop talking. I'm breathing hard, and my heart feels cold and shaky. I'm cold everywhere, actually, except where Travis is touching me. "Look at me."

I lick my numb lips and force myself to look up at him. He's standing a lot closer than he was before, and frowning at me like I'm a math problem he's trying to solve.

"Are you here because you want to get back together?" he asks.

"Yeah," I say in a tiny voice. "I mean, if you want to. Yes."

His mouth curves up. "Okay."

And then he kisses me.

And oh, *fuck*, but I've missed this.

His lips are warm against mine, and one of his strong, calloused hands is sliding over my neck, and the other is on my waist, pulling me into him. A strangled, happy noise slips out of my throat, and I kiss him back, rough and desperate.

After a minute—or maybe an hour, I don't know—I pull back. I'm almost crying, practically. "Hang on—hang on."

He leans back to see my face, but his hands are still on me. His thumb is pressed against the pulse point on my neck, and his breathing has quickened. "What is it?"

"I don't know." My breathing has gotten faster, too. It's really hard to think with him holding me so close. I can smell the soap on his skin, and feel the strength in his hands, and it's almost too much after so long without him. Too much and not nearly enough. "Don't you want to, like, talk more? I had this whole apology planned out—"

"Tell me later," he says, and then puts his lips to my neck.

Fucking hell, I forgot how good he was at this. Or like, I *knew* he was good, but I forgot exactly how it felt. Like he's lighting me up from inside, electrifying every single cell in my body. He's holding me so tight, I don't think I could move if I wanted to, and his mouth and tongue and teeth are moving over my ear, my neck, my throat. He pushes me backward until my back hits the wall, and then his hands are sliding under my shirt and dragging it off, giving him that much more bare skin to work with. I should probably be doing something, reciprocating in some way, but he's not really giving me the option. He's got my wrists pinned to the wall, which is just—insanely fucking hot—and all I seem capable of doing is panting.

He releases one wrist to grip me hard through my jeans, and that's when some useless moron who I'm going to track down and murder knocks on the door.

We both go still. Well, sort of still. My chest is still rising and falling rapidly, and his fingers are still squeezing me tightly. "They'll go away if I don't answer," he murmurs. And oh, god, his voice is sexy like that, all low and throaty.

We fall quiet, listening for any noise outside the door. The person knocks again. Travis quietly undoes my jeans with one hand, and I try not to moan as he shifts his hand to grip me through my boxers.

"They're not going away," I say (alright, whine), when the person knocks for a third time. Travis is moving his hand ever so slightly, and I seriously am going to kill whoever is out there.

He releases me suddenly and puts one finger to his mouth, telling me to be quiet.

"Who is it?" he calls.

I give him an imploring look, which he ignores.

A voice with a thick Swedish accent answers. "Stefan. Do you have a minute?"

Travis grimaces. Stefan is Harper's team principal. Fuck.

"Give me five minutes," he calls back.

The look I give him is probably a bit pathetic. But the things I want to do with him will take a lot longer than five minutes. "Thirty," I whisper, poking his shoulder.

His lips curl in amusement. "I can't tell my boss to wait thirty minutes."

I scowl (okay, maybe "pout" would be a better word) but I guess he has a point. We hear Stefan's footsteps head away, and I let my forehead drop onto his shoulder. God, he smells good.

"That's not enough time," I complain.

His lips brush over the shell of my ear. "Not enough time for me to fuck you, no."

He kisses my neck again and then pushes me back onto the padded bench behind me. I let out a strangled laugh. His words sound familiar. I think I said the same thing to him that first morning after we hooked up.

I open my mouth to say something in return, then all the words fly out of my mind as he drops to his knees.

Fucking hell.

All I can hear is the sound of my breathing, all I can feel is the heat of his mouth. It's been ten months since I've been with anyone, but even before the crash, Travis always had a way of dragging me to the edge embarrassingly fast. I tangle my fingers in his hair, gripping hard enough to hurt a little, because I know he likes that. Sure enough, he groans when I do it, and I can see his arm moving. He's touching himself while he moves his mouth over me, and *yes*, the knowledge of that is just enough to do it. My vision goes white at the edges, and I make a strangled noise as rings of pleasure burst through my frame.

Things are still hazy when I drop to my knees in front of him and push his hand away. He drops his forehead onto my shoulder and clutches my shirt as I touch him. I forgot how quiet he gets before he comes, and how fucking sexy it is when he finally makes this soft, desperate sound.

Then we're both just kneeling there, wrapped up in each other, letting our breathing settle. Impulsively, I pull him closer to me, and when his arms wrap around me, it somehow feels even more intimate than when his mouth was on me. I hug him hard enough to bruise, trying to get as close to him as physically possible. I feel sort of wobbly again, like I might fall apart.

Maybe he realizes it, because he leans back to look at my face.

"I really missed you," I mumble. It's hard to meet his eye again.

He drops his forehead against mine. "Missed you, too."

We stay like that for a few moments longer, then he gives a reluctant sigh. "I think it's been more than five minutes."

"Yeah." I pull back and quickly swipe the hem of my shirt against my cheeks. When I glance up again, he's looking at me so fondly, my cheeks go hot. I clear my throat. "Are you headed back to London tonight?"

He nods. "In a few hours, yeah. You?"

"Yeah." I glance at my phone. "Like now, actually."

Travis hands me some tissue and a bottle of water, and I stand up to clean myself off. "Where are you staying in London?"

"I moved in with my friend Kelsie, in Hackney. She was my girlfriend in high school. We're just friends now," I add hastily.

"Do you want to stay at my place tonight?"

I get this weird feeling when he says it, sort of like I've been running outside on a hot day and have finally taken a sip of cold water. Or like I've been carrying something heavy and finally put it down. I let out a long, deep breath.

"Yeah," I say. "I really do."

"Meet me there later?"

I grin. "Sounds great."

He takes out his phone. He has a new iPhone, I notice, and a fancy black leather case with his racing number on it. "What's your number?"

My grin fades. He knows my old number isn't mine anymore. That must mean he tried to text me after I changed my number in Albuquerque. God, I am a fucking idiot.

I fumble to get my phone. "I just got a new London number," I say. "I don't know it off the top of my head yet."

He waits patiently while I find it and then taps it into his phone. He types something, and a moment later, my phone dings. He's sent me a smiley face. Not a smiling emoji, like most people would do, but a smile made of a colon, dash, and parenthesis—:-)—like we've traveled back in time to when people used flip phones. I smile at it foolishly.

"I'll see you later," he says.

"Yeah," I say. "Sounds good."

We grin at each other like total idiots for a few more seconds, then he closes the distance between us and kisses me again, deep and warm. After a moment, he drags himself away. The moment the door clicks shut behind him, I collapse onto the bench and grin at the ceiling, fighting the urge to laugh hysterically. If anyone walks in right now, they'll think I'm nuts.

But I don't care.

I'm back together with *Travis*.

35
Different

AT ELEVEN P.M., THE DOORBELL RINGS. I DON'T THINK JA-cob's used the doorbell at my house since the very first time he came here. He always used to walk right in.

I scrub my palms over my thighs and pull open the door. He's changed into black sweats and a soft gray hoodie I've seen him wear before, and he looks pale in the moonlight. Pale and nervous.

It's a bit of a relief to see it. I feel nervous, too.

"Hey," I say. "C'mon in."

"Thanks." He steps inside and toes off his shoes. "Good flight?"

"Yeah, you?"

"Yeah." We look at each other a moment, then I clear my throat and gesture vaguely to the kitchen. "You want to—?"

"Of course, yeah," he says, and follows me down the hallway. "Did I see you got a dog?"

"Oh, yeah," I say. "Morocco. She's at Heather's place right now."

"Ah."

We reach the kitchen, and stand in silence for a few seconds. "You want something to drink?" I ask. "I've got beer, soda . . ."

"It's okay. I had, like, three sodas on the plane, so." He shifts his weight from one foot to the other. "Actually, can I use your bathroom? I've had to pee for, like, an hour."

"Yeah, of course," I say hurriedly. "You don't have to ask."

"Right. Sorry."

"No, it's fine." He tries to step around me at the same time that I try to step out of his way, and we both laugh uncertainly. "This is awkward," I admit.

He smiles. "Little bit."

"We'll get back into it," I say.

"For sure." He rocks on his feet a second. "Right, well, I'm just going to—"

"Of course." I wave him past me. "Go."

I drop my forehead against the fridge after he's gone. This is harder than I thought it would be. It was easy back at the track, when I was riding high on the shock of him showing up and wanting me back. Now, I feel like there's a ten-month weight hanging over us, and about a million unsaid things.

I hear the bathroom door open down the hall, but a few minutes pass and Jacob doesn't reappear. I finally peer down the hall and see him standing in the open doorway of the last room on the left, the third bedroom that I converted to a sim room for him.

"You okay?" I ask.

He flinches. "Yeah," he says. Then, with a strange little laugh, "No." He gestures feebly into the sim room. "You bought that for me."

"Um—yeah?"

"I never said thank you."

I open my mouth automatically to say "It's okay," then I stop myself. "No," I agree.

His lips turn up at the edges, but it isn't a happy expression. "I'm really sorry."

"Thanks." I hesitate, then add, "Why didn't you? I mean . . . if you want to talk about it."

"I want to," he says. Then he smiles crookedly. "Well, I don't want to, really. I hate talking about things."

"Really?" I say, in a tone of feigned surprise. "I never noticed."

He laughs. "I know, I hide it well." He licks his lips. "But I'll do it, this time. I promise."

His gray eyes are serious, and a coil of tension loosens in my chest. "Right now?" I offer.

He nods. "Right now."

He follows me to the living room and curls up on one side of the couch with his knees bent in front of him. I grab a blanket from the closet and toss it to him before I sit down, like I've done a hundred times before. I sit down on the other side of the couch, facing him.

"What do you want to talk about?" I ask.

"I'm in love with you," he says.

Just like that, with no preamble or anything. He goes a bit red after he says it, but he doesn't look away from me.

"You're—oh," I say, eloquently.

He clears his throat. "It's okay if you're not . . . I mean, if you don't feel the same way anymore." He drops his gaze and fiddles with the hem of the blanket draped over his knees. "I know we've been—you know, not together, for a while. I know things have probably changed."

I move my gaze over his face. His features are so familiar to me. The tousled blond hair, the tiny scar near his left eyebrow, the shade of his eyes, like a crystallized storm cloud.

"Nothing's changed," I say quietly.

His expression changes, like a flash of light leaping into his eyes. I try to remember if his face was so expressive before. Maybe it was, and I just didn't know how to read it. "Yeah?" he says, his tone hopeful.

I smile. "Yeah. But I don't think things can be the same, this time."

"I know." He rests his temple against the couch. "I messed everything up before. I'm no good at relationships."

"I mean, you're better than me," I point out. "At least you've dated people before."

He snorts. "No one I actually liked. Well, I liked Kelsie," he amends. "But I wasn't—you know. In love with her."

A pleasant shiver runs through me. That's twice now he's said the word. There's color in his cheeks again, and for a moment I'm tempted to change the subject, but Heather's voice is whispering in my ear, talking about being accountable.

"You didn't say it before," I say. "When I—" I gesture to the kitchen instead of finishing the sentence. I can tell by the look on his face that he knows what I mean.

"I know." He exhales heavily and shifts a bit deeper into the couch. There are faint smudges under his eyes, like he hasn't been sleeping well. "I wanted to. I just . . . I don't like giving up control."

I get the strangest feeling when he says it, like a puzzle piece has clicked into place in my mind. In the span of one heartbeat, my memories of Jacob reshape themselves. His plastic smile when I gave him the simulator. The stiffness of his fingers when I held his hand in the hospital. His strange jitteriness when he got back from his run with Nate, the day I tried to tell him I loved him.

I stretch my leg out and nudge his shin. "I don't want to control you," I say. "Idiot."

He laughs, and the air relaxes a bit more between us. We're

quiet for a moment, then I ask the question that's been haunting me for months. "What happened in the hospital? Why did you end things?"

"Because I'm an idiot," he says.

I snort. "Jacob."

He smiles a little, then sobers. "I was scared," he says, quieter.

"Of what?"

He shrugs a bit helplessly and casts his gaze around the living room. "I don't know. Lots of things. Never racing again. People finding out about us."

"That freaks me out a bit, too," I say.

"Yeah, well, it shouldn't," he says, his brow furrowing. "I mean, I don't want a bunch of strangers knowing our business," he adds, perhaps seeing the wariness in my face, "but there's a difference between private and secret. And I'm tired of keeping secrets."

One side of my mouth curves up. "Me too."

"Anyway, that's why I ended things, because I was a cowardly piece of shit. And I'm sorry. I'm really, really sorry."

My heart twists. "I'm sorry, too."

He frowns. "What do you have to be sorry for?"

"I should've fought harder for us. If I'd reached out to you sooner—if I hadn't given up so quickly—"

"It wouldn't have made a difference," he says. "I mean, if you'd messaged me a month ago, yeah, I would've been here in a heart-beat, but before that . . . I wasn't ready. I was a fucking mess, re-ally."

"You're not a mess."

He snorts. "Tell that to my therapist."

"You have a therapist?"

His cheeks color. "I did, yeah. It's kind of stupid."

"I don't think it's stupid," I say. "Was it helpful?"

"I don't know. Yeah." He shifts his weight and gives me a strange, uncertain look. "You really want to hear about it?"

I lean forward and take his hand, pressing my lips to the center of his palm. I know the taste of his skin just as well as the color of his eyes, but hearing him talk like this, it's almost like listening to a stranger. Or a new version of him, at least. A version I really want to know.

"I really do," I say, and sit back again to listen.

WE STAY AWAKE talking for another hour or two, until Jacob is practically falling asleep between sentences. I tell him about Heather and Matty and Mrs. Costa and Matty's parents, and he tells me about therapy and rehab and his first week with Crosswire. When he can't stay awake any longer, we migrate to my bedroom. He falls asleep with his head on my chest and my fingers threaded loosely in his hair. When I wake up around noon, he's sleeping so deeply, I have to check that he's breathing.

I know it's creepy to watch someone sleep, but I can't help doing it for a minute or two. I still can't quite believe he's here.

I grab my phone from the nightstand and flip through my texts. I told Heather and Matty about Jacob on the flight home, and clearly they (and by "they" I mean Matty) have told everyone else. I have texts from both of his parents and Mrs. Costa and Hunter, and even a text from Thomas (Happy for you! PS— Heather showed me a pic of your boy. DAMN. Any chance he has a twin brother? Asking for a friend).

I'm sending back a response when my phone vibrates again. It's a message in the group chat between me, Heather, Hunter, Matty, Matty's girlfriend Erin, his parents, and Mrs. Costa. Heather set it up to send us the time of our dinner reservation after the race in Brazil, but everyone's kept messaging in it since.

[12:07] **Matty:** so what are we all thinking

[12:07] **Matty:** dinner tonight to grill Travis' new boyfriend?

Oh, lord. I'm frantically typing a protest when Hunter answers.

[12:08] **Hunter:** oh HELL YES

[12:08] **Hunter:** I want to meet this asshole who thinks he's good enough for our boy

[12:09] **Heather:** agreed!!!! I can book it, just need a head count

[12:09] **Heather:** PS Hunter bring me coffee

[12:10] **Hunter:** ?? Come out to the kitchen and get it yourself

[12:11] **Alice:** Frank and I are on holiday right now, but we can't wait to meet him, Travis. Call us tomorrow if you get a chance.

[12:12] **Matty:** how come you never ask ME to call you, mom??

[12:13] **Mrs. Costa:** I'm home in Brasilia, but I would like a full report, please! I'm so happy for you, Travis. Sending you my love.

[12:13] **Matty:** are you sending me love too, Mrs. Costa?

[12:14] **Mrs. Costa:** Of course!

[12:14] **Matty:** see mom? SOMEONE loves me.

[12:14] **Alice:** Okay, dear.

I jump in as quickly as I can.

[12:15]: Do I get a say in any of this??

[12:15] **Heather:** No.

[12:15] **Matty:** nope

[12:15] **Hunter:** hahaha no

[12:16] **Erin:** Why don't we have dinner at our house instead of going out?

[12:16] **Matty:** ummm because neither of us can cook?

[12:17] **Erin:** Yes, but I can order pizza with the best of them

[12:17] **Erin:** Our place at 8?

[12:17] **Heather:** Sounds great!

[12:17] **Hunter:** We'll be there

[12:17] **Matty:** woooo

"Crap," I mutter.

"Mm." Jacob is waking up, stretching absently against me. He blinks up at me sleepily. "What's wrong?"

"It's nothing." I put my phone away as he shifts in bed to sit up next to me. "My friends want to have us over for dinner tonight."

"Ah." Jacob looks uncomfortable. "I guess they're probably not my biggest fans."

"It's not that," I say quickly. "I'm just not sure I want to spend our first night back together eating pizza with Matty."

He presses his forehead into the crook of my shoulder. "I thought last night was our first night back together."

"Yeah, but—" I cut myself off abruptly. It sounds a bit immature to say "Yeah, but we didn't even have sex."

But seriously, we didn't even have sex.

Jacob grins, like he knows what I was going to say. "Tell you what," he says. "Let's go get some food, then I'll run home and get some clothes for dinner, and then we can just . . . hang out here all afternoon."

"Mm." I snake an arm around his waist and pull him closer. "That sounds good."

"Right?" He grips the front of my T-shirt and kisses me deeply. A moment later, he pushes aside the comforter so he can throw a leg over my hips, settling all his warm weight on top of me. I run my hands up his legs, sliding my thumbs under the thin cotton hem of his boxers.

"You know what sounds even better?" I murmur, after a few minutes of increasingly heated kissing. He pulls back, his eyes very dark.

"Doing it right now?" he says.

I grin. "Fuck yes."

He laughs at me cursing—I guess I didn't swear as much around him before—and then kisses me again, deep and urgent.

I kind of thought the first time we had sex again, I would spend ages taking him apart, but now that we're here, I don't know why I thought I would have the self-control to do that. We're hurtling forward so fast, everything is happening in quick, breathless flashes. He's pulling my T-shirt over my head. I'm shifting on top of him and dragging his earlobe through my teeth. His warm, bare skin is sliding against mine; my fingers are working him open, making him cry out every time they curl. Then I'm sinking into him, all tight heat and pressure, and his eyes are on mine as I move.

And this, this is different than before. That layer of distance that used to live in these moments has been stripped away, and my name is slipping out of his mouth like a fucking prayer, and he only breaks eye contact at the very end, when his head tips back and the sexiest, most desperate sounds drag their way out of his throat.

I think it's the hardest I've ever come, watching him like that. It seems to go on and on and on, till I feel almost wrecked with it. Even the aftershocks kill me, little stabs of pleasure that have me clutching his hips like a lifeline. I think he's feeling it, too. He's holding my shoulders painfully tightly, and his head has tipped forward, tiny sounds almost like whimpers escaping his lips.

"*Fuck*," he manages finally.

"Fuck," I agree.

It makes him laugh again, a breathy, strangled sound.

"I can't believe I went ten months without you," he says.

And hell, if that doesn't cut straight to my heart. For a second I feel like I'm back in the ICU, pressing my lips to his skin and asking him not to die. I never want to lose him again.

I lean forward carefully and kiss him, my fingers digging into his thighs. There's a new scar on the right, stretching down from his hip. "I love you so much."

Color rises to his cheeks, but he smiles and says, "Love you, too."

We drag ourselves to the bathroom and shower together without having sex, a strange new intimacy. I trace the new scars on his skin with wet fingertips.

"Do they hurt at all?" I ask.

He watches my fingers move. "Not really. They're kind of ugly, though. There's some fancy laser therapy that could fade them."

"I don't think they're ugly." I run my fingers up and down the long scar on his thigh. "Think you'll get it done?"

He grins. "Not if you keep touching them like that."

Afterward, we get back in bed and laze around awhile longer, until my phone alarm goes off, reminding me of a stupid commercial thing I've got to do for one of Harper's sponsors.

"You can stay here as long as you want," I tell Jacob as I pull on my jeans. "I mean, you don't have to—"

"No, I will," he says. He leans forward in bed, crossing his arms over his knees. "Kelsie's working on this huge paper for school, so I've been trying to make myself scarce." He hesitates a moment, then adds, "Might use the sim a bit, if that's okay."

Warmth spreads through my chest. "Go for it," I answer. "It's yours."

He grins at me, a little crooked and a little shy, and I force myself to say goodbye and leave, because otherwise, I'm going to wind up climbing back into bed with him.

THE HARPER THING ends up running late—I'm no actor, and apparently my performance as "guy who genuinely likes Panther Soda" is highly unconvincing—and I arrive home past seven, after a quick detour to pick Morocco up from Heather's place. I grin a bit foolishly when she leaps onto Jacob's lap the moment she sees him, as if he's an old friend. I kiss Jacob on the lips and Morocco on the top of her head, then head for a shower. I emerge from my bedroom fifteen minutes later, pulling on a long-sleeve shirt, to find Jacob standing in front of my cabinets, both him and Morocco staring wistfully at the food inside.

"Hungry?" I say.

"Starving. I got caught up on the sim and forgot to eat anything."

I laugh. "So, eat something now."

He sighs and closes the cabinets. "Yeah, but then if I don't eat whatever your friends have, they'll think I'm a dick. Even more of a dick, I mean."

"They don't think you're a dick."

He makes a doubtful noise. "They should."

"Jacob." I curl my hands around his biceps. "You're not a dick."

He turns to face me, his mouth twisted a bit unhappily. "I was, though. I was the one who broke up with you. And I was a piss-poor boyfriend for a year before that."

I frown. "Do you really believe that?"

"I generally believe things that are true, yeah."

I tilt his chin up with my hand. "You weren't a bad boyfriend."

"Yeah, I was," he says impatiently. "You were so nice to me all the time and all I did was push you away and treat you like shit."

I take a step back and frown at him for a moment. "Did you lose your memory after the crash, or something?"

"What?"

"You know you were nice to me, like, all of the time, right?"

"I wasn't—"

"Shh," I interrupt, clamping a hand over his mouth. "I'm still talking. Like, remember Monaco last year, when I had that stupid flu?"

One corner of his mouth turns up slightly. "Yeah."

"Well, do you remember how you stayed at my hotel and made me take Tylenol and drink a bunch of water and soup?"

He shrugs one shoulder. "I guess."

"And do you remember when I lost the championship last year, and you stayed with me over Christmas?"

"You mean when you got me a really expensive present, and I didn't even say thank you?"

"I remember you making that gross mint hot chocolate—"

"Peppermint."

"—and making us breakfast, and falling asleep on my lap halfway through that weird cartoon."

"It was *How the Grinch Stole Christmas*, and it's a classic."

I run my thumb over his jaw. "I could name a thousand things like that. And it wasn't just that you did stuff for me." I search for the right words. "It was the way you made me feel. I didn't realize how lonely my life was until I met you."

Jacob looks at his feet. "You had a great life."

"Yeah, I did," I agree. "But I didn't have anyone to share it with."

I slide my hands down his neck and dig my fingers into the tight muscles of his shoulders. "Look, I'm not saying everything was perfect all the time. We both could've done things a bit differently. But I was really happy with you back then. And I'm really, really happy with you now."

He looks up at me, his gray eyes serious. "I'm not going to mess things up again. I'm in this, a hundred percent."

My lips curve up. "I know." I kiss him gently, a soft brush of my lips against his. "Now can we please go and eat something? I didn't eat all day, either. I feel like I'm going to die."

"God, yes," he agrees.

I shoot Heather a quick text on the way to the parking garage. On our way. Can you make sure no one's hard on Jacob? He's had a rough time.

My phone dings just as we pull into a parking spot near Matty and Erin's.

[7:56] **Heather:** I got you, babe.

I smile at Jacob before we get out of the car. "It's going to be fine, okay?"

He nods jerkily. It's really sort of cute, how nervous he is.

True to her word, Heather is waiting for us at the door with a smile and two drinks.

"An old-fashioned, courtesy of yours truly," she says, handing one to Jacob.

"Is that for me?" I ask, pointing to the second glass.

"This is mine," she says. "Obviously. You're not new and exciting." She clinks her glass against Jacob's and then leads us farther into the house, to the kitchen, where Matty, Erin, and Hunter are sitting around a large wooden island. Matty is unscrewing the cork from a bottle of red wine while Erin and Hunter are chatting over a stack of pizza boxes. I go a little lightheaded with hunger at the smell.

"Thank god," Hunter says when he spots us. "If I don't eat something, I'm going to die."

Heather rolls her eyes behind his back. "Vegans," she says. "They're all weak and frail from eating twigs and shrubs."

"Jacob, this Hunter and Erin," I say. "And you remember Matty, the guy who vaguely threatened you in Crosswire's motorhome the other day?"

"Hey!" Matty complains. "I was defending you, asshole. That's what a good bro does."

"Okay, please don't ever use the word 'bro' again," Erin says. "You really can't pull it off."

"Like you and the word 'girl,' you mean?" Matty shoots back. Then, in an exaggerated falsetto, "Hey, girl, call me later, okay? We can sip prosecco and play *Call of Duty*!"

Hunter snorts. "Is that what you think women do?"

"That's what Erin and her sister did all last night!" Matty says.

"Can we eat now?" I cut in. "Jacob and I haven't eaten all day."

"Whyever not?" Heather asks innocently.

I pretend I don't hear her. We all find seats around the kitchen island and descend on the pizza. It's insanely delicious, even the piece of Hunter's vegan pizza that I take by mistake, but there's a certain awkwardness to the silence as we take our first bites.

I shoot Heather an imploring glance, and she sits up a little straighter. "So—Jacob." She smiles at him. "On a scale of one to never, what do you think the chances are you'll break up with Travis again?"

I nearly choke on my pizza. "*I got you, babe,*" my ass.

"Heather," I snap.

"What?" she says sweetly. "I broke the silence."

"It's okay," Jacob says. "I'm not going to break up with him again."

"Good answer," Heather says.

"Can we get that in writing?" Matty asks.

I raise my eyes to the ceiling. "You two are the actual worst."

"We're just looking out for you, babe," Heather tells me. "Well, that, and we don't want to have to listen to you pine after him again. Months and months of this very sad, very self-indulgent obsession—honestly, Jacob, you should probably run away while you still can—"

"Ha, ha," I say flatly. The tips of my ears are hot.

Jacob squeezes my thigh under the table. "I can't imagine Travis obsessing," he says. "Are you sure it wasn't someone else?" He looks over at Matty. "Didn't you chase after a contract with Crosswire for, like, twenty years?"

There's a sputtering noise. Erin's snorted into her wine.

"He totally did," she says, laughing.

"Uh, it was two years, fuck you very much," Matty retorts. "See, Jacob, I knew I didn't like you. Travis, break up with him immediately. Go on."

Everyone's laughing, and Jacob's hand is still on my leg. Heather shoots me a little wink across the table. The atmosphere is much more relaxed, now.

Talk turns to everyone's jobs—Erin's got a photoshoot coming up in Alaska, and Hunter tells a funny story about one of his coworkers. Matty asks Jacob how things at Crosswire are going, and Jacob tells us a bit about the testing they're putting him through.

"You're all good from the crash now, though, yeah?" Hunter asks.

"Mostly, yeah. My hip gets kind of sore sometimes where I broke it, but it's nothing major."

"Physio must've been a bitch," Matty says. "I had trigger finger last year, and the physio was a nightmare."

"Yeah, his accident was exactly the same as your trigger finger," Heather says, rolling her eyes.

"It was kind of brutal, yeah," Jacob says.

Hunter takes a sip of wine. "Heather said you were living with your parents in the States?"

"Uh—yeah." Jacob's smile looks a little forced.

"They must be excited about your fancy new F1 job," Erin says.

Jacob tears a piece of pizza crust in two. "Maybe," he says. "I'm . . . not really talking to them right now."

I look at him. I haven't heard this yet. He hinted at how awful living with his parents was, but we didn't talk about how they left things.

"Why's that?" Heather asks.

Jacob hesitates a moment, looking around the table.

"Circle of trust here, babe," Heather says. "Nothing leaves the island."

He clears his throat. "It's not a big deal. They just aren't okay with the whole"—he waves a hand between me and him—"dating thing."

"Oh yeah," Matty says. "Travis told me they were being little shits at the hospital."

I glare at Matty. "I didn't use those exact words."

"Didn't have to," he retorts.

"It's fine," Jacob says. "It's not wrong."

I can hear the tension in his voice. "Did something happen?" I ask.

Jacob glances at the others again. "Ah—sort of." He lowers his voice a bit. "You know how you went to my house?"

"We all know about that," Matty says.

"I packed his suitcase," Heather adds cheerfully.

Jacob manages a tiny smile. "Yeah, well, my mother didn't even tell me you were there. The neighborhood kids told me, and when I confronted her about it . . . it got kind of ugly."

"Shit." My stomach tenses. "Sorry."

"Don't be," Jacob says. "They . . . aren't very good people."

"They're your parents, though," I say.

"Yeah, but does that mean I have to pretend all the shitty stuff they say is okay?" He lets out a humorless breath. "My dad said dating you would turn me into a laughingstock."

"Oh, hell no," Heather says.

"Fuck that asshole," Matty adds. "Seriously, that's total bullshit. If you and Travis ever go public, there will be, like, a hundred million girls falling all over both of you. And a hundred million gay guys. And at least fifty million bisexual guys. Or are there more bisexual guys than gay guys? Hang on, let me Google it real quick."

"I know it's bullshit," Jacob says.

"It still sucks, though," I say, watching him closely. "You were always so close with your family."

Jacob shrugs. "Was I, though? I feel like they were only happy with me because I never shared any of my actual feelings with them. Like, as long as I acted like this perfect cardboard cutout of a good son, they felt like we were one big happy family. I don't think they ever really knew me at all."

"Hear, hear," Erin says, raising her wine glass. "Matty has amazing parents, so he has no idea what you're talking about, but trust me, I get it. If they don't like you for you, you shouldn't feel guilty for not wanting them to be a part of your life."

"I don't feel guilty," Jacob admits. "Like, I know I probably should, but . . . I don't know. I mostly just feel relieved."

"I get it," Erin says again. "You and I should really have a bottle of wine sometime. I feel like we would get along."

"It's fifty-fifty," Matty announces suddenly, looking up from his phone. "At least according to this study. Although, I feel like these statistics are kind of nonsense, because if you're in the closet, you're not exactly going to tell some random survey person that you're gay, right?" He frowns. "Although maybe if they tell you it's anonymous, or if it's, like, a secret internet survey poll—"

"Put some more pizza in your mouth, Matty," Heather says. "Stop the words from coming out."

Matty tosses a chunk of pizza crust at her. "For real, though, that sucks about your parents," he tells Jacob. "If you ever want to borrow mine, just let me know. They love other people's children. They've already adopted Erin and Travis, but I'm sure they'd love a third child."

Jacob chuckles. "I'll remember that."

Erin asks everyone if they want more drinks, and the conversation turns to something else. I lean closer to Jacob and touch his hand under the table.

"I'm really sorry," I say quietly. "I didn't mean to mess everything up with your family."

"You didn't," he says. "It's their issue."

I squeeze his hand once, and he presses his shoulder against mine. He stays like that until we all get up and migrate to the living room, where we sit and chat awhile longer. Jacob and Matty get into a passionate and extremely boring discussion about track limits at the Austrian GP (they're both shocked I don't have a strong opinion on the subject), Hunter tells me about the great new guy Thomas is dating, which makes me feel a lot better about that situation, and Erin shows me some pictures she took in Canada for some nature magazine.

Everyone takes Jacob's cell phone number before we leave, and Heather says she'll text us all to set something up again soon. Jacob is quiet as we walk back to my car. He didn't drink anything except the old-fashioned Heather made him, but he's got a jittery, nervous sort of energy about him.

"Was that alright?" I ask.

"Yeah," he says. "It was fun." He hesitates a moment, then adds, "Do you think your friends like me?"

I grin. "I do."

He lets out a little breath, and some of the tension slips from his frame. "Good," he says, as we reach the car. He clears his throat and adds, "Kelsie will like you, too. She thinks you're super hot, which is a good start."

I laugh and pull open the driver's-side door. "That is a good start."

Jacob gets into the passenger seat beside me. There's a beat of silence, then he says, "I'm meeting up with my friend Nate next weekend, too. You could come with me if you want."

I go still, just for a moment. "Oh yeah?"

"Yeah. I think you'd like him. And he's bringing his fiancée, so." He leaves the sentence unfinished.

"So . . . you want me to come as a friend?" I ask, carefully.

He looks away from me to fiddle with his seatbelt. "I guess. Or you could just come as my boyfriend." He clears his throat again. "I mean, if you wanted to. I know we haven't really talked about it."

He gives me a small, slightly nervous smile, and a rush of fondness swells up in my chest.

I wonder if I'll ever stop feeling this way. I don't think so. He's as firmly rooted in my heart as he was that first week in Scotland. And as awful as I felt sometimes during the past ten months, I can't bring myself to regret it. It brought me my own family, Heather and Matty and Hunter and Matty's parents and Mrs. Costa. And it brought me this new version of Jacob, who's exactly like the boy I already loved but with all the layers of uncertainty stripped away. He said that he's in this, a hundred percent, and I believe him.

I lean over the handbrake to kiss him.

"Your boyfriend," I agree.

36

Home

I WAKE UP TO FIND TRAVIS' NEW DOG, MOROCCO, STARING at me. She's curled up on his abandoned pillow with her chin tucked between her front paws and a stern look on her face, like she's judging me for sleeping in so late.

I stretch my arms out and breathe in deeply. I forgot how good it feels to sleep through the whole night. All of my muscles are loose and warm, and my mind feels clearer than it has since the crash. I can hear Travis' coffeemaker gurgling in the kitchen and the faint sounds of music, a Mumford & Sons song I vaguely recognize. Hunter mentioned last night he was working on Travis' musical education. Or, as Heather put it, "trying to turn Travis into an annoying hipster, as if the world doesn't have enough of them already."

I really liked them, Heather and Hunter and Matty and Erin. I think they liked me, too, but I definitely get the sense that I'll be on probation until they're sure I'm not going to hurt Travis again. Which is fine with me, really. I like that he has people to be protective of him. And I have no intention of hurting him, now that we're back together.

Your boyfriend, he said.

I grin foolishly at the memory. I'm actually kind of excited to introduce him to Nate next weekend. I suppose there's a chance Nate will react badly, but I'm not that worried. He's a really laid-back sort of guy, plus he's a huge F1 fan. If anything, he'll probably just be annoyed I didn't tell him about Travis sooner.

Morocco bats impatiently at my hand. I pet her obediently for a minute or two and then roll over and reach for my phone. Kelsie's texted to see how things went last night, and there's a text from an unknown number that just says Sup bro!!, which is either Matty or Erin imitating Matty. I send back a string of question marks to see who it is and then scroll absently through Instagram.

My thumb stills over a post from an F1 news account. There's a photo of Tom Kellen frowning, with the caption "Kellen throws shade at Olsson after Crosswire dominates preseason testing."

My stomach twists unpleasantly. Olsson is Stefan Olsson, Harper's team boss.

"What's that face for?"

Morocco's tail thumps eagerly as Travis steps into the room carrying a steaming mug of coffee.

I hold my hands out eagerly. "Oh my god, thank you."

"This was mine, actually," Travis says dryly. "But you can have it."

He nudges Morocco out of the way to sit down beside me. I slide up in bed and take a sip of coffee.

"Fuck, that's good. Do you think it would be a bad idea to inject this directly into my veins?"

Travis grins. "Probably. So?" he adds, nudging my shoulder. "What was the face for?"

I shift uncertainly. "I'm just . . . not looking forward to going back to work tomorrow."

His eyebrows lift. "I thought you were liking it so far."

"No, I am." I hesitate. "I just don't know if I should tell Tom that we're dating again."

Travis pets Morocco's head. "Does he know that we were dating before?"

I wince. "Yeah. I sort of told him during my interview. Or, well, I didn't actually tell him it was you, I just said that I was dating another driver, and he guessed that it was you. And I know I shouldn't have told him that without talking to you, but that was when we were—you know, broken up, and he swore he wouldn't tell anyone else . . ." I trail off guiltily. "Sorry."

Travis shrugs. "I don't care. I told Stefan about you, when you were in the hospital."

"And he didn't care?"

Travis tilts his head thoughtfully. "Not sure. We never talked about it again."

My lips twist up into a wry smile. He sounds like he hasn't given it a moment's thought since.

"Yeah, well, Tom wasn't thrilled when I told him we'd dated. Or at least, he said it made things 'complex.'" I look down at my coffee cup. "He'll probably fire me when he finds out we're back together."

"Why? What does it matter?"

I look at him in fond exasperation. "I don't know if you're aware, but there's a bit of a rivalry between Crosswire and Harper."

He laughs. "I vaguely remember hearing something about that, yes. But what does Tom think you're going to do? Find out all their secrets and pass them on to me?"

"Er—basically, yeah."

"Hm." Travis takes the coffee cup from my hand and sips it for a moment, staring at me. My cheeks go slightly warm under his gaze. I forgot what it felt like, to have all his focus and attention. "Let me talk to Stefan," he says. "There must be some sort of nondisclosure agreement we can sign to stop them worrying."

I hesitate. "You mean, like . . . something they'd work out together?"

He shrugs. "Why not?"

"Because they hate each other? Or because it'd be way easier for Crosswire to just replace me?"

Travis rolls his eyes. "Who are they going to replace you with? They don't have any good drivers in their academy right now."

"They have their reserve driver—"

"Who, Farin Leblanc?" Travis shakes his head. "He isn't half as good as you."

I pull a face. "I don't know if that's true. Even if it is, there are plenty of other drivers."

"No," Travis says, simply, as if the idea that Crosswire might pick someone other than me is insane. "They're lucky to have you. And if they want to keep you, they'll have to put up with us dating."

I roll my eyes, flattered and exasperated in equal measure. "That's easy for you to say. Harper will never fire you. You've just won them the championship."

"And I'll remind Stefan of that when I tell him to set up a meeting with Crosswire."

I scrub a hand over my face. "And what's going to stop Crosswire from firing me?"

"Besides the fact that you're the best driver to take Mahoney's place when he retires?"

"Yeah."

Travis grins. "Maybe the fact that my contract with Harper is up at the end of this year. Crosswire's been after me before. I don't think they'll risk pissing me off, not if they want any hope of signing me in the future."

I stare at him in surprise. "You'd really leave Harper?"

He chuckles. "Probably not. But they don't have to know that."

He puts the coffee cup back in my hand and kisses me swiftly, then pulls his phone from his pocket and starts dialing.

"Wait, you're calling Stefan *now*?"

"Of course."

I groan. "Travis . . ."

He waves away my protest and heads into the hall with his phone to his ear. His voice echoes back to me, polite but firm. "Stefan? Hi. Yeah, good, thanks. Look, I've got a bit of a situation—"

Morocco bats my thigh with her paw. I put my coffee aside to rub her ears.

"Insane," I tell her quietly. "Your owner is *insane*."

But as I reach for my coffee cup again, I'm smiling.

A WEEK LATER, Travis and I sit in a conference room along with Stefan, Tom, and five well-dressed lawyers. Two of them are from Crosswire, two are from Harper, and one is the monstrously expensive, slightly terrifying lawyer Travis hired to represent our interests—mine and his. It's taken them seven days of what sounds like nonstop work, but they've all finally agreed on a nondisclosure agreement for Travis and me to sign.

It's without a doubt one of the most uncomfortable situations I've ever been in. Tom and Stefan really, really don't like each other, but they're clearly trying to out-civil each other. They did this strange thing at the start, where they were each trying to flex how supportive and principled their team is compared to the other's. Like, Tom said he "fully supports" our relationship, so Stefan had to one-up him by saying he'd be "perfectly happy" to support us going public. Which we aren't—we talked about it, and we both want to keep things private, for now—but I've been thinking about how I would feel if the news leaked someday, and it doesn't give me cold stabs of panic like it used to. In fact, I kind of think it would be easier, after the media shitstorm settled.

Anyway, Tom and Stefan bragged about their anti-discrimination policies for a while, then the lawyers jumped in and said we should probably get started. I don't know why it takes fourteen pages to say it, but the agreement they've drawn up basically boils down to this: whatever Travis and I share with each other will stay between the two of us. I can tell Travis about Crosswire's new brake ducts, but he can't then run and tell Harper about them, and vice versa.

It just seems like common sense to me, and I take no issue with signing until we reach a little note on the last page, which says that neither team will ever hire the opposite team's driver. My stomach twists a little, but I'm thinking I'll just ignore it, until Travis speaks up.

"Remove that," he says. "That's unreasonable."

He's the only one in the room who isn't tense or red-faced. I know him, so I know he does occasionally get nervous about things—although, now that I think on it, it's only ever stuff to do with me, like how he handed me a key the other day without any explanation, and it took five minutes of wheedling to get him to explain it was a key to his place—but clearly he isn't nervous about this. Looking at him, you'd think he's lounging on a beach in the Maldives. Which, incidentally, is a holiday we're planning with Heather and Hunter for the F1 summer break.

He's got one arm on the back of his chair and the other stretched out on the table, his fingers resting next to his phone. It's his old iPhone, the one he was using when we first met. Heather and Hunter bought him a newer model, and Matty and Erin bought him a fancy case for it, but he hasn't used them since I gave him the Christmas present I got him last year, the wooden phone case with the picture of the cabin in Harris etched into it. I kind of wish he'd keep it in his pocket, because every time I see it, I remember the look on his face when I gave it to him, and I want to grin like an idiot.

Instead, I bite the inside of my cheek and try to mimic his calm, unbothered expression.

Stefan clears his throat. "Well, now, our lawyers feel that it's important protection for the team. What's to stop Crosswire from poaching you from us to steal all our secrets?" He sort of laughs after he says it, like he's trying to keep things light and friendly.

Travis raises an eyebrow. "They could do that now. And why would you sign something that could keep you from hiring Jacob?"

Oh, lord. The tips of my ears light on fire as Tom and Stefan turn their critical gazes toward me. Travis makes it sound like I'm some sort of prodigy, like they'd be insane to pass up the chance to work with me.

The crazy part is, Tom and Stefan are frowning at me like they might *agree*. I can practically hear their brains whirring.

Tom gets there a little faster. "I have no issue with removing it," he says. "We've always supported our drivers to do what's best for their careers. If a better opportunity arises for Jacob, of course we would want him to take it. Although," he adds, "I have confidence our team will only improve with the new regulations."

I stifle a smile. He's really put Stefan in a corner with that one.

"We are *equally* supportive of our drivers," Stefan says stiffly. "And I'm just as confident in our team." With obvious effort, he puts on a smile. "Who knows? Perhaps one day the two of you will be teammates."

I glance at Travis, and I know he's trying to imagine it, just like I am. He and Matty are a bit of an exception—most teammates in F1 aren't close friends. Or if they are, they usually don't stay that way.

But I don't know. I think Travis and I could hack it.

The meeting drags on for another hour after that, then everyone finally agrees on the final language, and the lawyers whip out brand-new copies for us to sign. It feels sort of weird signing a contract with Travis, almost like we're getting married or something.

And I know it's not the same thing, obviously. But it's still something of a statement. It's saying we think we'll be together for as long as we're with our respective F1 teams, and I hope to hell that's longer than a few years.

I think he must feel the same way, because he takes my hand on the car ride home and grins at me in that fond, easy way that makes my skin warm.

"Kind of cool, yeah?" he says.

I nod, biting into my grin. It definitely is. Just like it was cool last night, when I was telling him a story about Kelsie and he said, sort of offhand, "Have you signed a lease for her place yet?" And when I replied just as casually that I hadn't, and asked if he thought I should, he shrugged and said, "Maybe just for a month or two. It would suck to be stuck in a lease for too long."

And then we sort of grinned at each other for a while, pretending like we both didn't know what we were getting at. I swear, if I saw a couple acting like this on TV, I would roll my eyes and call them both lame.

But it turns out it's really fucking nice when it's happening to you.

Travis turns onto the highway back into London, and I watch the countryside roll by. It's one of those perfect spring days, when it seems like all the leaves have come out overnight, and the sky is a bright, unbroken blue. The city is silhouetted in the distance, filled with things I want to do and places I want to see. Kelsie made a whole list for me, three hundred and forty-two items long, and Travis and I have slowly started picking them off. Sometimes we go with Kelsie and Heather, who met a few days ago and hit it off straightaway, or Nate, who likes Travis just as much as I hoped he would, but most of the time, it's just Travis and me. A few days ago, we went to the Tower of London, and a bunch of people recognized Travis and asked for his autograph.

A year ago, I wouldn't have gone anywhere alone with him, in case something like that happened. I would've felt sick worrying that someone would wonder why we're always spotted together in London without any girlfriends in tow. Now, I can't bring myself to care. Let them wonder, let them talk. I've already decided I won't live my life to please my parents. I'm sure as hell not going to do it to please a bunch of strangers.

Travis rubs his thumb over my palm. I smile at him and squeeze his hand.

When I look back over the last year, it sometimes feels like one single, endless bad day. It would be easy to wish it had never happened or call it a waste of ten months of my life. But it did happen, there's no changing that. And now that I'm on the other side of it, I can't bring myself to call it a waste. It was hard, and sometimes horrible, but it led me to where I am now.

Driving toward my new home, with Travis beside me, and a lifetime of good days ahead of us.

Acknowledgments

AS EVER, I FIRST WANT TO THANK YOU, THE READER. Whether you loved it, hated it, or something in between, thank you for giving this book some of your time.

Enormous thanks to Tessa Woodward, Madelyn Blaney, and the rest of the Avon team. My books are so lucky to have found a home at Avon, and I appreciate all of your hard work so much.

To my agent, Josh, and Anna at Adams Literary—thank you both for your endless support and enthusiasm.

Finally, a huge thank-you to my friends and family, with a special shout-out to my sister, Gillian, to whom this book is dedicated. It is always a comfort to know that at least one person in the world will like your book, and I am reasonably confident you will like this one.

About the Author

AMY JAMES is the author of *A Five-Letter Word for Love* and *Crash Test*. She lives on the east coast of Canada with her husband and dog.